BACKWARDS
into the future

Bronwyn Elsmore

flax
roots

Backwards Into the Future is a work of fiction,
any resemblance between the characters and actual
persons, living or dead, is coincidental.

ISBN 978-0-9922491-4-4

Published by Flaxroots, Auckland
www.flaxroots.com

Design and cover by Aaron Elsmore.

Contents

Na Ranginui taua, na Papatuanuku taua.
Ko ahau tenei, ko koe tena.
Taua tahi.

You and I are from the same beginnings –
the Sky Father and Earth Mother.
We are one.

— ONE —

You Can't Go Back

"Don't do it," they said, "everyone knows you can't go back."
Everyone except her apparently, because here she was.

"It can never be the same again." Her friends pressed the
point to persuade her to drop the plan. Mary knew the argu-
ments, but at the same time a voice competed with them. A
very special voice from the past, telling her something else. The
way to move forward is to walk backwards into the future.

Some things in her old hometown remained, of course – a
fact confirmed by her visit six months earlier. The river, the
layout of the streets with their familiar names, the major buildings of the past, side by side along four blocks of the Esplanade.
The house in which she grew up.

1

"You'll miss your friends." That one was a better argument against the move, but in her most honest moments she admitted to herself the relationships filling her leisure times were based more on habit and familiarity than anything truly deep. Yes, she assured them with a smile, but she was sure the internet reached Waimamae, so they could email or chat online. And the town was only a four-hour drive away – if they missed her they could come and stay.

"Do you still know anyone there?" Linda had looked at her over the mug of soy cappuccino. Plenty, Mary considered replying. Her parents, Uncle Elwyn, Hemi, the McCaskills, Hortons, Watts, Rawiris, and dozens more. But she knew Linda meant live people, and she couldn't come up with any specific names. What about Kui, who talked to her most days now – did she count?

"Ana. My best friend when I was growing up," she said. Not a deliberate lie. Ana mightn't be there right now, she'd been gone from Waimamae for as long as she had herself. If Kui had her way, though, Ana would be coming back too.

Now Mary stood on the grass embankment separating the street from the river, assessing the structure that linked one side of the town to the other.

This bridge was set higher above the water, the span rising in the middle instead of level all the way across the way she remembered. The sides were concrete instead of painted iron. It used to look substantial, solid, green.

The width of the river hadn't altered. Its banks, still in the same place, looked much as they did the best part of half a century ago. She knew then just how many slabs made up the pedestrian pathway, the number of steps it took Ana and her to cover the crossing. In those days they competed to see how many of the bolted-together iron side segments they could hop past on one leg before they lost their balance. Or, more likely, had to stop to allow someone coming in the opposite direction to pass. If her memory served her well, and she had no reason to believe otherwise despite the years, Ana made the complete crossing twice, the chosen lean brown leg never looking less than confident in its solo performance. Mary's own attempts were less spectacular, though once she came close, as she consoled herself at the time, and Ana was kind enough to confirm.

After all these years people might try to say her memory let her down – and what she remembered decades on was an imagined perspective formed by childhood thoughts. They might say it made sense for an object to look bigger then, because at that time she viewed it through a child's eyes. Her sightline was lower to the ground, and the steps she took to cross it were shorter, so the span appeared longer. She knew the theories – she had no doubt expounded them to others in similar circumstances. But the fact is, this bridge was not the same as the one she used to know.

The one she remembered disappeared more than a decade earlier – a mass of metal collapsed into the waters below. This one, its replacement, spanned the same stretch – its deck rising in the middle so the centre stood further above the water, out of the way of floods which washed over the edges of its predecessor and covered the roadway. And this one was concrete grey rather than the green the other had been – deep leaf green, overlaid with a greying film from time and weather.

She imagined little fingers – her fingers, but much smaller, smoother, than their present more worn state – running across the half-hemisphere braille-like bumps that studded the heavy iron panels separating the walkway from the twin vehicle lanes.

She wondered if children still tried to hop all the way across, changing from one leg to the other in the middle. Or if a pair of girls, their pink and brown hands clasped, now ever stood at the half-way point of the span looking upstream to catch sight of the ripple in the flow which marked, still marks, the underwater den of the taniwha.

As she watched, two figures on the pedestrian path moved toward the centre then, with increasing speed, receded to the other side. Too fast, and their gait too even for walking – no doubt they were on skateboards or scooters. If Ana and she had been born another generation or two further on, perhaps they'd have done the same. No perhaps about it – they would have done the same.

Dear Ana,

It's me – Mary. It's been a long time. Too long.

Guess what? I'm back in Waimamae. For good, after all these years.

I wanted to come back.

I had to come back.

TWO

You Can't Keep Anything Private

The woman behind the checkout counter passed the first half-dozen items across the scanner before she spoke.

"Getting the old house in order, are you?"

"Pardon?" Mary wasn't sure she'd heard correctly and, if she had, what the intention of the query was.

"I hear you've moved back into your old house."

Mary paused momentarily, wondering if the woman in the blue smock had mistaken her for someone else.

"I've just moved into a house in Sutherland Street," she said. It seemed a response that would answer the earlier comments satisfactorily whatever their intention.

"The house you grew up in, yeah. I don't think the previous people did much to it, so you'll have a bit of work to do." As if to illustrate her point, the woman slid the next two items Mary transferred from her trolley – a pair of rubber gloves and scouring cloths – across the glass pad. As she reached for the next she added, "You can't keep anything private in Waimamae – you should know that."

Mary looked at the name-badge pinned over the woman's left breast, then up to the face.

"Amiria. I know you, don't I?"

The woman laughed. "Kia ora Mary."

"Amiria…" She searched for a name to follow the first.

"Waihape when you knew me. I heard you were back

in town."

"Amiria, of course. You lived in Ruakumara Road."

"Still do. I haven't gone far. Same road, about half a kilometre closer to town." She pressed the foot pedal so the belt brought the next items to hand.

"You're Ana's cousin."

"Now you've got it." Amiria laughed again. "Her little cousin. The little nuisance you two had to look after when my parents went off to tangis up north and I stayed at Kui's."

Mary thought back. There was a distant memory of straining to ease an old pushchair over the banks of shingle on the road between the two houses, but she couldn't come up with a clear picture of the child in it. Then glimpses of another girl, getting progressively bigger but always younger than they were, sitting watching them play during interval at school, being doubled on the carrier of Ana's bicycle, tagging along to the pictures on a Saturday afternoon.

"Do you know where she is?" There wasn't an immediate reply, so Mary carried on, "I've been trying to find her."

Amiria scanned the pack of espresso coffee and didn't appear inclined to answer.

"I need to find out. She has to come back."

Three items from the greengrocery section passed from Amiria's right hand to the left and into the waiting bag before she spoke again,

"Ana hasn't been back in all this time."

"She's got to come."

Amiria's head moved from one side to the other and back again in a slow sign of disagreement. "She won't."

"I've got a message for her."

"She didn't even come for Nanny Peka's funeral." Amiria's voice was even, but there was an undertone – disappointment perhaps, or censure? "Do you know why?" Amiria looked into a paper bag containing half a dozen lemons.

"You don't want these," she said, putting them behind her on a ledge that already held another item waiting to be returned to the proper place down one of the aisles.

"But I do." Mary was surprised at the other woman's action – one she'd never encountered in a supermarket before. She started to say what she was going to do with them, but Amiria over-ruled her.

"They're imported. Trust me. They're not as good as real ones, Waimamae lemons. I'll bring you some from off my tree. A welcome home present. You can make me a cup of that coffee. And we'll talk."

BACKWARDS INTO THE FUTURE

THREE

A Fair Share of Characters

Mary handed the mug to her visitor who was standing with her back to the cupboards lining the inside wall of the kitchen, facing toward the appliances on the opposite side. A generous sized bag sat on the table where Amiria had placed it as she entered. Yellow shapes of fruit showed through the plastic.

"Do sit down," she started to say, then hesitated, remembering the lessons learned in another kitchen so many years ago. "Let's drink our coffee here," she said, "and we'll go into the lounge to talk."

Amiria gave her a look, and grinned. "It's okay," she said, "at home we talk in the kitchen all the time. It's where everything happens – my mum knits, the kids do their homework, I pay the bills. We've even had kohanga meetings. It's not like in Kui's time any more." She pulled out one of the chairs and sat, pushing the bag of fruit aside, and nudging the plate of gingernuts into the middle of the table so they could both reach.

"Now, let's have that talk, and I'll catch you up with what's happened in Waimamae while you've been away. Who do you remember from the old days?"

The town had its fair share of characters. Perhaps all small towns do. Or maybe they are more obvious in little places where they can't disappear among the mass.

Characters like old Miss Purdey!

Not that she was often called Miss Purdey. Either Miss Purity, or Miss Prudey, was what she usually got – sometimes even to her face, as people forgot her real name. The lady herself probably wouldn't have minded the alternative – Miss Purity, at least. On the odd occasion when she was addressed as 'Mrs' – obviously by someone new in town – she quickly put them right.

"It's Miss, I'll thank you to know."

On one occasion, so the story went around – and it certainly did go around – she added some elaboration.

"It's Miss, I'll thank you to know. I've been a good girl all my life."

Then there was old Bottler Bob. Few people knew his surname – he was only ever known as Bottler Bob. Bob walked around Waimamae, Monday to Saturday, but on Sundays too if there was any special event occurring, pushing a wheelbarrow and collecting bottles. Clear glass soft drink bottles went straight to the cordial factory to be exchanged for coins. With the barrow stacked full of brown beer bottles, Bob would go to the back door of the pub and cash them in. Then he'd walk around to the front door and spend his earnings on beer, specifying he wanted it served in the bottle, not by the glass. When he'd finished drinking, he'd collect his empties from the side table where he always sat, plus any others left behind elsewhere, and take them out with him. Once outside, he'd place them in the wheelbarrow waiting by the door. With the new bottom layer already begun, he'd pick up the barrow and start his rounds again. People in the town left their empties outside their gates, confident they'd be gone within a day or so without having to go to the trouble to dispose of them themselves.

Bottler Bob provided such a good service, the local Scout group gave up trying to hold bottle-drives for funds, and had to resort to chopping and selling firewood. Thanks to him, Waimamae had a kerbside recycling system well before the cities thought of it. Even before most of the town's streets had proper kerbs.

Another of the local characters, just as memorable to Mary as the others, was Myra Salmond who worked at the bank. She was just the opposite of Miss Prudey.

"I'm Mrs, love, not Miss," she'd say, in deliberate contrast to Miss Purdey.

But no Mister shared the Foster Street house. If there had ever been a Mr Salmond, no one knew of him. No word of such a person had filtered into the local network since Myra transferred to the Waimamae branch, and views on whether she qualified as an ex or present wife were only speculation. Without doubt, these days she'd insist on 'Ms', as Mary usually preferred for herself now, but that term was then still decades further on.

Myra had left an indelible impression on Mary's young mind. In a town where the norm was to let one's hair and other natural features appear much the way they were, or "how the good Lord intended them" as it was put then, Myra Salmond employed art. Her hair, always kept to an impeccable ash blonde, fell in stylish waves to her shoulders. It was, however, the lack of eyebrows that so interested Mary. No natural ones, anyway. Every facial hair was carefully plucked, and a fine brown line drawn in high on the beautifully made-up forehead.

It so happened Miss ("not Mrs, I'll thank you to remember, I've been a good girl") Purdey also lived in Foster Street, the two being near, though not good, neighbours. While the women couldn't have been further apart in their moral outlooks, they happened to live just across the road and a little along from each other. A story about a reported encounter between the two, whether apocryphal or true, spread like melted mutton fat throughout Waimamae one March.

"Miss Salmond, I'd appreciate a word if you don't mind."

"Not at all, Miss Purdey, and I'm Mrs if you don't mind."

"I have happened to notice a car, which I understand belongs to the new doctor at the hospital, was parked outside your house on Tuesday night." The tone in Miss Purity's voice left no doubt this was a matter of censure rather than cordiality.

"Perhaps I had a headache."

"It did not leave till 2.13 a.m."

"If that's so, what of it?"

"This has always been a moral street, until you moved in."

Myra didn't intend to be preached to by the Foster Street Foxhound.

"I suggest, Miss Purity, you mind your business and watch your own behaviour." She delivered her curt response and continued along the footpath toward town.

Sure the matter wouldn't rest there, everyone waited with eager anticipation for what was to come. They didn't have to wait long.

Three mornings later, Myra Salmond, immaculately groomed and made-up, stood at her gate pointedly drawing the attention of passing workers to an equally distinguishable vehicle outside Miss Purdey's white-painted fence.

"Will you look at that. Miss Butter-wouldn't-melt-in-her-mouth Purity. And look who she's been entertaining all night."

A superbly manicured finger pointed triumphantly

to – Bottler Bob's barrow!

The story goes that when Bob went into the Police Station to report his missing wheelbarrow, Sergeant McIndoe was laughing so much it took five minutes to tell him where he could pick it up.

Amiria put her mug on the table and looked at the espresso machine on the bench beneath the window. Mary took the hint.

"Another cup." She made it more a statement than a question, rising at the same time. Impatient as she was to get the information she needed from her visitor, she knew it could not be rushed. Another cup, probably other cups on further days would be needed. It took time to establish trust. She turned and reached out to unlock the filter holder.

"It's as good as you get at Jack and the Bean," Amiria said with a grin, "I'll know where to come in future when I've got spare lemons."

"Any time." Mary emptied the spent grounds into the new compost bucket and refilled the scoop measure from the screw top jar in which she kept the ground espresso. You said you'd tell me about Ana, she thought of saying, but paused before she began. It wasn't strictly true. They'd talk, was what Amiria said, and Mary knew the other's decision would not be made lightly. That's all right, she thought, she had the time. After several decades of working life it was a relief not to have to meet externally imposed deadlines. On the other hand, she had to answer to Kui, and Kui was pushing her.

"Jack and the Bean?" she queried.

"The café on the corner of the Esplanade and Day Street."

Esplanade was a rather pretentious title for the strip it designated, she'd thought as she drove along it on her first day back
in Waimamae. On one side was the straight stretch of the river,
its bank admittedly much better landscaped and inviting than
in times past. Where once a narrow raised stretch sloped down
to a thin muddy flat, years of flood-deposited silt had built up
the area to form a wider and higher bank, now grass-covered,
with seating and shrubs. Day Street – that was the one she used
to cycle up when her mother sent her to the bakery. She located
the corner in her mind.

"You'll remember Jack Warren," Amiria prompted. "You
know, he and his sister went to our school…"

"Rabbit and Bunny Warren?" She dredged up those names
from a long way down.

Amiria laughed. "That's them."

"It's what we used to call them."

"Everyone did. It's Jack's café. He used to call it just 'Jack's', but
then he got this fancy coffee machine and people started calling
it Jack and the Bean, so he changed it."

Mary made herself a mental note to have a look next time
she was in town.

"Jack married Wendy Galbraith – you should remember her."

Mary thought. She wasn't sure, but a mouth with metal
wires across the top teeth came to mind. Such dental work was
a rarity in Waimamae in those days, and had to be done in
Robertstown, so the Galbraiths must have had more disposable
income than the average family.

"Business must be good – they've built a big new house in
Whites Road."

Whites Road – Mary did remember that area, not that she'd

been in the street much. "Stay away from Whites Road," her mother, Ruth, had told her on more than one occasion. Her questions as to why the ban was imposed were never answered satisfactorily. "It's just not a nice part of town," was the best explanation she ever got.

"Rupena lives on the corner of Whites Road," she'd said once while setting the table for dinner, "and Georgie goes there."

"Rupena lives in Cork Street," Ruth ruled, as though a gate and letterbox on one side of a corner rather than the other made all the difference. Her father, William, folded his newspaper and took his spectacles off the table to make room for his knife and fork.

"The Rawiris are a good family," he confirmed, "they're all right."

Mary's memory of the lower end of Whites Road might have shown on her face. Amiria grinned. "It's not as rough as it used to be. You remember those old houses down the end? Most of them have been bulldozed and there are big new ones there. It's different now. Go and have a look."

Mary let her talk as she heated the milk. So far Amiria hadn't mentioned Ana. She wanted to prompt her, but it wouldn't pay to push her for the information she needed. Not yet – it could have the opposite effect. It had waited long enough; a little longer would make no difference. As long as Kui could be patient too. Meanwhile, this talk about people she used to know was reaching within her and stirring places long left undisturbed – recapturing old memories, reassembling them as pictures in the album of her mind. It would all help her work things out.

I've been thinking a lot about you lately Ana – about the things we shared as kids, and all that has happened since. I've got all our school photos, from when we were five right up to sixteen.

— FOUR —

For All the Time It's Been

Mary sat on the lowest of the three concrete steps running the breadth of the block of classrooms. Behind her, the folding doors that formed a full side of the room were opened right back, the glass-paned sections stacked at each end, exposing it to the sunlight and any breeze that might flit through to freshen the air.

Her right hand pulled her left elbow into her waist in an effort to avoid her arm being hurt any further. She shouldn't have worn a short-sleeved blouse today because the lower edges of the ring of tender red showed on her upper arm, inviting action from the bigger boys who revelled in their reputation for toughness. Yesterday was 'jab day' when the district nurse visited, laden with stocks of iodine, swabs, needles and vials of vaccine. When the messenger arrived at the door to the classroom and announced it was their turn all forty-two desks were vacated, varying degrees of anxiety showing in the faces of those who sat at each. Once again this year Mary's pleas to her parents for her to be excused the annual typhoid shot had been refused. All it took was a note from one of them, she begged, then played her trump card – she'd never heard of anyone at school who'd had typhoid fever.

"Quite right, it's because everyone gets vaccinated," came the unarguable reply. Mary knew if she persisted there'd be talk of Dad's Uncle Arthur, which wasn't fair because that happened a long time ago, back in the olden days and things were different now. Georgie, with the superiority born of his two years and two months seniority, called her a sissy so that left no chance of looking for support there. Once, when their cousins visited from Wellington soon after a previous jab day, Mary sought sympathy from Jennifer, the closest of the three to her age and just a year ahead in school, but Jenny looked at her without comprehension.

"What do you mean?" she asked, "We don't get them at our school."

So here she was today nursing her arm and trying not to give way again to tears. They'd already sprung from her earlier when Ben, the largest boy in the class, spied her favouring her left side and administered a well-aimed punch. He and Tipene ran off laughing – their own injection sites obviously not causing them any concern.

It looked as though Georgie was right once again, because a group of girls skipping on the concrete in front of her were laughing and chanting in rhythm – apparently they weren't troubled either. As far as she knew, she was the only one with a large red wheal and an aching arm. Ana's two black plaits, longer and thicker than those of the others, were bouncing as she jumped. Join in, she called out, but Mary shook her head. It's true, she was a sissy, she admitted to herself. She should have worn a jersey or cardigan the way she noticed Ana and some of the other girls were doing, then the raised red circle wouldn't have been seen, and she might not have been targeted. The rope caught Mihi's bare heel and, eliminated from the game, she dropped onto the step beside Mary. She panted lightly.

"Take off your cardy – you must be hot," Mary said to her, but gained no response.

The rope rotated faster and faster and within a minute the remaining girls dropped out. All collapsed onto the steps laughing and out of breath.

"You've got your jerseys on," she pointed out again. When no one made any move to shed themselves of their covering, Mary asked, "Aren't you all hot? Take them off."

Mihi looked at Aroha and Ana and grinned, but none of them moved to take the advice. Mary realized she had often seen them covered this way on other warm days. If it wasn't a matter of protecting their arms, as she should have done, they were obviously in on something Mary wasn't party to. She looked at them, puzzled.

"Nah," said Mihi, "I'm dark enough now. I don't want to get any darker." The girls laughed, and started to talk about something else, the moment gone for them. Here was another thing Mary didn't understand. She couldn't get brown even if she wanted to, or no matter how she tried. All she got was red and blistered, and then her skin peeled leaving her looking like an undercooked piece of flaky pastry.

The primary school still looks much the same, Ana.

The weekend after I came back I went there and looked around. There's a new staff room, but otherwise it hasn't changed a lot.

The concrete where we used to skate in the weekends. The swimming pool where we learned to swim – when I think about it, I can still smell the chlorine. Actually, the pool does look different – it's a lot smaller than it used to be when we had to swim lengths, and it's hard to imagine we couldn't touch the bottom at the deep end.

I walked by the classrooms – they're much the same too. Except some have carpet. Carpet, imagine – not in our day! And the walls are brighter with more coloured posters. But overall they haven't changed a lot, for all the time it's been.

FIVE

Going Up in a Parachute

At the beginning of the new school year pairs and groups of children made their way, more or less willingly, down Fergusson Street to the north entrance to the primary school. Or along Wiremu Road to the south gate. Older children charged with delivering a younger brother or sister, or perhaps a five-year old neighbour, to the new entrants' class made sure their impatience showed on their faces till they could release their responsibility to the Infant Mistress and join their friends. Knots of girls and clumps of boys formed outside classrooms – the girls showing each other pocket-sized treasures obtained over the holidays, the boys stubbing the toes of new shoes into the edge of the concrete before discarding them altogether.

Mary's spirits rose a notch as she looked into the room allotted to their class. They'd been told on the last day of the previous term, before the bell rang to release them into the hot December day, who their teacher for the coming year would be. Even though it was anticipated, her hopes for more welcome news were dashed.

Throughout the weeks of the summer holidays she'd spent time imagining, and then trying not to imagine, how she would cope under the charge of the teacher widely reported to be the strictest at Waimamae North.

Georgie didn't help. "You'll have to mind your Ps and Qs,

now," he kept repeating, laughing at her.

Mary didn't understand, but didn't want to admit it by asking. Georgie often took great delight in showing his greater knowledge. Last time their mother's brother visited, Georgie whooped with joy as he told their uncle how once, when the two of them were playing in the back yard, Mary suggested they go up in a parachute. "Up in a parachute!" He rolled his eyes upwards to accentuate how ridiculous he found the idea.

"That's not fair," Mary protested, turning away in shame, "it was years ago, and I was only little then. I bet you thought the same too, when you were little." She was stung by her brother's laughter, especially in front of Uncle Elwyn. He was their favourite uncle and she didn't want him making fun of her too.

"Did not," replied Georgie, "I always knew."

But Uncle Elwyn didn't laugh. He stepped behind her and put his hands on her shoulders, turning her to face Georgie. "Going up in a parachute? That's a really good idea – I wonder why someone hasn't invented an up-parachute before now! I'll tell you what – if we can come up with a prototype we'll patent it."

Mary idolized him even more after that. She didn't know the words prototype and patent, but they sounded important and positive. She'd look them up in her junior dictionary when Georgie wasn't watching. He didn't know them either, she told herself, and she might be able to use them in front of him some time.

It was another thing her brother laughed about – when she'd asked for a dictionary for her birthday. Girls her age asked for dolls' furniture, or skates, not dictionaries. Her mother seemed puzzled by it too. There was the Oxford Dictionary on the bookshelf in the sitting room, she pointed out, but Mary found it big and heavy to pull down and use. Besides, she wanted her own – one she could write in, and underline words with a pencil. Georgie shook his head and laughed again when she repeated her wish. He didn't know why she wanted one. No one did, thank goodness. It was Mary's secret – one she wouldn't tell anyone. It went back to something that happened a few weeks before her birthday.

"Georgie." Ruth called but there was no response. She went to the back door and repeated the call. She was sure he and Andy were playing at the end of the backyard, but there was no sound from down there – they must have gone elsewhere. Darn it, she'd started to mix a biscuit recipe and found she was short of an ingredient. She wanted him to get something from the dairy.

"I'll go for you," Mary volunteered. Ruth looked dubious, then relaxed. Georgie had been running such errands for two or three years, and there was no reason why Mary couldn't do it now. She'd probably be more reliable, though not as fast – Georgie always ran there and back, wanting to get back to his play.

"I need a tin of condensed milk," said Ruth, wrapping a two-shilling coin in Mary's hanky and putting it in her pocket.

Mary set out down Sutherland Street. It was a block to the corner, turn to the left, then just one more block to where the dairy stood on the corner of Patterson Street. She stopped to stroke the ginger cat lying in the front garden of Hall's house, and rounded the corner. Someone had left a hopscotch grid chalked on the concrete. She hopped through the squares, careful not to touch any lines, and spotted a display sign standing outside the dairy. It showed the familiar Peter Pan ice-cream logo with its red curling letters and the boy blowing a pipe. What was it her mother wanted? Some sort of milk. In her mind she could see the can, with a picture of a man in a Scottish kilt and a tall black headdress on the label. Highlander... Highlander... what was the word? Densed? That was part of it. Densedcon milk! She was relieved to have remembered. In the shop she looked up and, feeling the importance of completing her first solo errand, put her request.

"Densedcon milk, please."

The woman behind the counter smiled at her. "Condensed milk," she said, reaching to a shelf behind her and handing Mary a can. There was the tartan-clad man she recognized, so it was what her mother wanted.

"That's what I meant," she said, head down, holding out the coin Ruth had given her. She carried the can home reciting all the way – condensed, condensed, condensed.

Since then, it was something Mary had worked on. Every time she heard a new word, she tried to remember it so she could look it up in her own dictionary. Each time she looked up a word she underlined it – now there were pencil marks on most pages. The problem was, many of the terms she heard in the playground at school weren't there – her book listed English words only, not Maori.

On the two blank pages at the back of the volume she added those she knew were missing, with their definitions.

ae = yes
apopo = tomorrow
haere mai = come here
haere ra = go
hoa = friend

hui = social gathering
kai = food
kao = no
kehua = ghost
mahi = work
manuhiri = visitor
marae = meeting place complex where hui are held
nui = big
puku = stomach
tangi = funeral
tapu = sacred
umu = earth oven
waka = boat
weka = brown bird
wharepaku = lavatory

The entry for taniwha remained undefined. When she'd added it, Mary had paused thinking. A taniwha was a taniwha, there was no other word for it. Some people said it was a monster, but that wasn't right. Not really. Never mind, she knew what it was anyway so it could just stay as it was.

In her last school report the teacher wrote, "Mary has an above average vocabulary for her age," and her mother beamed and pointed it out to her father. Georgie could laugh all he wanted, Mary felt vindicated – she'd looked that one up too, and underlined it.

Now Georgie said it again, taunting her. "You'll have to mind your Ps and Qs in Mrs Flint's class." Mary couldn't leave it this time.

"What do you mean peas and queues?" she asked. Georgie hesitated, then increased the volume of his mirth, adding a note of scorn to the mix.

"You know," he said.

"I know what they are," she said doubtfully, "but not what you mean. What is it?"

"Mary doesn't know. Mary doesn't know," Georgie chanted in the singsong rhythm that so annoyed his sister. He batted a tennis ball against the wall next to the glass doors leading into the dining room, retrieved it and repeated the action. "Mary doesn't know."

"George," came their mother's voice from inside, "you'll break a window."

"I don't think you know either."

"I do so."

"Then tell me, or I'll know you don't." It was a response she had learned often worked.

"You know what pee is, don't you." From the tone Mary knew her brother wasn't referring to what their father grew in the vegetable garden along the side fence in the back yard behind the house. But pee in the other sense she'd heard of wasn't a word spoken in their home. The term for that was wee, or wees. Pee was what Mum would call vulgar and ban from their vocabulary, along with bum for bottom and dunny instead of lavvy – words she sometimes heard at school but wouldn't dare use at home.

"It's not that at all." She thought she'd heard the saying before, uttered by grownups, and they wouldn't say it if it was what Georgie was saying it was.

"'Tis so!"

"Then what's Qs?"

"It's what goes with pees." Georgie ran around the side of the house laughing, and Mary went inside for another opinion.

Ana, I swear some of the desks were even the same ones that we sat in. I stood there, looking in, and I could see us sitting there – listening to Mrs Flint reading us a story about squirrels and badgers. There were no stories about tuataras and kiwis then.

You and I liked to sit in the row by the windows, remember? You know, the ones right along the side, which opened out like folding doors. You liked to be first out into the playground.

I liked it for another reason.

— SIX —

All Present and Correct

When school restarted and they saw their allocated classroom was furnished with new single desks, their varnished lids untouched by pen marks or gouges that could affect one's printing, Mary allowed herself a surge of hope for the year to come. In the past the pupils in her class had been paired, with each two sitting side by side at a twin desk. The fact of being one of a pair wasn't a problem – sometimes a partner would whisper an answer, or share a pencil when a lead tip broke and you didn't want to go to the front of the room and use the sharpener fixed to the teacher's desk. But the old double desks were constructed as a solid unit with built-in fold-down seats, and with each year that passed, it became more difficult to squeeze into the space.

The year before, Ana and Mary shared a double unit. Now the new desks and chairs stood in single rows, one behind another, with a gap across to one's neighbour on each side. The chance to prompt one another with an under-breath word was lessened, the opportunity to pass things between each other behind the security of the wooden barrier now gone. Anything of the sort must be done behind the teacher's back and, as they were constantly told, teachers had eyes in the back of their heads. As much as Mary felt the thrill of moving up to the next level, indicated by the change of furniture, a tinge of panic welled up as she realized she was no longer one of a pair. She took Ana by the arm and drew her up the steps to the windows, to inspect the new layout inside.

"Where shall we sit?" Her eyes went toward the place they'd occupied the year before, near the centre of the room. Ana glanced at the new setup.

"Here," she said, pointing at the desk in the middle of the closest row just through the folding glass doors which formed the full side of the room nearest the playground. "We can be first out to play when the bell goes."

On hot summer days small breezes skipped up the steps that ran the full length of the rooms, and tickled the bare feet and arms of those in the first row of seats. Leaves and the occasional abandoned lolly paper being tumbled along outside in the current might catch the eye, but the girls needed to try hard to ignore any movement. Reports about the teacher proved accurate. Mrs Flint, even when seated working at her own desk on the far side of the room, spotted the slightest sign of inattention. Such lapses when detected never escaped comment – at best exasperated, more often blistering.

On a Wednesday morning in April, before morning break, the classroom shuddered.

The Reverend Matthews had just ended his weekly half-hour Bible-in-Schools lesson with a closing verse from the Gospel of Matthew – prompting Mary to wonder, once again, whether his frequent reference to this book suggested some relationship between it and his family. Mrs Flint returned from the weekly staff meeting to again take charge, and smiled as she noted the lack of noise, and saw that order prevailed. The children, in the main, sat quietly at their desks, most looking straight ahead but with eyes not focussed on any specific point. That was a welcome change – the elderly vicar wasn't known for his ability

ALL PRESENT AND CORRECT

to control a classroom full of youngsters, and she usually had to reprimand one or two for talking.

After the two adults greeted each other, the clergyman eased himself down the three outside steps with the help of his walking stick and walked in the direction of the Fergusson Street gate to where his Austin A40 was parked. As he disappeared from sight, and before Mrs Flint had a chance to instruct them to open their spelling books, a hand was raised in the middle row.

"Yes, Jeffrey?"

"Is the world really going to end?"

A moment's silence passed as all in the room considered the weight of the question. Mary, along with the other seated children, waited. She wanted an answer too, but at the same time she was scared to hear what it might be.

Mrs Flint opened her mouth, and shut it again. She turned to the blackboard and rubbed at words erased by the blackboard monitor at the end of the day before, and which were no longer there. For several long seconds Mary thought she was not going to respond, but then the teacher turned to face the class again.

"What did Reverend Matthews tell you?" she asked.

"There'll be a harvest at the end of the world, and angels will be doing the reaping."

Mrs Flint looked at the wooden-backed duster in her hand and turned back to the blackboard to set it on the grooved ledge below. It toppled off and landed on the platform at her feet. At the same time, the vertical sections of the glass doors, which were folded back on themselves, rattled against each other, and desks shifted and shook. The teacher, her body caught in the act of twisting, with one foot moving and the other pivoting on a toe, tottered and reached out to grip the ledge. She steadied herself and, prompted by the looks on the faces of the children in the front row, realized the cause was not her own lack of stability. She issued an order.

"Get under your desks."

She didn't need to repeat the instruction. The forty-one chairs occupied that day scraped backwards on the wooden boards – a sound that usually provoked a reprimand – as the class scrambled to obey. Earthquake drills were held each term, so the class was well prepared as to what to do in case of a shake. But this was no drill, the movement was sharp and real, and the event wasn't preceded by a warning bell coming through the speaker mounted in the centre of the front wall above the blackboard. The shaking continuing around them told them this was not an exercise, but the real thing.

Mary crouched beneath the supposed safety of her wooden shelter. Someone a few desks away made a whimpering sound. Her own stomach felt knotted and queasy, but she didn't dare open her mouth. She looked through the legs of her discarded chair toward Ana behind her. Ana grinned back at her, and the knotted feeling eased somewhat.

"Just as well we're not in our old desks, eh?" Mary heard Ana's whisper and nodded in response. With each drill over the past year or two she and her growing classmates found it more difficult to get under them, and even harder to wriggle out again when given the all clear.

This time though, the situation was real. The windows near them continued to jiggle and scrape, and a movement near the ceiling, visible between their row of desks and the one beside them, caused Mary to glance up. The suspended centre light swung in an arc between the front and back of the room. She remembered the story her mother told about being in what was now popularly called 'the Robertstown quake' even though it was more widespread, and affected several other towns in the province too.

"I was eighteen and working in an office. It was a two-storey building and we were on the upper floor. We'd felt earthquakes before, enough to make the place shake, but we knew right away this one was different. I heard a rumbling noise first and looked out the window thinking a big truck was coming along the street. The building jumped up and down again, and as I watched I saw the footpath on the opposite side of the street come right up. It lifted about a yard above the roadway," Ruth demonstrated the distance with her arms spread apart, "and a gap opened between them. We couldn't get out the door to go through the hallway and down the stairs because something fell behind it and blocked it. One of the men forced open an emergency exit, which was never used, and we climbed down the fire escape."

Mary looked outside to see if any part of the playground had risen or sunk, but the concrete and grass seemed as flat as usual. This wasn't what people often referred to as the coming 'big one', then. It was big enough for her, though, so if there was a much larger one on the way, she hoped she wouldn't be around when it came.

When the swaying movement that followed the first jolt eased, and the classroom settled again, Mrs Flint issued a further command.

"Stand up, and in an orderly fashion go outside. Don't take anything with you. I said orderly!"

By the time Mary stood Ana was already out the open side of the room and jumping down the steps onto the concrete strip. She led others at a run onto the field beyond.

"No running. I said in an orderly fashion," came the call behind them.

As the class assembled at a spot designated a safe distance from objects that might be expected to fall from the buildings, Mrs Flint came to the door of their classroom, then turned and disappeared inside again.

"She didn't get under her desk," someone said, and giggled responses including references to her size followed.

Mrs Flint reappeared, clutching the folder holding the class roll. She instructed them to sit on the grass and for the second time in the morning she recited the names from A to Y, comparing the ticks. "All present and correct," she announced, then walked away to speak to another teacher, her overburdened shoes crushing upstanding stalks of paspalum till she regained the steadier surface of the concrete.

"Perhaps it's the end of the world," someone suggested. Everyone else laughed, though not all with confidence. The Reverend Matthew's lesson was still disturbingly fresh in their minds.

"Nah," said Daniel, who Mrs Flint always called Raniera when she called the roll, "it's just Ruamoko moving in his mother's puku."

Mary heard the ripple of giggles around her. Ana's voice was among them. She didn't want to appear ignorant by speaking up now and asking what it meant. People might laugh at her, the way Georgie did. She'd ask Ana at lunchtime.

As I looked in the glass doors I could see us. You, me, Wiki, Theresa and Lynne in the row by the window. Maxine, Aroha, Josie and Mihi in the next row, with Derek at the back.

Looking at our class photos I find I've forgotten the names of some of the boys.

But I'll never forget Derek.

BACKWARDS INTO THE FUTURE

SEVEN

The Way Things Were

Derek wore built-up boots, and callipers on his legs. He ran after the others in the class with a stumbling gait. It was obvious to them that Derek's arms and legs often didn't behave the way he wanted them to, and every awkward movement was an extra effort for him. Though she wouldn't have said so aloud, and certainly not to him, Mary admired the way Derek would try to keep up at phys-ed. And how, after school, he staggered along the sideline of the football field, urging on the bigger and fitter boys in the school team; squinting to focus even with the help of the thick lenses of his glasses. Apart from just passing references, she and the others didn't discuss his differences – they didn't even think too much about them. That's the way Derek was, and it's the way they accepted him. None of them, as far as she was aware, had ever asked Derek himself why he was not able-bodied like the rest of them. In Waimamae disabilities in others were handled by not referring to them, or pretending they didn't exist.

"Don't stare," Mary's mother warned her when they walked down the street and saw the boy at number twenty-nine leaning over the gate, his face pulled into weird grimaces. Dribble came from his mouth, and he called out to them in unintelligible words.

"But Mum, what's the matter with him?"

"Hush," responded her mother. "He can't help it, he was born that way. Keep your voice down and don't keep looking at him."

On another occasion when Mary pointed and said, "Look at the man on the bicycle. He's got little short legs. He's got to stand on the pedals because he can't reach the seat," her mother repeated the lesson.

"Don't stare, it's not polite, and don't ever talk about such people."

Maybe that was the reason no one asked Derek. Or perhaps they didn't because none of the class imagined he would know any more than they did.

Derek's mind didn't keep up with the rest of his classmates either. It was another thing they accepted about him because, again, it's just the way things were. Derek was always bottom of the class – a position he accepted with good humour.

Mrs Flint, though, was another matter. Sharp tempered and authoritarian, she had no patience for mediocrity of any sort. Education equated with knowledge, and the acquisition of knowledge was her pride and purpose. She bestowed praise on those who knew an answer already, and punishment on those who didn't.

Rather than promoting a love of learning, Mrs Flint provoked in her pupils a paralyzing fear of not knowing. Roving through the desks as they worked, she would descend on an error or a smudge, pick up the offender's ruler, and deliver sharp slaps on the legs. The tears that blurred the eyes of the one selected after she moved on were less for the pain of the physical blows than for the humiliation of the stinging criticism.

"Wiki, what is eight times seven? I'm waiting. It seems Wiki doesn't know her eight times table. Come to the front of the class."

"Three spelling mistakes in one page of your story, Joe. Hold out your hand."

"Stand up Jacob, Christopher and Perry. Look at them everyone – these boys could not give an example of an oval ball in their test. Can you believe it? Perhaps we should not let them play with their oval ball at lunchtime and after school."

Instead, out on the playing field, the three took out their anger on younger children unfortunate enough to be in the way.

"Mary, Mary, quite contrary – if I gave you two and sixpence for something costing one and sixpence, you'd give me only ten pence back, would you? Well, class, if Mary ever gets a job in a shop, though I doubt it will be the case, don't go in there because you'll get the wrong change."

After school Mary sought her mother's sympathy. Ruth shook her head and continued sewing bias binding around the neckline of the summer dress she was making.

"You should be nice to Mrs Flint. She suffers from rheumatism and she's often in a lot of pain."

What was it about parents? They always supported other grown-ups, even against their own children. If Mary ever had children, she vowed, she wouldn't do the same – she'd believe them, especially if they had a crabby teacher like Mrs Flint. Her feelings splintered further by not receiving the supportive outburst of righteous indignation she thought was her due, Mary remembered the pain of the humiliation. On many occasions afterwards, while seated in the classroom and noting the teacher's stiff movement, she found some measure of the consolation she wanted at the time. Not in the way her mother intended, but in the knowledge of their teacher's affliction.

As sorry as Mary felt for herself, and for anyone who suffered from Mrs Flint's slashing tongue and strap during that year, it paled into insignificance compared with what she felt for Derek. Of all the class, it was he who most bore the brunt of the teacher's intolerance of ignorance.

"More spelling errors, Derek. Will you ever learn? Come to the front of the class."

"Derek, this page looks as though rats have used it to make a nest. Hold out your hand."

His disabilities found no empathy with Mrs Flint. Rather, they seemed to give her even more incentive for spite, as though she saw in his thin crippled limbs a reminder of her own imperfect body.

Mrs Flint's handicap was, in contrast, her over-generous size. Whereas Derek stumbled along, weak and uncertain, on his callipered legs the teacher tottered, heavy and ponderous, on hers. She was fettered not by iron shin supports, but by her bulk. An over-large bosom pulled her woollen dress tight. Between that and her corseted hips, a wide belt strained to hold it all in check. A pair of unattractive black shoes constricted her feet so balloons of flesh bulged out beyond the edges. As though in compensation for the rest of her body, she possessed one redeeming physical feature. Her hair, which reached to her shoulders, was a dark honey colour with silver threads just beginning to show through. Two or three decades ago, and several stone lighter, she might have been judged attractive, but if that were the case, such a time was long past.

Now Mrs Flint used her weight to crush compliance into her pupils. She would stand behind someone seated at their desk and lean over to correct some part of their work, her outsized bosom pressing them down so their nose was right on their book, her own nostrils breathing heavily from the effort. When it happened to Mary she wanted to scream and fight her way out from the oppressive constriction. It also left her with a lifetime refusal to put on excess weight. Mrs Flint, Mary realized decades later, was instrumental in shaping her life in more ways than one.

The climax came one Thursday afternoon. It was almost three o'clock, and for Mary the day had been better than most because she got all the words on the spelling list right, even 'government', which gave her anxious moments as she agonized over whether or not to put an 'n' in the middle. She and her classmates were clearing away their books, ready for the signal of the bell when an awkward figure lurched through the rows of desks to the front of the room. Derek faced the teacher, a triumphant smile pulling his face into a picture of happiness.

"Mrs Flint, you haven't strapped me today!"

Mary looked up, happy to share Derek's delight and his invitation to the teacher to join in his success. Mrs Flint wasn't. Her face, normally mottled red, went purple as she struggled to contain her anger at what she saw as impudence. Ponderous and purposeful she moved to her desk and picked up the strap.

"Hold out your hand," she ordered.

Derek's shoulders slumped. He stood in front of her, his broken figure a complete contrast to hers. He held out his hand.

How lasting an effect the incident had on Derek, Mary couldn't tell. Whenever she recalled the event during the years and decades later, she remembered only the horror she felt at the time – the flush of revulsion for the action, and for the one who acted, followed by the ache of empathy for the one so misinterpreted and mistreated.

"It's not fair," she told others after the event, and repeated to herself for years to come, refusing for a long time to learn the most important lesson her teacher no doubt knew, and could have taught her.

That life itself is not fair.

Do you recall when we were at High School, in the sixth form, and Mrs Williment asked me to put in an application for teachers training college? You'll remember my reaction – you had to calm me down afterwards.

EIGHT

All On Her Own

In spite of Mary's problem with Mrs Flint her life, as for others, centred on the school. The swimming pool, dug out and constructed by a group of fathers, was open for bathing on weekends and holidays. The playing fields hosted sports events. In lieu of a hall, large folding doors that separated two classrooms were opened up in order to accommodate concerts and the break-up function held at the end of the school year.

Public health concerns were catered for as well. The district nurses made regular visits for reasons other than giving typhoid injections. Again Mary and her friends were lined up and called forward one by one to where two women in starched white waited – this time with their hands in rubber gloves and holding what looked like a pair of wooden sticks from ice-blocks.

"Ice-block sticks," laughed Georgie. "Haa-haa, Mary thinks they're ice-block sticks. Do you think the nurses go around eating ice-blocks so they can get the sticks for cootie inspection? They're called spatulas, dumb-dumb."

"At least I haven't got them!"

"Neither have I."

"You did though – you had cooties."

"Did not."

"You did so, Georgie. It's why Mum put kerosene through your hair. You ponged of kerosene for days."

"Mum, Mary says I've got cooties!"

"Mary! Never talk like that. And don't you ever mention it outside this house."

Mary let the reprimand skip past her. She had paid Georgie back for calling her "Mary Hairy". She was trying to grow her hair so she could wear it in a long plait down her back, the way Ana wore hers. But it was already clear hers would never look as good. Mary's fine fair hair was not the same as her friend's. It was thinner, wispier, and even if it did become long it would be a skinny plait instead of thick and sleek. Already, even though it was just past her shoulders, getting the knots out was a chore every night, and she knew it wouldn't be long before she'd ask to have it cut short again.

"Guess what Georgie had," Mary invited Ana as they sat side-by-side on the forms outside their classroom eating their sandwiches. Everyone brought sandwiches for lunch, the only variety was the fillings: lettuce, egg, jam, or cold meat. The two girls had just swapped one of Mary's lettuce and Marmite for one of Ana's blackberry jam. Ana offered suggestions between bites.

"What Georgie had? Ah, measles? Fish and chips for breakfast? A ride in an aeroplane?" With each guess Mary shook her head and laughed. Ana always thought up fanciful ideas.

"Try again."

"Ants in his pants?"

"No, but you're closer."

"Cooties."

"Yes, he had cooties in his hair!" she laughed with delight, expecting her friend to join in.

Ana shrugged. "So what?" she asked.

Mary felt deflated. She'd ignored the firm instruction not to mention the subject expecting, wanting, a reaction of horror, and it didn't come. So why was her mother so insistent she shouldn't talk about it to anyone else?

"Everybody's had cooties," Ana added in a bored tone.

Mary didn't answer. Here was something else everyone had done and she hadn't. Sometimes she felt all on her own.

It's crazy, the things I remember, Ana.

I have a memory of us at school at lunchtime, sitting on those forms outside the classrooms, where we had to stay till we'd eaten our lunch and the bell rang to release us for play. I was eating my sandwiches, and I had brown bread – my mother always gave us brown bread. You and Wiki and Theresa had white. Wiki laughed as she noticed.

"Look, Ana, the white girl has brown bread, and the brown girls have white bread." You and Theresa joined in the laughter.

At the time I wasn't sure how to react. Now it's my turn – I laugh about that even today when I buy my wholemeal loaf.

— NINE —

Call Me Kui

Georgie stopped pedalling at the end of the sealed road, and put his foot on the edge of the tar-sealed surface to steady the bicycle.

"That's far enough with you on the back," he said. He looked at the furrows formed by car tyres in the shingle laid on the part of the road stretching ahead. "We'll come off in the gravel."

Mary unhooked her hands – to his annoyance she'd kept them clasped around his waist since they set out from their own house – and climbed off the carrier. Ana, holding the handlebars of her own bike, pointed to a white house with a red roof fifty yards away.

"It's not far. It's that one there."

"Right, then. I'm off." Georgie turned his front wheel back in the direction they'd come.

"Are you coming back for me? Mum said you had to bring me and take me home."

Georgie shrugged. He hadn't wanted to come at all. He had better things to do than to look after his little sister, but at least agreeing to take her to Ana's meant he was allowed go to Andy's in the meantime. "Quarter to five, you be ready," he said, and set out.

Ana walked her bike along the left-hand channel in the stones, and Mary followed. She'd wondered what Ana's house was like. After all the times her friend had been to her place after school, this was the first time she'd returned the visit.

A woman in a long dark green skirt, and a checked shirt that looked as though it might have once belonged to a man, sat on the edge of the verandah at the back of the house. A broad-brimmed hat sat beside her, and a pair of old shoes was discarded on the grass. Her bare feet rested next to a garden fork and a machete.

At the sight of the girls, she smiled and gave a slight upward lift of her head.

"You must be Mere. Nei?"

Mary wasn't sure how to reply. She presumed it was how the woman pronounced her name, even though she made it sound more like merry. And she was trying hard not to stare at the lined and marked face. Before she could say anything the woman reached out and grasped her hand in both of her own.

"I'm Ana's grandmother."

"Hello." Mary wasn't sure how to address her. She saw lines of amusement form in the other's face, pulling the blue-darkened lips upwards.

"You can call me Kui, as Ana does."

Kui. That's the name Ana used when she talked about home. At first Mary imagined an elegant immaculately groomed lady with a crown on her head, sitting upright and regal on a large gold chair. Ana laughed when she asked more about it.

"Not like queen," she said, "it's Kwee with a K, and no N. She's my grandmother. I live with her."

Now Mary saw that her imagined picture could hardly be more removed from this very different stooped figure relaxing on the edge of the verandah.

Ana looked across the back yard. "The boat's gone," she said,

"I thought Hemi was going to help you plant kumara."

Kui gave a small sideways movement of her head.

"He heard the fish were biting. But we got it done first. It's hoata – a good day for both." Ana nodded, she obviously understood.

The old woman looked at Mary again and stood up, grunting as she straightened her back. "Ana talks about you," and she motioned toward the door into the house.

Ana – you remember it all, don't you? Those days?

I've never forgotten. You and your house.

Kui. Hemi.

And Uncle Elwyn.

TEN

That Sort of Guy

Whenever Uncle Elwyn came to stay, not only Ruth and William, but all the adults of the neighbourhood, trod warily and counted the days till he decided to move on again – whereupon he would leave just as abruptly as he arrived, and sometimes with just as little warning. On the other hand, Mary and Georgie, together with their friends, looked forward to these visits almost as much as they waited for Christmas.

With good reason. Take the case of that memorable Guy Fawkes day so many years ago. There was no doubt at all about who was considered the guilty party.

At the time, Uncle Elwyn denied it vigorously. Well, as vigorously as he could while laughing so much he had to sit on the ground holding his side and groaning about having the stitch. This proved a fairly common sight when he was about, and the children loved him for it. Other grown-ups gave a slight smile, or at the most a short chuckle, when something amusing occurred, but Uncle Elwyn really let himself go.

Not that he needed to wait for something funny to turn up – each time he made an appearance in Waimamae anything was likely to happen. And it usually did. Like the time their mother was working in the kitchen preparing dinner and Elwyn hovered nearby talking to her. Ruth filled a saucepan with cold water and put it on the stove. A while later, she reached out and turned on the element. Elwyn's eyes gleamed. With a contrived casual air he crossed the room and whipped the lid off the pot.

"What delicious dish are you cooking for us tonight, sister? Ah, Sam and Selina. But surely there's not a lot of meat on two goldfish." Ruth banned him from the kitchen for some time after that.

With Uncle Elwyn in the area Mary and Georgie got away with tricks they wouldn't dream of attempting otherwise. He was often their scapegoat, Georgie's especially, and they adored him for it. And that's the way it turned out to be that memorable Guy Fawkes night, the year of the biggest neighbourhood fireworks party ever held in the town. Rightly or wrongly, Uncle Elwyn had to be the obvious choice for the one who put the jumping-cracker in their father's pocket.

William never once considered it could be anyone but Elwyn – especially since his brother-in-law was the one who organized the event. Till Elwyn turned up the day before, there'd been only the usual interest in celebrating the occasion. Just the kids of the area doing their own thing with the few crackers they'd been able to buy with their pocket-money, or beg by wheeling a couple of sacks dressed in old clothes through the streets asking for "a penny for the guy". But with the arrival of Uncle Elwyn came the best array of fireworks ever seen in Waimamae. Within a few hours he had it all arranged.

"Jack Painter said we can use his paddock by the river. Sis, you and the kids' friends' mothers can put together a picnic tea. Georgie, round up a couple of your pals and see if you can…" his voice dropped and he delivered the rest of the sentence directly into Georgie's ear. "We'll make a night of it," he promised.

And a night of it, it was. While the children made swirling patterns with sparklers and applied lit matches to the blue touch papers of cardboard cylinders bearing names such as Mount Vesuvius, Golden Rain, and Bridal Shower, the adults stood around chatting.

"Hey Bert, the guy on top of the bonfire's got a jacket just like the one you wear duck-shooting. Come to think of it, the cap looks familiar too. It's mine, by God. Andrew!"

Georgie and Mary's father's opinion was that Uncle Elwyn staged the whole elaborate affair for the sole reason of seeing the fool he made of himself – no, the fool someone else made him look – leaping around Painter's paddock, the jumping-cracker in his pocket providing the stimulus. It made him, he claimed, the laughing stock of the town.

"Say, Bill," he was addressed by more than one of the other men, "I guess you'll be putting your name down for the hop-step-and-jump next sports day."

To make the matter worse, the story went around that Myra Salmond arched her pencilled eyebrows at him in the reception area of the Borough Council building the following afternoon. In front of the office staff she said with a wink, "I like a man who's a good mover – you know where I live." For him, the Town Clerk, to be put in such a position was unforgiveable.

When William arrived home from work, obviously steaming, things in the house were even more strained. After a word from their mother, no doubt at the insistence of their father, Uncle Elwyn decided to move on. Mary saw him collecting his shaving gear from the bathroom and ran to spread the news, so when he made his way down the road to the bus depot he trailed a straggly retinue of children, all reluctant to see him go.

"He'll come back," her mother consoled her. "We're his family. We're all he's got now Gran and Gramps have gone."

"But you told him to go! How could you?"

"It's just till your father cools down. Besides, he had to go back to Robertstown tomorrow anyway, to work. He'll be back, just wait and see."

Mary's theory about what Georgie thereafter referred to with glee as "The Infamous Guy Fawkes Incident" accompanied by the four notes associated with the *Dragnet* radio show he loved – dum di dum dum – was never proved any more than her father's. After all, it was dark when the event took place, and anyone could have slipped up to where the adults stood in a loose group. She, however, always believed it was her brother, not her uncle, who did it.

"Now he's gone, Georgie, and it's your fault."

"Why?"

"You know why. It wasn't him, it was you."

Ana, too, had no doubts, and backed her up. "You did it, Georgie."

"Me? Everyone knows it was Uncle Elwyn."

"There were only two jumping-crackers in the box when Uncle Elwyn showed it to us, and you and Andy grabbed those. I saw you."

"Two? Nah, there were more than that."

Mary insisted. "I saw only two. And you were right there, behind Dad, just before it went off."

Georgie gave the girls a grin. "Look at it this way. Even if you're right, and I'm not saying you are, Uncle Elwyn's the sort of guy who'd like to be known as the man who put the jumping-cracker in Dad's pocket."

And he was right, of course – Uncle Elwyn was that sort of guy!

They were good times, Ana.

The pictures on a Saturday afternoon – remember the crush you had on Marlon Brando after you saw him in The Wild One!

Those kittens we found and tamed in the empty section next to your house.

And the lavatory down the path behind your shed. Do you know, in all these years since, I've never heard or seen a reference to an outhouse without thinking about the first time I came to your place.

BACKWARDS INTO THE FUTURE

ELEVEN

The Two of Them, Together

The sizes and layouts of Mary and Ana's houses were fairly similar – much like the majority in Waimamae. Most times when Mary went to friends' houses or visited others with her parents, she found things looked much the same.

Most often, the front door opened into a long hallway and passage that ran through the middle of the house linking front to back. The best room, on one side at the front, faced the street. It was known as the sitting room or front room in most families though Mary heard her friend Fenella, who lived in a larger more modern house than most, refer to their 'lounge'. Opposite it, on the other side of the hall, was the largest bedroom, invariably occupied by the parents in the family.

Mary knew of only one person at their school who didn't have two parents. Jeanette, called Jinny for short, lost her father when she was four, when his tractor overturned pinning him under it. Jinny and her mother moved into town and every day after school, unless she went to play with friends, Jinny walked to the library where her mother worked. Mary thought it would be great to have access to all those books whenever she wanted them, but Ruth always sighed and referred to her as "poor little Jinny". Then, of course, there was Ana. The one time Mary asked where her mother and father were, Ana just shrugged, and the two of them never referred to the matter again. But Ana had Kui, and Hemi, so it was sort of the same.

Behind the two front rooms, in the middle of the house, were two smaller bedrooms and a dining room. At the rear stood the bathroom and kitchen, with the back door through the kitchen leading out to a porch or verandah – depending on the direction the house faced. Verandahs were placed on the north-facing sides where they took advantage of the sun in the changing seasons, and provided protection from it in the heat of summer. Porches were smaller structures built to give shelter to south-facing doors.

Always at the back, attached to one side of the verandah, or in a separate detached building erected a few yards away from the house or along the fence line of the neighbouring property, were two other facilities essential to everyday living.

The washhouse, constructed in weatherboard similar to the main house, or sometimes a less substantial structure of corrugated iron, housed laundry equipment and served as overflow storage.

Ruth considered herself fortunate. She no longer needed to fill the copper with water and light a fire under the bowl, then transfer it bucket by bucket into the washing machine when it steamed, as other women had to do. Some, perhaps the majority, those without a machine, still boiled the clothes in the copper itself – hooking them out with a well-worn wooden laundry stick, hauling them across to the tub for rinsing, then turning the handle of the wringer to squeeze out the excess water. Whites were always rinsed twice – the second tub of water turned a shade of blue by a block of Reckitt's blue-bag, a dab of which also served as the treatment for bee stings. When the task of dealing with the second lot of baby napkins, plus keeping a mischievous toddler away from the fire, proved too much for Ruth, a fully electric system – washing machine and hot water tank – was installed in the washhouse at number 17 Sutherland Street. For a while it stood out as the model laundry in the area, and the envy of many other women who still had to light the copper fire every Monday.

But that was decades ago now. Some time in the past the back area of the house had been remodeled by a later owner, with a new laundry incorporated into the main house along with a larger modernized bathroom and a bigger kitchen with room for a dishwasher and other appliances. Mary wished her mother could have enjoyed such amenities. These days, Ruth's model laundry would be considered substandard.

Back then, Sutherland Street was fortunate in another way too. It was situated in one of the early areas of Waimamae to benefit from the new sewage system – a matter of geography rather than his position in the town management, William was quick to point out whenever the subject came up. Some outer parts of the town still relied on a weekly night-cart collection in which full cans were swapped for empties – the inspiration for some humour among young males. Georgie once, when he thought no adult was within hearing, recited a short verse that included the rhymes honey, money and runny along with the forbidden 'dunny'. "George!" came their father's voice from around the corner of the house, followed by the bristling figure himself. He hauled the boy off by the ear to meet the inevitable punishment.

With Number 17's lavvy now incorporated into the bathroom, a trip outside the back door was no longer necessary, and 'going to the bathroom' became a more genteel though less precise term than it had been previously. At other houses, the improvement took the form of a small room off the back porch, sometimes combined with the laundry.

But elsewhere, in areas further from the town centre and more sparsely populated, a 'run down the garden path' was still required. Ruakumara Road, situated on the outskirts, still had some years to wait before the sewage line reached far enough in that direction.

"And this here's the wharepaku," said Ana on Mary's first visit, waving a hand to indicate a tiny wooden shed sitting behind the large garage-sized building at the end of the drive that ran beside the house. She had already mentioned someone called Hemi lived in there – Hemi's whare, she called it – but he was out in his boat fishing.

Now Ana opened the door of the place she called the wharepaku and motioned Mary to mount the step and look in. Mary wondered why, but it seemed important to her friend, so she complied.

"Be careful in here," Ana instructed, "you see these nails in the walls?" Mary looked. Overlapping weatherboards made up the sides of the tiny room, and set against the back wall was the bench seat containing the usual oval shaped hole with a wooden lid. At what appeared to be random spots, large nails had been partially driven into the wallboards, so they protruded several inches. Apart from the fact one held a bundle of small book-sized squares cut from copies of the *Waimamae Guardian*, she could see no reason for the projections. Ana, however, apparently considered them important.

"Don't, whatever you do, pull any of these nails."

"Why not?" Mary had an awful vision of one of them coming out in her hand and the structure collapsing – a bit like when

Georgie flicked the key tile in his carefully constructed domino run, resulting in the sequential disintegration of the whole pattern. The truth however, if she could believe it, turned out to be far worse. Ana, a serious look on her face as she did so, revealed the reason.

"There's one of them that, if you pull it, will make the can fly out!"

"No it wouldn't." Mary's reaction of disbelief was instant. It sounded like the sort of thing Georgie would tell her, and she knew better than to believe him. Well, most of the time now, anyway.

"It will so."

Mary looked at her friend. The look on Ana's face intensified – her head jutted forward and a pinched look formed about her eyes as she insisted. Mary still couldn't believe any of the nails would have any mechanical connection to the can. On the other hand, had Ana ever lied to her before? Not that she knew. She stood in the doorway of the tiny room thinking, weighing the two sides of the dilemma; Ana's apparent fear together with her greater worldliness and apparent trustworthiness, against what Ruth would advise her when asked to rule on one of Georgie's similar claims – "use your common sense." Much as she wanted to be loyal to her friend, her mother's counsel won.

"I don't believe it," she said, and reached out her hand to the closest nail. Ana backed a couple of paces down the path.

In spite of remnants of doubt remaining, Mary touched it lightly. Nothing moved. She tugged at the nail. It stayed firm, as did everything else in the structure. She tried another, then another, till she'd pulled them all. Unless she'd missed the vital one, it looked as though she'd been right. She stepped back down onto the path and said, "I pulled them all, nothing happened."

Ana just shrugged. But it seemed to Mary that she looked at her differently, and from that time on the two of them were best friends.

It was after the circus came to town when Mary and Ana first planned what they'd do in their lives.

"I'm going to be a trapeze artist," Ana said, throwing one hand above her head in a gesture of graceful triumph and inclining from the waist in a slight bow to acknowledge the future applause.

Mary believed her. She could imagine Ana flying high in the air, ankles hooked around a slender silver bar, her hair trailing beneath her so far above the sawdust-covered ring. She saw her friend launching herself from the relative safety of a tall platform, making daring leaps between one swinging bar and another. She heard the gasps rise from the spectators as Ana released herself at the peak of her arc, completing a somersault before being caught by the reaching hands of a precision-timed partner swinging toward her, and the sounds of release of tension as she regained the platform. She could see Ana in short glittering costumes – pale blue, silver, gold – setting off her friend's slim brown body. Best of all, she could hear the applause, the whistles and roar coming at the end of the performance as Ana stood once again on the safe surface of the circus ring, her glittering cape again around her shoulders, one arm held aloft to invite and acknowledge the audience's appreciation of yet another flawless performance.

"And a tight-rope walker."

Mary could see that too. She longed to say she'd be one too; they'd both do it together. They'd be twin stars of the flying trapeze and daring champions of the high wire. But underneath the thrill of the dream she knew it wouldn't be for her. It couldn't be. She wasn't talented in the same way as Ana – she'd have to settle for something less daring, less glamorous.

"I'll be the ring-master. I'll announce you." Mary threw out her arm in a flamboyant gesture. "Ana, the most graceful, the most daring of the aerial artistes in her death-defying routine."

"Ring-master? You?" scorned Georgie. "You'll be lucky if they let you be the clown who follows the elephant with a broom and a scoop."

Wasn't that like Georgie, always spoiling things for her. Mary felt the familiar feelings of annoyance and frustration, which often went along with their times together – when she made the mistake of sharing with him her hopes or dreams. She stood staring at her brother, trying to think of an equally crushing retort, but nothing suitable came.

"Mary Glary," he taunted further, laughing at the look on her face. "Mary Glary, oh so scary." But Ana linked her arm in hers and drew her away. After a minute or two, when she'd calmed down, Mary knew it didn't matter, not really. Somewhere in the circus there'd be a place for her. Whatever it was, there'd be the two of them – Ana and her – they'd be in it together. Let Georgie laugh, he didn't know, but she did. With Ana, she could do it – the two of them could achieve anything they set out to do. She turned away and walked off with her friend.

Along with Ana, she held onto their dream throughout the rest of the year, despite Georgie's laughter.

Playing in the school grounds, skating, swimming in the river. The school and church galas.

You and I, Ana, we did them all. Together.

TWELVE

It's Your Number

Mary giggled as she lay on her back, hands stretched behind her head so they just touched the raised edge of the concrete, her toes pointing downward in an effort to gain a further half-inch. A stalk of paspalum tickled her right foot. Beside her, a yard away on her left, Ana lay in a similar position, also stretching in her attempt to bridge the space between the concrete pad in front of Room Three and the board marking the edge of the pit of sawdust containing the jungle gym. Saturday afternoon pretty much guaranteed they'd have the climbing frame to themselves, without having to give way to children from the younger classes and today, as far as they could see, they had the whole school grounds to themselves.

"We're closer than last time," Ana raised her head to peer at her feet. She sat up and bent forward, her hand easily reaching past her toes. Mary stayed lying down – she knew her arms didn't stretch all the way.

"I've got this far to go." Ana spread her thumb and forefinger to specify the distance, then extended the gap, "Last time it was this much."

"How far for me?" Mary knew the span between Ana's fingers would widen still more. Perhaps two hands spaced apart were still needed to indicate the difference in her case – Ana's longer limbs gave her many an advantage.

The two relaxed and flopped back again, each using a bent

arm to shield their eyes from the brightness of the early afternoon.

"I can hear an aeroplane, but I can't see it."

"Me too." Mary used both hands to form binocular-type circles around her eyes and searched the sky.

"There it is – almost straight above us."

Mary adjusted the lift of her hands and located the speck that was the source of the drone.

"It'll be Johnny Lamb in his bi-plane." Mary didn't really know, but she'd heard her father make a similar statement and knew there weren't more than a single handful of possibilities. Most of the planes using the aerodrome were working machines used for topdressing. Sometimes when they were operating close to town she'd seen them, scooting not far above the hills, a trail of fertilizer spreading out in their wake and drifting down slowly to settle on farmland. This one, though, was high and making a slow circle directly above the town.

"What's the silver...?" Both girls sat up and shouted simultaneously.

"Leaflets."

They leapt to their feet, their eyes not leaving the sight of the tiny tumbling objects catching the light as they turned and twisted on their slow descent. At ground level there was just an occasional lazy breeze, enough to cause a few hairs to brush across Mary's face and to riffle the sticky fronds of the paspalum grass on the surface of the field. Higher up, the glittering specks were drifting a little to the north. They needed to judge the landing area just right.

"I think that patch is coming our way."

"Stay here till we're sure." Three times before, in Mary's

memory, there'd been a pamphlet drop above the town, and the falling sheets were subject to the whims of the wind – at one moment apparently certain to land at one place, then being whisked away to alight a distance further in any direction. Once, they held an advertisement for the Agricultural and Pastoral show held each year at the show-grounds in Farm Road, and on another occasion each bore an individual number that might prove to be a lucky one when presented at the ticket box outside the big top of the visiting circus. The third time, Georgie scored a free ice-block when he'd retrieved a specially marked leaflet from the top of Mr Gladstone's hedge.

Being already in the grounds of the school gave the girls a large catchment area, and at present they had it on their own. It wouldn't stay that way, they knew. As children around the town spotted the falling sheets the shouts would go up, spread, and there'd be feet running and bicycles pedalled in the direction of the apparent drop zone. Any open space looking as though it could be a likely landing place would quickly attract many others. Mary knew that as the leaflets dropped the final few feet her efforts were unlikely to yield a reward if there were larger contestants, particularly more agile boys, ready to launch themselves upwards to snatch away the prize she'd been targeting. But today, the thought came to her, some of the likely opponents would be at the picture theatre because today's matinee was a western. A week earlier, when the printed list of movies showing at the Majestic for the current month arrived in the letterbox along with the day's post, Georgie gave out a whoop, and said "Apache – I'm going to that one." At the same time Mary knew she'd give it a miss. It was an easy decision – they were each allowed to go to just one session a month and The Belles of St Trinians sounded a lot better to her than Georgie's choice.

"Stay here, I think we'll get some." Ana's eyes remained on the tumbling papers. A rush of sound came from behind as two bicycles sped in the Fergusson Street gate and were dumped on the grass. Two boys came toward them but Ana waved them off. "You go over there," she ordered pointing to the opposite side of the field and, to Mary's surprise, they moved off without a word. If she'd said it, they wouldn't have listened.

The pamphlets descended twisting end over end, side over side. Mary and Ana moved a dozen paces in order to intercept the first, then scrambled to retrieve a further few landing nearby.

"What's this?" Ana pointed to a number printed at the bottom right-hand corner.

"Esplanade shops festival week. Match your number with one in the window of a participating shop, and win a prize," Mary read. "Hey, we could be lucky." Georgie, when she showed it to him, would be sorry he'd decided to go to the pictures. Or perhaps not – you never knew with Georgie.

The boys returned to pick up their bikes. One held what looked like a single piece of paper in his hand.

"How many did you get?" Ana asked.

"Just one."

"We got five," said Ana, "here you are." She held out a sheet to the one with empty hands.

"I hope it didn't have a lucky number," Mary said as the boys walked off.

"We've got two each," Ana replied, "it's enough."

Of the shops along the Esplanade, only the Black and White

Milk Bar was open. A quiet spell between customers allowed Jenny Gibbs to mop the alternating lino tiles that inspired its name. The two girls parked their bicycles in the stand outside and started along the footpath.

Despite the closed doors, the owners of several shops were in their windows setting up displays for festival week. In the double width frontage of McConnell's Drapery stood Nancy McConnell, still better known to most of the residents of Waimamae as Nancy Turner, which she'd been till two months earlier and her marriage to Wes, the eldest of the three McConnell boys. As Mary and Ana arrived on the other side of the glass, Nancy pulled the jacket of a mushroom-coloured costume from a standing model with its bottom half already stripped. She looked around at the two girls, grinned, and slipped a blue floral summer dress over the bare form. The talk around the town said Nancy was under orders not to leave denuded figures on display for more than a minute at the most, and not at all if possible. The ruling came about after a recent episode with a group of boys commonly described as larrikins, and a subsequent complaint from Miss Purdey who happened to be on the Esplanade at the time.

Nancy saw the leaflets clasped in the girls' hands and pointed to a tiered stand in the middle space of the window. Usually it held smaller items such as sewing and craft goods – thread, skeins of wool, embroidery kits – as well as accessories such as handbags and belts. It also served to keep the genders separate – women's wear on the right, men's on the left. Now Mary and Ana saw printed numbers on strips of paper set in front of some of the items. Together they leaned forward to try to spot a match.

Window-shoppers along the Esplanade were generally few on a Saturday afternoon unless there was a regatta on the river or some other event brought people to town. Otherwise, an occasional carful of people broke their travel between Robertstown to the south and Shipton to the north, stopping to visit the public toilets and get a soda; or a pod of motorcyclists clad in wool-lined black leather jackets, some sporting a silk scarf, roared up to the Black and White and stood outside sipping milk shakes before remounting and weaving off down the strip and across the bridge. Local lore also had it, probably reliably, that Miss Purdey had recently bailed up the Mayor at the entrance to the Bank of New Zealand and demanded he take action about the latter. Milk Bar cowboys should not be permitted to ride through the streets of Waimamae, she stated in a tone leaving no room for argument, so Mr Stevens assured her if she would write to him about it he would be sure to put the matter on the agenda for the next meeting of the Borough Council.

Today, other pamphlet-waving children and one or two adults had also arrived at the main street and were working their way along from shop to shop. The usual quarter hour rush before the matinee at the Majestic was already well past, and the corresponding burst of picture-goers back out onto the street when the film finished wouldn't come for another hour and a half, but the added groups made the scene look as though it were a weekday morning.

By the time they'd checked several more windows Mary and Ana knew their numbers and could move on after a quick look.

"Probably some of the shops haven't put theirs in yet," Mary said after their check of two side by side failed to reveal any numbers, and only one other person also looking confirmed they'd found a match. That was all right – if necessary they could repeat their search on Monday after school.

The window of McKenzies, who stocked just about everything and where the girls sometimes spent any money they received on birthdays, didn't reward them today. They moved on to Quarto Stationery & Books, and Harvey's Hardware 'The haven for the home handyman', which were next to each other near the corner of Day Street.

"Isn't that one of yours?" asked Ana, pointing. "Haven't you got 429?"

Mary nodded. "I think so," she said.

"It's what you've been saying. Look, you've won something."

Mary crouched so she was almost level with the floor of the window and held out one of the sheets so she could compare the two printed numbers. "They're the same," she said, still not believing the object behind the numbered strip could be hers.

"Told you so."

"It's an autograph book," said Mary, reading the ornate curling word written in silver on the dark red cover, a feeling of wonder sweeping through her – she'd won something. There was something to tell Georgie, and it was better than an ice-block too. But Ana didn't have anything. "We can share it if you like," she offered. Ana laughed.

"Don't be silly, it's yours."

"But you saw the number first."

"It doesn't matter. It's your number. Besides, I'm going to win my own."

"Yes, you will," agreed Mary, "you have to, you're the lucky one! Let's find your prize."

The two looked through the marked items – a pencil box with sliding top, wooden rulers, packets of rubber-bands, a small address book – but none of the attached tickets coincided with the figures they wanted to see.

"Maybe yours is here," said Mary, moving to Harvey's. Ana would be the first person invited to write in her autograph book, she decided, but that wasn't enough. Now she had her prize she was even more determined her friend should find one too.

Ana spotted it almost right away. "Neat-o!"

"You've got one too?"

Ana pointed to a postcard-sized picture surrounded by a narrow wooden frame.

"Who is it?" Mary didn't recognize the people standing in front of a green car, the peak of a high mountain rising behind them.

"Nobody," said Ana, "it's just a picture. You put whatever you like in the frame." Of course.

"What will you put in it?"

"I'll give it to Kui."

THIRTEEN

The Cleverest Person in Waimamae

Kui, she knew everything about Waimamae. It seemed she was familiar with all of the long-established families in the area and where each of its members fitted into the social fabric of the town. At the same time there were probably very few in the community, the Pakeha or non-Maori side at least, who would have recognized her – even fewer who could come up with a name.

She knew all the stories about the town, would fill in details when the memories of others faltered, and provide elaboration to make a sketchy account come to life. Kui could describe the best places along the riverbank to wait for whitebait, and what days and times to be there. How to strip and treat flax for taniko weaving, how and when to plant the garden for best results.

And a lot more besides. Including every plant and what it could do. How it should be picked, at what time of day, in what location, in order for it to effect a cure. Every time Mary visited Ana's place there was a pot on the stove with leaves or bark being boiled in it.

"Kahikatea for Nanny Henare's water," Kui would tell them.

"Miro, for Mr Ratapu's leg."

"Koromiko, and never you mind why, or who for!"

"Kui?"

"Yes, Mere?" Kui looked at her, and sat down on one of the wooden kitchen chairs and indicated Mary should sit next to her. She wasn't like other grown-ups. When you talked to her she stopped working and looked as though she intended to listen; but perhaps this time she just needed a rest.

"Nothing," Mary said. She had taken some time to get up the courage to ask her question, but as soon as she addressed Kui, she changed her mind. She didn't want anyone else laughing at her, the way they'd done at home when she talked about the worry niggling at her.

Kui looked at Ana. "Put your cup in the sink and go and see if you can find me an onion in the garden."

"There are some in the vegetable box," Ana replied, starting to move to the shelf under the bench.

"Never mind those. I want a fresh one. Kia tere, hurry up now," she added as Ana hesitated.

Mere pushed back her chair to join her friend, but Kui put out her hand to stop her. "You stay here and finish your drink." There was only a small mouthful left, but Mary sat back down.

"Now," said Kui when Ana had leapt off the back verandah and they could hear her steps running across the back lawn, "what is it, little Mere?"

There was no pulling out now – Kui knew something worried her. Mary couldn't imagine her laughing at what she would say, and perhaps she could help.

"Do you have anything," her eyes went to the row of jars on the top shelf, "to heal leprosy?" She was right about Kui, the old woman's deep brown eyes didn't as much as blink as she looked back at her.

"Let me see, I might do. Who is it for? You or someone else?" A sense of relief rippled through Mary's body. Kui knew of a cure. She'd been sure if anyone did, it would be Kui. Ever since Mr and Mrs Field talked to them at Sunday School the thought of the dreaded disease had eaten at her. The pictures the missionary couple showed the group of horrified children weeks before were still vivid in her mind. Perhaps they were even more graphic than the ones displayed at the time, because those were in black and white and Mary could see them now in full colour. Dark brown limbs crippled, covered with ulcerated sores. Twisted feet without toes. Deformed hands with no fingers, faces with lumpy patches stripped of their colour. Mary's shaking hand took one of the envelopes printed with "Leprosy Mission – your donation can make a difference to the lives of sufferers of leprosy." At home she emptied her purse of the few coins it held, and asked her parents to add more. The following Sunday she put the envelope, along with the regular three-penny coin, into the offering plate. It should have satisfied her conscience, but the pictures didn't disappear from her mind. She imagined what it would be like to be one of the children hopping along on a tree-branch crutch, one leg dangling footless and useless. It so horrified her she tried to banish the sight, but it refused to go, and she started to examine her skin for the first sign of lumpiness or erosion. It was infectious – whole families got it – she might pass it on to her mother and father, and to Georgie. Or to Ana.

"Lots of people in the Solomon Islands have got it," Mary said, tears threatening to overflow her lower eyelids, "it can't be far away because Mr and Mrs Field have been there."

Kui reached out and gently removed Mary's right hand from

her opposite arm where she scratched at a spot near the elbow.

"Of all the things I've been asked for help with, over all the years, I never saw a case of that yet." Her voice was steady and calm, matter of fact. "It's lucky there's none of it here in New Zealand, nei?"

"Are you sure there's none here?"

"As sure as there are stars in the sky, and I looked up at Te Rangi just last night." Mary could hear Ana running back to the house, and felt the weight of worry lift. She would be safe – her friend wouldn't be left without her toes, or with stumps for hands, because of her.

"I'll tell you what," Kui had something else to say, "if you ever find someone who does have it, tell them to come to me – I reckon some of my manuka mixture would be just the thing. Ana sprang through the door holding a green onion.

"Does have what?" she asked.

"Anything," said Kui, "manuka's good for lots of things."

Mary knew she'd been right. Kui had to be the cleverest person in Waimamae. She'd heard her mother and Mrs McCaskill say after Mrs Wickham's funeral the doctors could do nothing for her. Now she wondered why everyone didn't go to see Kui.

There was always something new to see at Ana's place. Quite often a bird sat in one of the cages hanging from one of the beams supporting the back verandah – sometimes with a wing or leg strapped up, or a pad of leaves over an eye.

"Kui, there's a mynah bird in the big cage today. It's got a bandage on it."

"Ae, Mere. It's hurt its wing."

"Will it get better?"

"Ae."

"The tui is still there."

"That one's just about ready to go. Another day or two." Kui let out a chuckle. "Unless the two of them talk each other to death first."

It seemed to Mary, of all the people she knew, no one else understood as much about so many things.

"Kui, we climbed up Puketapu and we found a cave. The entrance is just a hole you have to crawl into. It goes right down into the ground."

"Ae, I know it. It is Mahuika's place. Mahuika, nana te ahi. She of the Fire. You keep away from there – she does not welcome visitors."

"Rupena and Georgie went in."

"Whakarongo mai! Listen to me. Never go in that cave."

It was a funny thing about Kui – despite the fact she knew so much about the people of the town, Mary knew she seldom went out. Except to the places where she picked her plants, or to the marae just down the road. But she knew every spot, every road and street. If you talked about any place in the district she'd close her eyes, appear to concentrate for a moment or two.

"Ae. I can see it," she'd say.

FOURTEEN

But Georgie Went

A noise rose in volume and pitch – the drone sounding throughout the late August afternoon.

"Fire siren," whooped Georgie, "hot dog!" and ran out the kitchen door. A moment later he tore back in, raced through the house, threw open the front door and stood on the verandah. "I can't see any smoke," he said, running back to lift the receiver hanging on the left side of the wooden telephone box mounted on the wall of the passage near the kitchen.

His mother slid the biscuit tray into the oven and wiped her hands on the half apron tied around her waist.

"George, what are you doing?" she called.

Georgie didn't answer and Mary wondered once again how come her brother got away with more than she ever could. Failure to respond immediately to a question put by an adult was enough to lead to a reprimand from either of their parents, but Georgie flouted small rules with apparent impunity – at least as far as his mother was concerned. With his right hand he grasped the handle on the side of the box and wound it around several times.

"Georgie, Mum's talking…" Mary began, but her brother waved his hand to hush her as he concentrated on listening, the earpiece of the receiver clapped hard to his left ear.

"Okay," he said into the mouthpiece, "no, that's all I wanted. He went to replace the receiver, then said as an afterthought,

"Thanks," before replacing it on the hook.

"George, what are you up to?" Ruth tried again.

"The fire's at McNaughton's shed," said Georgie, as though the response provided sufficient answer.

"How do you know?" asked Mary.

"The woman at the telephone exchange, of course," said Georgie, "the operators always know where the fire is. They take the calls and put them through to the fire station. You don't even have to ask – if you ring after the siren's sounded they tell you as soon as they answer." He ran through the kitchen. As he did so, he reached out and pulled at the apron strings dangling behind his mother's back.

"George…" she tried again, but he was out the door and picking up his bike where he'd discarded it beside the garage.

"…be careful," his mother said, calling out a futile warning as Georgie threw his leg over the bar and started down the drive, leaving in his wake a clacking sound that increased in frequency as he sped up. The day before, he'd taken Mary's Snap cards, saying some were missing so it was no use as a game anymore, and threaded them through the spokes of his wheels. Now when he rode he could be heard for half a block in either direction.

"Is it true, Mum? If you ring up, do they really tell you where a fire is?"

"Probably," her mother answered. She'd heard stories about how 'the girls on the exchange', as they were usually referred to no matter how old they were, often anticipated the needs of Waimamae subscribers.

"You're calling the Watsons? They're not at home, they're at Mahoney's. I'll put you through there."

"Doctor Anderson is already on a call-out. If it's urgent I'll put you through to Doctor Cullen. Otherwise I'll give him a message to call you when he gets back."

So Georgie was right.

"Mum, can I go to McNaughton's too, to see the fire?"

"No, you stay here. They don't want a lot of people looking and getting in the way."

"But Georgie went."

"All the more reason for you to stay – that'll be one fewer." As Ruth reached up to the top cupboard to take down a tin of Golden Syrup, her apron slid down her body and fell to the floor. She shook her head, as she stooped to receive it, "When will that boy grow up?"

— FIFTEEN —

By Hook or by Crook

As Mary said goodbye and went to leave through the kitchen door, Kui passed her the small book.

"Have you put something in it?"

"Ae. You can look at it when you get home."

She'd have to. Mary knew she was already late. She and Ana had been playing *Tour of New Zealand* in Ana's bedroom. They'd each won a game and were onto a third as the decider. The blue button selected from Kui's sewing basket to serve as Mary's counter had just got onto the top level of the track when she noticed the alarm clock on Ana's dressing table showed it was almost five o'clock. She was supposed to be home by five, and the cycle ride between their two houses took her ten minutes even with a good tail wind. She hesitated, not wanting to give away her present advantage of half a dozen squares, but Ana picked up the two buttons and the die, and lifted the sides of the board, folding it.

"You won. You were ahead."

It was generous of her, Mary knew. And lucky for her. Ana had a habit of throwing a six and surging into the lead in the home straight.

As she left the house, Mary took the book Kui held out to her and slipped it into her pocket.

"Thank you," she said, but Kui dismissed it with a movement of her hand and the slight upward jerk of her head she used as wordless acknowledgement.

"Haere ra, Mere. Hoki mai ano."

"E noho ra, Kui." Mary took pride in the fact she knew the correct response to the farewell. After the first time getting it wrong Ana explained it to her. She was the one going; Kui was staying.

She had to wait till dinner was over, the dishes washed and dried, and she could go to her bedroom, before Mary had the opportunity to take the autograph book from her pocket and leaf through the different coloured pages.

Right in the top corner of the first page – the yellow one pasted on the inside of the hard cardboard cover – in Ana's printing were the words *By hook or by crook, I'll be first in this book*. When Ana first wrote it, Mary looked at it with admiration. She wouldn't have thought of anything as clever as that – Ana always knew what to say. But Ana dismissed her praise.

"Nah. I didn't make it up. I saw it somewhere before."

"You didn't sign it. You're supposed to write your name in an autograph book."

"I don't need to. You know who I am." But Ana took the book and added a capital A below the words. Then she said "Hold on," and flipped through the pages. When she handed it back there was a further entry – this time squeezed into the bottom outside corner of the sheet pasted onto the back cover. *By hook or by crook, I'll be last in this book too.*

When Mary gave the book to Georgie with the request for his contribution, he opened it, saw Ana's words in the front and thought for a moment. He turned to the back and frowned when he saw the matching verse.

"I'll think about it," he said, and disappeared into his bedroom.

When she got the book back a day later, the two middle pages were used. On the left he'd printed a verse –

The night was dark and stormy
The billy goat was blind
He backed into a barbed wire fence
And scratched his never-you-mind.

The facing page held Georgie's signature – his full name and the date.

"Keep that," he told her. "One day, when I'm famous, it will be worth a lot of money."

But now she could see what Kui had recorded. Mary turned the pages with expectation. The words penned in dark blue ink stood out on the light blue page. The handwriting was immaculate.

E Mere.
Haere atu koe. Kia kaha to ako.
Ka hoki mai ki te mahana o te kainga.
na Katarina Te Amo

Oh! Mary's first reaction was disappointment, followed by a sense of shame. Within the dedication there were words she knew. Haere atu was go away, hoki mai meant come back, and kainga was where you lived. She knew what they meant on their own, but she couldn't put them together into something she could understand. She took the opened page to her father and handed it to him without saying anything. William studied it, then gave it back.

"It's nice of Mrs Te Amo to write in your book."

"Kui wrote it," Mary informed him.

Her father nodded, and pointed to the bottom line. "Katarina Te Amo. It's her signature."

"Is that her name?" Mary had only ever heard her called Kui. Perhaps it was short for Katarina. She'd ask Ana about it. "Do you know what the rest says?"

"No. Perhaps Ana can tell you."

Of course, she'd ask her tomorrow. Mary was glad he didn't advise her to ask Kui herself. Somehow it didn't seem appropriate to do that, and she'd have to admit she didn't understand. But her father was right. Someone would be able to tell her.

Ana looked at the words during morning interval.

"I don't know," she said and went to return it, but Mary pushed the book back into her hands.

"You must know. Look – there's haere, and hoki mai like in the song…" The two of them, and other girls in the class, sometimes sang that song along with other ones as they sat cross-legged on the grass, a pair of short ti rakau sticks in their hands passing from one to another in time to the beat of the tune.

"Yeah, it's something about going and coming back, but I don't know what it means all together." Ana closed the book, passed it back to her, and skipped off to join Wiki and Aroha who were bouncing a tennis ball between them. "Ask Mr Paratai," she called back.

That was a good idea. Mary went to Room Six and looked in the door. The teacher held a duster and was rubbing words off the blackboard. He saw her and beckoned her in. Mary handed him the book opened at the right page.

"Can you please tell me what this means?"

Mr Paratai looked over the words and didn't reply immediately. He read them over several times and Mary's hopes raised – he must be working out how to translate the message in the best way. Then he returned the book.

"Sorry," he said, "I'm not sure. I don't know all the words. You'd better ask the person who gave it to you."

Mary left the classroom disappointed. She still didn't want to ask Kui and admit she didn't know.

"One day," she told herself, "I'll find out." She could ask Hemi, but somehow it seemed the same as asking Kui. "I'll learn how to read it myself," she decided, and feeling better at having made her decision she went back to where the other girls in her class were playing.

Ana flopped down onto the step beside her, breathing fast from the exertion of the game.

"Mr Paratai didn't know. He said he doesn't know all the words."

Ana gave one of her shrugs. She didn't look surprised.

"You'll have to ask Kui."

"It's okay. I've got another idea." Mary thought for a moment. "I didn't know her real name. I thought it was Kui. It's what everyone calls her. You, Hemi, me too – she told me to call her that."

"But she's got to have a name," Ana answered. Do you think she goes to the bank and says she's Kui?"

"Why not?" Mary was confused. "Isn't it short for Katarina?" She expected Ana to confirm it, but her friend shook her head.

"Nup," she looked amused by the idea. "It's short for kuia. It's what you call old women."

Mary looked at her. She didn't know whether to believe it. Why would anyone want to be called old woman? But Ana didn't appear to be joking.

"Then isn't it rude, to call her that?"

"Nup. It's like grandmother. It's like…" Ana thought, "a compliment – to their age, and all they know."

That wasn't so bad then. Mary remembered her mother's mother once pointing to her white hair and telling Georgie she wanted respect because of it. Now Gran was gone and Mary seldom saw her father's mother who lived near Wellington; she'd sometimes considered Ana lucky to have a grandmother.

Kui. Kui. She repeated the word in her mind. Yes, it was nicer sounding than Grandma.

The bike-rides we went on – all around Waimamae.
Cycling along the old Waimamae Coach Road
and climbing to our favourite place on the hill
overlooking the town.

You came to my birthday parties.

Remember me and birthdays? They never went well
with me, did they?

It's no wonder they're not something I've ever looked
forward to particularly eagerly.

BACKWARDS INTO THE FUTURE

SIXTEEN

Mary Peary's Doom Day

The bell clanged and Mary stopped turning her end of the rope. It dropped from the peak of its arc and the two girls jumping tangled in the aborted circle.

"You can have first turn at lunch time," Wiki promised. Mary nodded. Since it was her skipping rope they were using she should have gone first this time, but she didn't care – she'd passed over the opportunity willingly. The half-pint of milk they all had to drink at playtime every day sat uneasily in her stomach.

Others didn't mind the rule. In fact, most appeared to relish it. Many of the boys in the class always ran to grab theirs from the crate, pulling off the cardboard cap and drinking from the bottle. Some of the girls were just as keen, but Mary followed a lot less readily. She'd have left it altogether but for the watchful eyes of this week's milk monitor who was charged with the responsibility of ensuring everyone got theirs whether they wanted it or not.

Today, as she usually did, she'd poked her finger into the middle of the top, depressing the small circle inscribed in the centre, and pushed a straw right to the bottom. It was the method she used in the hope of avoiding the thick cream forming the top inch and a half in the neck of the bottle. If the milk was kept cool, the way she could have it at home straight from the refrigerator, it wouldn't be so bad. But by the time the crates of half-size bottles were transported from the dairy factory to the school, and waited till morning playtime, it was always warm, and the band of cream sat there – a plug of almost jelly-like consistency that must be endured if it couldn't be escaped. "Shake it," she'd been told over and over, "mix it through and you won't notice." But she did notice, she always did, so she drank with the straw at the bottom and hoped to be able to replace the bottle in among the empties without the remaining amount being noticed. Sometimes, when one of the larger boys acted as monitor, he'd punch out the top, tip back his head, and finish it off for her, often adding she'd left the best part. But today the self-righteous Eric was on duty and, since the responsibility of the position meant he'd had to finish his own, she'd been told to suck up the clotted remnant. Right now it taunted her from the pit of her puku.

With the noise of the bell fading, Mary took the two wooden handles of the skipping rope and wound the length of the cord around them as she ran up the concrete steps and into Room Eight. One of the larger boys racing past bumped into her, knocking her off balance and sending her flying sideways. In the half-second before she hit the front desk she glimpsed a pair of bare feet close to her face, then felt the numbing thud of what Georgie later referred to as wood on wood.

The Headmaster's face was uncomfortably close to her own, and someone must be holding her head because it didn't move when she tried to shift it.

"Good, you're awake. Don't try to sit up. It's best you stay there. We've called your mother, she's on her way to take you to the hospital to have it looked at." 'It', apparently referred to her head – she could feel stinging at the back.

A ride in a taxi was an unusual occurrence – the whole family usually biked everywhere – so such events were all the more memorable. This one, though, barely registered. She sat in the back seat as the car moved quickly through the streets, across the bridge, and up the incline toward the hospital. Ruth's arm supported Mary's neck, her hand holding the towel that was wrapped around her head. The taxi driver kept turning around to check on them. He appeared anxious to get them there.

"Is it hurting?" asked her mother.

Mary nodded her head. "I feel sick." The driver increased the speed even more, and the car thumped into a pothole as it turned into Gordon Road.

"It's the shock. You'll feel better when they look at it."

"No, it was the milk," Mary put her hand on her stomach and tried to keep the nausea down. When the car door opened and her mother helped her out she brushed off the steadying hand on her arm, headed to the nearby strip of garden, leaned over and emptied the half-pint over a patch of petunias. Now she felt better.

"It's the shock," Ruth repeated, dabbing at Mary's mouth with a handkerchief as they walked to the entrance. Mary started to respond then let the denial slip back into her throat. It was no use. She'd tried before to convince her mother, and the teachers, to no avail. Everyone knew milk is good for you. She wished her stomach knew it too.

The waiting area was overwarm and smelled too much like the school dental clinic. The chemical smell set up an uneasy feeling in her teeth, adding to the throbbing at the back of her head and the sharp taste of vomit in her mouth.

"No, I meant her birthdate, not today's date," a woman in

a starched uniform explained to her mother. When Ruth responded, the woman looked over at her and spoke in a tone similar to the one used by other middle-aged women when her mother introduced Mary as "my baby".

"You did this on your birthday! What a shame. It's not fair, is it? I suppose it will stop you having a party."

It didn't. The after-school event went ahead, though with Mary spending most of the time sitting watching as her guests played games on the back lawn. When she woke the following morning she found she couldn't remember much about it. All she could come up with was a faraway memory of girls asking if she'd had stitches in her head, and how many. She saw a row of birthday cards displayed on the mantelpiece in the front room, and some new books and ornaments were placed on her dresser.

The following year wasn't a lot better. The dozen guests at the afternoon party searched the back garden for pennies secreted in gaps between fence boards and under leaves and stones. Mary, once again excluded from participating, but this time because she'd planted the coins before going to school, stood advising "cold, warmer, hot," as her friends moved about. Georgie and his pals Rupena and Andy, removing themselves from association with such an event as a little girls' party, armed themselves with an iron club apiece and were at the end of the quarter-acre section near the plum tree knocking golf balls to each other. Taking a stance more suited to a fairway than a back lawn, Georgie sent one whizzing down the middle of the space, toward the house. Once again on her birthday Mary found herself prone, this time clutching her left eye.

The year after, Ruth insisted on Mary and her friends meeting at the Majestic for the Saturday matinee. Although that one went off without any major incident, on each subsequent anniversary for some years the day was greeted with a mixture of celebration and trepidation. Georgie teased her with a daily countdown from a couple of weeks out from the date.

"Only two weeks away. I wonder what you'll do this year!"

"Just seven days to go to doom-day." He'd extend the double vowel and put a fearful intonation on it.

"Mary Peary's doooom-day – now just a day away!"

Georgie had a nickname for everyone. Especially teachers. None of the pupils ever thought of Mr Brown as anything other than Broomhead Brown after Georgie dubbed him with the term because of his short bristly hair. Spearmint Spencer got her nickname because of Miss Olive Spencer's disgust for chewing gum being chewed in the playground. And Teddy-Bare Edwards earned his after Mr Edwards once took off his shirt at the school sports. Those ones stuck too – to be used ever after. Perhaps others also had a hand in introducing them, but in Mary's recollection of the times it was always her big brother who came up with them first.

Mrs Flint, however, was only ever called that. Perhaps it suited her so well no one felt the need for anything else. To Mary's secret delight, Georgie once called her 'Fatso Flint' at home, but his mother heard him. She forbade him to ever say it again, and he didn't – at least not in her hearing. It probably wouldn't have stuck anyway. For one thing, Mrs Flint's girth didn't need commenting on – it was self-evident – and the implied levity of the particular epithet didn't sit well with the steely reality.

Georgie. He always called you Ana Banana. He used to laugh when he saw us together.

"Here they are – Mary Peary and Ana Banana, the fruit salad sisters." You got your own back, though, by calling him Georgie Porgie. He hated it, because it stuck.

Georgie died on my birthday. It's years ago now.

SEVENTEEN

Dreams of Gold and Silver

The girls' flirtation with circus life was relatively brief. In spite of Georgie's scorn Mary and Ana rigged a trapeze made of rope and an old vacuum cleaner tube from a horizontal branch of the plum tree. After school and in weekends they'd take turns hanging upside down by their ankles, and swinging each other. A single trapeze, though, simply added to their frustration, and the dream faded further after the next visit of the big top the following year. What they remembered as romance and glamour didn't look the same. The glitter wasn't as sparkling, the colours not as bright. Had they missed the tired look of the costumes the first time around, and the mend in the Amazing Mitzi's tights?

Or perhaps they, Ana in particular, had other goals by then. Dreams of gold and silver. At the very least, expectations of bringing home the bronze.

The school film projector was large and noisy and, at best, generated flickering grainy images, some jumpy, in black and white. It also broke down at frequent intervals, and did so at least once on the occasion the replacement plan for their great career came to the two girls. This was supposed to be a sports day, but turned out to be the day following a three-day southerly. While the boys were out on the field watching Waimamae North play a visiting rugby team despite pools of water still lying on the ground, the girls – a combined group from two classes – were inside, permitted to watch a film on the old 16 millimetre machine.

"Six, five, four, three, two," they chanted as the lead-in numbers counted down to the start. Then the title flashed onto the screen – "Golden Girls".

A javelin arced across the sky, followed by a discus skimming through the air, and a shot put ball thudding into the ground. Then there were long legs running, gaining speed, taking off in a tense leap to land yards further on, sending sawdust scattering. Best of all, there were women, New Zealand women, on the winners' dais, having medals hung around their necks.

The trapeze was all but forgotten – abandoned for other equipment, usually just as makeshift. A broom handle for a javelin, a paint tin lid for a discus. Ana strained her ankle long jumping in the school grounds without a sawdust pit, but it didn't keep her down for long.

Together, with the aid of a treasured chart pinned to the wall of Mary's bedroom and pored over on many an afternoon after school, they learned the winning names and events.

Empire Games, Auckland 1950 – Yvette Williams, gold in the long jump, silver in the javelin. Jean Stewart, silver medal for 100 metres backstroke. June Schoch, silver in the 80 metre hurdles. Patricia Woodroffe, silver for individual foil. Silver medals for teams of New Zealand women in the 440 yards running relay, the 440 yards freestyle swimming relay. Bronze medals for more of the nation's women athletes in long jump, javelin, 80 metres hurdles, and high jump.

Helsinki Olympics, 1952 – Yvette Williams, gold for women's long jump. Jean Stewart, bronze medal for 100 metres backstroke.

British Empire and Commonwealth Games, Vancouver, 1954 – Yvette Williams, golds for shot put, long jump, and discus. Jean Stewart, silver medal for 100 metres backstroke.

They recited them as they practised the events in weekends and after school in the empty school grounds.

Mary was aware that Ana's discs soared when hers went flump. She knew her leg of the relay race always proved the slow one after Ana passed her the skipping-rope baton. After a while she settled mainly into being Ana's support person, content to measure her friend's leaps by means of Ruth's dressmaking tape measure – or a ball of knotted string after being forbidden to borrow the tape again.

"This is way past the last knot," she shouted, feeling even more excited than Ana showed at her own success. No doubt came into Mary's mind. Ana was the next Golden Girl – on her way to the top. Not the next Olympic Games, and probably not the one after, but definitely the one following that. Without doubt. Ana would be there, representing the nation. And, she, Mary, would be there too, to support her.

Ana – Do you remember the time something disappeared from our classroom? I remember because of something you said. I don't recall what was taken – perhaps someone's lunch money, maybe something as little as a missing pencil – but I've never forgotten your reaction.

Do you remember, Ana, what you said?

EIGHTEEN

Shark-tooth Earrings

Mrs Flint stood on the low platform at the front of the class-room. It had been stolen, she announced. Stolen. She repeated the word with all the gravity it demanded.

"Class, we have a thief in our midst."

Swollen feet planted a hip-width apart, moustache hairs quivering in indignation above her tight-set lips, she repeated the allegation, trying to shame the person responsible into owning up. Mary looked straight ahead, not daring to even glance around the room at her classmates, and hoping no one responded. Perhaps it was just lost. Maybe it would turn up, and they'd find nothing had been stolen at all. The way Mrs Flint put it, pointing out the loss as a failing within the class, Mary felt involved in the guilt. Judging by the silence around her and the few lowered heads she could see, her classmates, her friends, felt the same. Certainly no one would want to see another of their number so identified and exposed.

It wasn't until the bell released them into the playground for morning break that she felt she could breathe easily again. She was glad the person who did it, if anyone had done it, didn't speak up. Mrs Flint's verbal branding would have been as bad as a mark on the forehead saying 'THIEF'. Or having a hand cut off.

A small group of girls gathered, and Mary saw Ana standing with her head down. She went to join them, slipping into the circle next to Ana, their arms touching.

"Who do you think did it?" asked one.

Mary opened her mouth to voice her hope, "How do we know it was stolen?" when Ana spoke, a mutter directed at her feet.

"Dunno." Then she added, "I bet it was a Maori."

"Ana," Mary turned to her friend, about to protest, but Ana pulled away, put her arms around the shoulders of Wiki and Theresa and walked off. Mary started to go after them, but stopped. Without being able to put the realization into words, she knew for this time at least, she was shut out.

It was the same as when, in the following year, Mr Daniels asked how many of the class spoke Maori. No one put up a hand. The teacher looked puzzled, paused, then tried again.

"Nobody?"

Silence. Such a complete lack of sound was rare within the classroom. Usually there'd be something – someone shifting a piece of paper, pushing a pencil across a desktop, or moving in their seat.

"Surely some of you speak Maori? At least a little?"

Mary turned her head to look around. A good number of faces were lowered, eyes stared at desks, bodies were still – as though they were wooden figures carved as one piece along with their seats.

Mr Daniels smiled, as though the answer had come to him. "All right, if you can't speak it yourself, then how many of you can understand it?" Still no response and again he repeated his question.

Mary heard the silence continue, and wondered. On the foot-path outside the shops on the Esplanade, she'd see the old men in suits, carrying a walking stick; stooped women dressed head to foot in black, some with a tattooed chin, and wearing shark-tooth earrings. She'd hear them talk, and longed to understand their words, to know what they were saying. Then, of course, there was Kui. And Hemi. She looked at Ana. Ana knew – she could understand. Yet she didn't say. She wondered why she didn't speak up. Mary felt excited for her, and started to put up her own hand and volunteer on her behalf.

"Ana's grandmother speaks Maori – Ana understands." But Ana's head dropped as she saw Mary looking at her. She too stared at her desk without meeting her eyes, and Mary, her excitement for her friend fading into confusion, let the moment pass.

You couldn't have known then how much I ached too, how much I shared those hurts with you. I couldn't tell you then because at the time I didn't understand it myself – why I felt that way.

Ana, you'll remember Mr Daniels who taught us in standard 4. He's dead now – I heard he died a very old man a couple of years ago. I wonder if you recall something that happened in his class, the way I do.

He was telling us some legends, especially the one about how Maui went down into the underworld and tricked Mahuika into giving the power of fire to the human world by pulling out her fingernails.

Kui talked of Mahuika. You remember. She warned us not to go into the cave on Puketapu. The one Georgie and Rupena went into.

Mr Daniels told us why.

NINETEEN

A Boon and a Curse

"E toku tipuna, my ancestor. Grandmother. Ko Maui ahau. I am Maui, son of my mother Taranga.

The figure before him, immense in its presence though not much larger than the lad in physical stature, turned toward him and straightened. Maui forced himself to look into the piercing eyes of Mahuika.

"Grandmother, I come from the upper world with a request from your descendants. We have no fire on which to cook our food. I beg you, as keeper of fire, to supply the world with this gift for our use."

The figure regarded him for a long moment. It was a severe look that would have had others cowering in fear, but the young demi-god did not flinch. The woman saw his resolve, and judged his courage.

"Maui-Potiki, Maui-tikitiki-a-Taranga. Because you are my kin I will give you fire." She lifted her hands, brought them together, and from her outstretched fingers pulled out one of the long nails. "Take this, my fingernail, which will be a flame for you. Guard it carefully."

Maui took the gift out through the entrance to the underworld back into the world of light. He walked to a stream, plunged it into the water, and doused the flame. As it spat and lost its magic heat he turned and re-entered the domain of Mahuika.

In front of the forbidding presence once more, Maui adopted a look of apology overlaid with entitlement.

"Grandmother, I dropped it into a stream and the flame you entrusted to me has gone out. Your descendants are still in need of fire to cook their food, please again take pity on them."

Mahuika, having no reason to doubt the young man's story, plucked another of her fingernails and put it in his hands. Maui retreated from the dark of the underworld and again extinguished the flame in the water.

"Grandmother," he wailed again, repeating his story and renewing the request.

Once more the keeper of the fire granted his plea, and again Maui repeated his action. Time after time he plunged each succeeding nail into the water and doused the flame. Mahuika, her suspicions and temper rising at his growing insolence at each new approach, had soon given up all her fingernails and was persuaded by the pleading of the demi-god to pull out her toenails also.

"Grandmother, it has happened again. How can I return to my mother, your kin Taranga, and your descendants, without the fire they so desperately need."

By now, Mahuika was in a fury. She tore off the last remaining nail and flung it far away, beyond Maui's grasp, out of the entrance to the underworld, into the bushes beyond, where it set alight to the upper world – the forest, the land, and all things. So it was that fire came to the world of humans, proving to be both a boon and a curse.

We all laughed at the story, remember? Of course we did. Maui, the young lad, tricked his elder. We were children, and it wasn't often kids got one over on grown-ups.

Mr Daniels misunderstood. He got mad about it and told us the creation stories of any culture are not funny – not to be laughed at. They're serious explanations of how things came to be. There's no difference, he insisted, between those stories and the ones in the Bible.

I've thought a lot about that since.

I'm glad we had him for a teacher after Mrs Flint.

BACKWARDS INTO THE FUTURE

— TWENTY —

My Mokopuna Too

Mary remembered what she'd been meaning to ask Ana. The idea had come to her when she and her mother went into Stert's Jewellers after school the Friday before. As Ruth handed over the watch with the broken strap, then examined a tray holding possible replacements, Mary went along the glass-topped counter and looked down at the other goods on display inside the case.

A black velvet pad sat on a raised stand in the most prominent place, holding a dozen rings stuck into slits so they stood upright. She knew the stones were diamonds and they were most precious. Ruth had one – one diamond set above a gold band, a solitaire she called it – which Dad gave her for their tenth wedding anniversary. She remembered how her mother burst into tears as she opened the box, and how her father said he hadn't forgotten he'd once told her he'd give her one when he could afford it. Mary, though, preferred the blue stones. One day she'd have a sapphire ring. She couldn't imagine anyone buying it for her, so she'd save her own money.

Bracelets made of silver and gold, pendants on fine gold chains – in each case she picked the one she liked best before she moved on to the next section.

She looked at a tray of gold earrings, each pair pinned onto a card covered with dark blue velvet. They had hooks at the top, for people with pierced ears. Next to it, on a similar stand, the sets had no hooks but a rounded shape to go around the earlobe, with a tiny screw to tighten to hold them on. Her mother owned some like it but she didn't wear them often. She couldn't, she said, not for long, because they pinched her ears and made them hurt. If she put them on to go to church, they'd come off again as soon as the family got home.

Mary thought the ones with the hooks were nicer. They had more intricate designs – little crosses, hoops, things hanging, which would swing and dangle. They were more attractive than those that just sat on the ends of the ears. But then you'd need to have a hole put through your earlobe. There were girls at school who had it done. They came with a length of wool dangling on either side and told how someone – their mother, aunt, or older relative – heated a darning needle and poked it in till it came right through and stuck into a cork held on the other side. They said it didn't hurt much, but their lobes always looked sore and red for a while. They made Mary squirm by pulling the ends of the wool back and forth through the hole.

Kui's ears were pierced, so she must have had it done once. From one of her lobes swung a long pendant of polished greenstone – pounamu, Ana called it. From the other dangled a shorter triangular shape, which looked like a sharp pointed tooth. A shark's tooth, Ana confirmed it to be, from a mako shark. Mary wondered if she wouldn't rather have a new pair – a pair that matched.

"When is Kui's birthday?" she asked Ana the following day. Ana shrugged.

"You must know." Mary knew Ruth's birthday was on the twenty-fifth of May. She always made her mother a card, and Dad would take Georgie and her to Quarto Stationery to buy a book or some pretty writing paper and envelopes in a box.

"Kui doesn't know it either. She says she doesn't have one."

Mary couldn't believe there was someone who didn't know their own birthday, and next time the three sat around the kitchen table in Ruakumara Road it was impossible to keep the thought to herself.

"Are you sure you don't know what day you were born?"

Kui responded with an amused smile. "I was too little to remember," and laughed at her own joke.

"What does it say on your birth certificate?" The family photo album held Mary's certificate, and she wondered where Kui kept hers.

"We didn't have those when I was born. Not in our village. At that time no one in our area had their birth registered."

"Kui doesn't even know what year it was," Ana said.

Mary sat stunned. She couldn't imagine not having a birthday – no specific day you looked forward to, on which you were treated as special. She thought while she drank her glass of water and nibbled at the watercress sandwich. Kui looked at her face and smiled. She reached out and patted Mary's hand.

"Never you mind about that, e hine. I've got along all my life without one," she reassured her.

"You can choose one! You pick a day and it can be your birthday." She felt excited as the idea came to her. Perhaps it was even better to choose your own rather than have it chosen for you. A boy in their class whose birthday fell on Christmas Day always complained about it – she bet he'd like to choose his own.

Kui still looked amused. "Would it make you happy, Mere? My mother said the pohutukawa was starting to flower," she said, when Mary nodded, her face brightening.

"When is that?"

"It depends on the weather – how warm it is. Here in Waimamae if it's an early summer it can begin in November, even October. Further south it's later. If it's a bad year it mightn't be till December."

"Not December. Pick one before then," Mary urged, jiggling up and down in her seat. Ana too looked interested now. She unhooked the calendar from where it hung near the light switch and put it on the table. Kui put her left hand over her eyes and put her right index finger onto the page.

"October the nineteenth," the two girls said together. Kui uncovered her eyes, but kept them closed.

"Ae," she said, "it's a good date. That will be my birthday."

"Neato!" With the matter decided, Ana looked as pleased as Mary felt. She made a circle on the calendar around the number nineteen.

It seemed a good time for Mary to ask the question on her mind. She'd been wanting to for some weeks, but always pulled out before the words emerged, just in case it didn't go right. Now Kui looked really happy, so she put aside her fears and went ahead.

"Kui?"

"Ae, Mere?"

"Would you be my grandmother too? As well as Ana's," she added quickly in case there was any misunderstanding.

Kui looked at her, the lines in her face crinkling even more than ever. She pulled Mary to her and kissed her check.

"I already am," she said. "You're my mokopuna too. My little white-skinned grandchild, my mokopuna kiritea."

Mary smiled as she cycled all the way home. What a great day it had been. It wasn't fair that Kui didn't have a birthday, and she'd helped make it right. And now she had a grandmother. A kui.

Hey Ana, the other day on the radio they were playing Blue Smoke, *and do you know what images went through my mind? I saw the two of us walking together to your Sunday School.*

TWENTY-ONE

Welcome to One and All

Te Oranga Road stretched further than Mary could see ahead even if the air had been clear and not filled with the fine dust that hung in the breezeless morning above the unsealed roadway. She and Ana trod single file in the furrow formed at the side by vehicles forcing their way through the thick layer of fresh shingle. They'd left their bikes at Ana's place – in such conditions the narrow wheels of bicycles were treacherous. Once, when they heard a car coming from behind, they had to step out of the way and wait by the blackberry bushes at the side of the road till it went past, holding their breaths as long as they could to avoid inhaling the grey cloud left behind by the black Chevrolet. They stepped back across the bank of shingle edging the road and resumed their walk.

By the time they reached the hall Mary's once white sandals and socks were putty coloured, and she thought of how her mother insisted she use the whitener on her shoes before she set out. She could have saved herself the bother – it wouldn't have mattered.

The board set above the small porch read *Whare Rongopai*. Mary knew the first word, but the other was new to her. She thought of asking Ana, but remembered the lowered head, the refusal to meet Mr Daniels' eye when he'd pressed the class about speaking Maori, and said nothing. Ana noticed her looking.

"House of good news," she said. A man in a dark suit and a clerical collar stepped out from the doorway.

"Good tidings, the Gospel, the New Testament – all of those things. Morena Ana. Ko wai to hoa? Who is your friend?"

"Good morning, Minita. This is Mary."

"Mere. What a good name for a visitor to Whare Rongopai today. Welcome Mere." He held out his hand. Mary was not accustomed to shaking hands with a grown up – her parents' friends generally just said hello, though sometimes the men patted her head in a paternal gesture. She started to extend her left then her right. The minister laughed and took them both, enveloping them in his large brown hands.

"Uru mai," he gestured into the hall, "there are seats near the front."

Ana led her to a row with two empty chairs on the middle aisle. She stood aside and motioned to Mary to take the one next to a woman wearing a blue floral dress. The woman reached out and patted Mary's hand.

"Nau mai, welcome," she said, and acknowledged Ana with an easy upward movement of her head.

When people stopped arriving and were seated, the Minister stood before the gathering and gestured to some of the children to come forward, "We'll start with our welcome song for our guests." Ana got up and stood with about two dozen others at the front of the hall.

Welcome to one and all
This is our welcome song
Welcome to our Maori Sunday School.

The first bars of the tune rolled toward Mary and slid around her, wrapping her in a warm wave of molten melody. She didn't remember ever hearing it before, but at the same time it sounded as if it was already there within her, so perhaps she had. For the rest of the hour and a half they were in the room it replayed over and over in her head.

To Mary, the walk home took about a quarter of the time they'd taken to make the journey to the hall. The tune accompanied her as the girls retraced their steps along the length of Te Oranga Road, the liquid-sounding movement of the melody giving ease to her steps whereas before her gait seemed clumsy. *Welcome to one and all… welcome to our Maori Sunday School…* the words kept repeating, impressing themselves in her mind so they couldn't be forgotten.

It was some time before she heard the tune again and learned its name and the original words. Over the decades that followed, whenever she heard *Blue Smoke* played on the radio the lyrics were altered in her mind, and the images invoked were of a dusty road, a small church hall, and Ana surrounded by the warmth of her own surroundings.

She never took Ana to her own Sunday School, even though the leaders always encouraged the children to bring others. Ana could have stood alongside her and sung *Jesus wants me for a sunbeam* and dropped her penny into the plate with the rest of the children, but Mary didn't suggest it. After her experience at Whare Rongopai and the welcome she received there, she knew it wouldn't have compared.

Ana, when you come back, you'll see how much it's like we knew it then, and how different.

The hospital's still open, but it's just an outpost now. When I went to get my head stitched up, and you had your operation there it was a busy place. Now you'd be transferred to the city. If it had been like that then, I couldn't have come to visit you. And perhaps I still wouldn't understand.

It's a long time ago now, Ana.

I guess you heard about the new bridge, and do you know they're extending the Esplanade?

TWENTY-TWO

The First Taniwha

With the river running right through Waimamae, its course and changing conditions defined and ruled the life of the town in many ways.

In times long past it was the very reason for the settlement's existence. First, a waka of new arrivals, paddle-weary from weeks at sea, found the way inland from the coast up the water-road to the promising tree-clad land within. Much later, schooners, ketches, then small steamers brought a different race of settlers attracted by fertile acres of alluvial soil on which to run their stock.

Once into the channel, and the safety of the broad reaches of the lower river, each group found the surface generally placid, a marked change from the perils of the rough water of the Pacific Ocean. In their own way all gave thanks they'd survived a sea that spent the energy gained throughout its journey westward from South America by pounding against the steep shingle-covered beaches.

Such sanctuary was not given to all who asked. Applicants for entry were first tested at the bar, a treacherous bank of gravel guarding the mouth of the river. Far from constant, the bar shifted according to the pressure and currents of water coming down from the high hinterland; though there were always some who were inclined to believe it to be an agent of judgment, acting for either the atua or, later, the great Atuanui who replaced the former gods.

In more recent times the waterway was a place of entertainment. Yachts tacked up and down. Water-skiers glided, and often wiped out. Speedboats roared up and down in the annual regatta. The town's children gathered to play and swim on both sides of the banks. The stretch downstream from the marae Wharemamae, a short distance up Ruakumara Road from Ana's, where willow trees trailed their branches into the water at high tide, was the favourite spot of many. Georgie and his friends, and some of the local girls knew which branches to trust as swings. They would run, leap up to grab the hanging branches, swing out over the river, and drop. From time to time Ana tried to get Mary to follow her lead flying through the air, and though Mary longed to be able to throw herself off in the same carefree way, she always stopped short on the edge of the bank.

Most important of all, the river gave its name to Waimamae.

"Why Waimamae?" Everybody asked, why Waimamae? Everyone understood Wainui, Wairoa, Wairere, Waimakariri, Waimate, Waikare. Their names – big water, long water, fast water, cold water, dead water, rippling water – they all made sense. But Waimamae?

"How could the water be in pain?"

"Perhaps the river itself was a pain! The early travellers and settlers going overland would have thought so. It blocked their route up and down the coast."

"It must refer to the pain caused by the river, surely. Think about the floods that sweep down after rain up-country, inundating farmland and homes, sweeping away stock. Think about the lives lost in its waters."

Every adult in Waimamae could name a list.

"The Johnson boy who jumped off the bridge and hit a snagged branch."

"Three of the crew of the *Moana-Hau*, when they were crossing the bar."

"Those two city children, remember, who were staying up at Mangamuka Station and got swept away when a piece of the riverbank collapsed."

"Heni Porter who went in after her whitebait net wearing her gumboots."

"Don't forget the body found by the Mangaiti inlet. They never discovered who it was, did they?" And it could go on.

Kui, though, when Mary and Ana asked her about it, of course she knew.

"Ae, the river has caused a lot of pain. He tika, that's true. However, it's not the reason for the name. Waimamae moteatea rau is its full name. Waimamae of a hundred laments. Hine-Toa moteatea rau it was originally." Kui closed her eyes and broke into a chant.

> *Me mihi ki a Hine-Toa*
> *Toku taniwha, Toku tipuna*
> *Toku tipuna o Hawaiki*
> *I nga ra o mua koe e tu ana*
> *Kua tangi hotuhotu mo te wahi*
> *Kua hoki atu ki te Hawaiki.*

Kui remained silent for several moments, her eyes still closed, her fingers fluttering in her lap. Then she opened her eyes and continued.

"The first taniwha to come here was Hine-Toa, my ancestor. She was the kaiarahi, the guide, for the first waka that brought our ancestors to this region in the old times, long long ago. Across the ocean, Te Moana Nui a Kiwa, moving through the water in front of the canoe, she led the way. She was our protector and our guide – she led us without mishap, right to this place. Here we stayed. First we named it after the homeland. It was different here, nei? But we got used to it, and we stayed.

Hine-Toa, though, she missed the old place. As time went on she came to yearn for it more and more – till the longing became an agony within her. Ae, it was the aching pain consuming Hine-Toa that became the agony of Waimamae.

It was the old people who told her to return. She resisted, of course. A taniwha kaitiaki, a guardian taniwha, does not abandon the people it guards and protects unless they betray the trust of the kaitiaki. But the people saw the agony of Hine-Toa, heard her moans and lamentations.

'Your heart is in the homeland,' they said. 'Go back. Return to the remainder of our people and yours, the ones we left behind. When you get there, send us another guardian to protect us.'

So Hine-Toa left the place of her pain, and it has had the name in remembrance of her, from that time.

Taking farewell of those she was leaving, she swam down the river and out to sea. It is said, as she made her journey back across Te Moana Nui a Kiwa the people could see the swell of water she created. When the backwash from the swell reached the shore, all manner of things were washed up on the beach. Gifts from the homeland – coconuts, tubers for planting, and flowers such as we knew before in the old place."

Kui stopped, drew breath, and smiled at the two girls.

"That is why the present taniwha is called Tiaki Hou, new guardian. He has been here for going on a thousand years, nei? But he will always be Tiaki Hou to us because he was not the first, but the replacement."

Ana – Kui is calling for you. She says you must come back to Waimamae. She told me to find you and make sure you return.

She's here, Ana. I feel her so strongly. As soon as I arrived I could hear her laughing – you know, in that way of hers.

Now she's with me all the time.

TWENTY-THREE

At the Heads

At the end of its fifty-mile journey down from the high country the river met the ocean at a place known locally as 'the heads'. There the people of Waimamae walked wind-smoothed banks of sand, and picnicked. Children clambered through the forts on the nearby hills – concrete remnants of fears they didn't understand, but which their parents did, and were grateful had not been realized.

The beach was the resting place of all the treasure and trash the river transported in its rush from mountains to sea. Pieces of pumice, evidence of violent volcanic forces in the earth's interior, were picked up to be taken home for use in the bathtub, or to be trodden along with broken shells into garden paths. People filled trailers with the water-worn driftwood that covered the length of coarse sand, carting it off to fuel their open fires and chip heaters. Others, with a more artistic bent or less need, examined the shapes of the larger pieces before making their selection – to be displayed in the front gardens of many of the town's sections. An occasional dead cattle-beast or sheep, which had fallen into the river somewhere way upstream and been carried down to rest eventually among the wood and seaweed, was viewed with grisly fascination.

"Why don't we take a run out to the beach," suggested Ruth. William didn't respond, though she knew he heard because he took his eyes off his newspaper and pushed his glasses back up his nose. She hesitated, unsure whether to repeat the request. He'd gone out the night before on Borough Council business, this morning he had put in a couple of hours working in the vegetable garden, and after lunch settled into his chair with yesterday's *Robertstown Courier*. But this Saturday afternoon had several more hours to be filled in, and she was sure it would pass more pleasantly if they were out of the house with other things to think about.

"I don't think Elwyn's been out there. Have you, Elwyn?"

"Nope, Dotty, I don't believe I have."

Ruth frowned. Much as she loved her only brother, she wished he wouldn't be so annoying. The reason she now used her second name was to avoid the contraction she disliked so much throughout her childhood. It's not that she minded Dorothy as a name, but Dotty made her sound silly, brainless, and she hoped people didn't think of her like that. She hoped her husband hadn't heard, but the newspaper shifted to allow William to eye his brother-in-law.

"You know she wants to be called Ruth."

"Sorry, Sis!" He didn't sound at all repentant.

"What about it Will? You've got the car…" Ruth spoke to her husband, then picked up a tea towel and dried a couple of plates standing in the dish rack as she let him think about it.

Although it was permitted, William didn't like to use the council car for too many personal trips. Even though he was scrupulous about paying for the petrol when he did, he believed it best to avoid any criticism on those lines. So on the occasions he brought it home for the weekend it often sat, unused, outside the front gate while the family walked or cycled when they wanted to go somewhere within the town. Today, however, it would be good to get out and, William thought to himself, it wouldn't do his brother-in-law any harm to see he did indeed have the right to use it if he wished. At a pinch he could justify a trip to the heads on work grounds. He was expected to be aware of all parts of the district, and a good while had passed since he'd been out that way.

"Please Dad," said Mary, and at his nodded agreement went to the back door to call down the garden to where Georgie and Rupena were throwing rope quoits over a wooden stake they'd hammered into the lawn. Earlier, Elwyn told them he'd challenge the winner and both boys were competing to better the other for the honour. The kudos attached to being able to say they'd beaten Uncle Elwyn was too great a prize to take lightly.

Twenty minutes later Mary shared the front seat with her parents; and Elwyn, Georgie and Rupena clambered into the back. Georgie perched on the front of the seat between the others so the three of them just fitted.

"Breathe in, boys," Elwyn instructed, "these cars aren't made for comfort." Ruth turned in her seat to give him a warning look. When William wound down the driver's window and stretched out his arm to indicate a right-hand turn into Rimu Street, Mary opened her mouth to ask why her father didn't use the electric indicators. A few days earlier she'd heard Georgie telling their mother that Dad still used hand signals when most cars these days had at least side indicator arms, and some even sported indicator lights to flash on and off. In response, Ruth explained he'd once had a near miss when a trafficator stuck and failed to show, and since then he was extra cautious. Ruth nudged Mary, and gave her a look to say leave it – now, with Uncle Elwyn in the car, wasn't the time to bring it up.

Fortunately Georgie and Rupena were waving to someone on a bicycle so the incident passed without comment.

A few minutes later, as they turned from Lancewood Avenue into Fitzroy Road, Mary spoke the next question on her mind. "Dad, why do you call the beach the heads?"

Her uncle's voice came again from behind. "Good question. I've been wondering about the same thing. Aren't the head-waters of a river the beginning – its source?"

Ruth, always aware of having to stand between the two men and smooth the path of their conversation, looked toward her husband to judge his level of irritation. To her surprise, she saw a smile appear, and could sense, not a rise but, a release of tension from his face.

"Quite right," William announced. He felt pleased to be able to display his knowledge to the children whom, he suspected, were inclined to think him a rather poor option when Elwyn was around. And he was even happier to demonstrate it to the man himself. "But it's not the headwaters it refers to. When it's a coastal term it means the headlands at the mouth of a river." He could have added some elaboration but knew it was better to leave it there. In his children's tolerance, Georgie's in particular, there was a narrow gap between an explanation and a lecture. He suspected the gap wouldn't be a lot wider in the case of his brother-in-law.

Even before the car stopped, Georgie and Rupena threw open the back door and took off up the path to the fort dug into the hillside above the stretch of sand. They ducked out of view behind the grey concrete, then their hands appeared waving through the gun slit set into the seaward face. The hands disappeared, to be replaced a few seconds later with sticks, accompanied by stuttering akakakak sounds. William snorted.

"Machine guns! That'll be the day! The men stationed here back in the war were probably lucky to have old rifles. And there wouldn't have been many of those to share between them."

"Did they really think the Germans would attack our coasts?" Elwyn sounded dubious. "Weren't they too busy trying to take over Europe?"

"Not the Germans. It was the Japanese who were the threat." William and Ruth spoke together making the correction, William adding, "They got this far all right – their submarines were in our waters, and their planes over our cities."

"If the war hadn't ended when it did…" Ruth left the sentence unfinished.

"Do you wish you'd gone overseas with the forces?" Elwyn looked at William who hesitated while he tried to decide from the tone whether the question was seriously intended or designed to needle him.

"You know he couldn't, because of his eyes," Ruth jumped in, "He would have, but for that. He did his service here, and got a lot of other men signed up."

"Yes, I would have gone." William's voice was firm. "If I could have. Why don't you go and have a look," he pointed up the hill at the fort.

"Yeah, I will." Elwyn started up the path worn through the grass.

William watched him climb. "There's one man who would have been improved by army discipline."

Ruth put her hand on her husband's arm, "Remember how young he is. I'd turned thirteen when he was born. He's only that much older than Georgie." William offered no response, so she continued. "He knows you were in the recruiting office. He wasn't being rude."

"Maybe not. Perhaps in another ten years when he's…" A renewed burst of simulated gunfire, akakakak, sounded from up the hill. Georgie burst out from behind the concrete pillbox, the stick weapon in his hands jerking as he aimed at an imaginary line of attackers. He stopped suddenly, dropped the stick, clutched at his chest, and fell sideways into an exaggerated pose. Ruth shuddered.

William shook his head, remembering his comment about discipline. "And there's another one," he said.

TWENTY-FOUR

Pumice Duck

"It's for you," said Mary, holding out her palm on which rested the pale grey shape. Kui looked at it and smiled.

"He parera pungapunga, nei?"

Mary was unsure what the old woman meant. "It's pumice. It looks like a duck. I found it on the beach."

Kui nodded. "A pumice duck. Thank you, Mere."

"You can use it in the bath," Mary said as Ana filled two glasses of water from the tap and handed her one. "It's from a volcano – it used to be right down deep in the middle of the earth."

"Pooow!" Ana made a noise of an explosion and threw her hands in the air in explanation. There'd been a story in the *School Journal* about how rock was heated to a fiery temperature and filled with bubbles as the gas burst out when it reached the cold air above ground.

"I will keep it here." Kui placed the light stone shape on the sideboard beside the wooden picture frame the girls had found in the window of Harvey's Hardware on the day of the leaflets. Now it held the photograph of the two girls Mary's father had taken outside the big top when they went to the circus. "It will remind me of the story of Te Rongo-Kahere, my ancestor."

Mary felt a burst of pleasure. Not only did Ana's grandmother – her grandmother – like the gift, but it meant something special to her. Even better, there was a story – she loved listening to her tales about the past. Kui looked at her face and smiled.

"E noho," she said – touching the chair beside her. Mary sat, giving Ana a look she hoped would persuade her friend to join her. The girls had been going to search through the long grass of the empty acre next door to look for any walnuts left under the trees. That could wait – she wanted to hear Kui's story now, in case she changed her mind or started to do something else. This sounded as though it might be more than the short snippets she shared with them whenever they were together. It promised to be one of the longer ones, the sort she liked most, one telling of days gone by. Nga ra o mua, as Kui often referred to those times with a sigh. Mary knew from other such occasions there was likely to be intrigue as someone tried to outwit another or even the atua, drama when battles between peoples or monsters were involved, or jokes as a trickster tried to get the edge over a rival.

"Te Rongo-Kahere," Kui closed her eyes and smiled, "ae, it's a long way back." She paused, and Mary had a moment of doubt that the story would be told.

"Do you remember…?" she prompted, stopping short as she realized she wasn't sure if Te Rongo was a him or a her.

Kui gave a little laugh but kept her eyes shut.

"She belongs to nga taima tawhito, the ancient times. Even I'm not old enough to remember her," she laughed again.

"They say she was beautiful. So beautiful all the men wanted her. Not only that, she was an expert in the fine arts – her weaving second to none in the whole district. Many men, from her own people and visitors who saw her, tried to win her. And if she had been an ordinary girl she would have made her choice from among them. But Te Rongo-Kahere was a puhi, a virgin being kept for a special match. Any ordinary man could not hope for her as his wife. It was more important than just between a man and a woman, this joining would be between peoples. Hers would be a marriage planned to unite two tribes and cement peace between them. Until this was arranged she must be kept pure, with watchers and attendants to make sure she stayed that way.

One day a party of visitors arrived from Te Tatu – a village two days walk to the north. Among them there was a young warrior called Pokia. You can guess what happened, nei?" Kui opened her eyes and looked at Ana, then Mary.

"They fell in love?" Mary asked.

Beside her Ana gave a small snort. "They ran off together."

"Ae," Kui looked at Mary. "They did fall in love." Her eyes shifted to Ana. "Kao. They didn't run away together. Not then, anyway." She leaned against the back of the chair and her eyelids closed again.

"People noticed their eyes meeting, the looks passing between them. When the party of visitors was farewelled and went back to Te Tatu, they saw how Te Rongo-Kahere lost interest in her arts, and her eyes were often fixed along the beach to the north. For fear she would try to go off on her own, they decided to take her to Motukohu – you know the island, nei? She was left there with two companions – kuia, old women like me," Kui laughed.

"She took a canoe from there!" Ana could see where this was leading, but again Kui shook her head.

"Kao, kao. Her people knew better than to make that mistake. The waka that took them there went back to the mainland.

There was no boat left there, and it was too far, and too rough, to swim. Those three were to stay on the island till the time came for Te Rongo's marriage. And time enough had passed for her to forget Pokia."

"So what happened?" Mary put her question at the same time as Ana asked, "How did she get away?" Kui smiled at the looks on the two faces.

"She was a clever one, Te Rongo. After a time when she stood on the shore looking out to sea and throwing sticks to drift with the tide, she pretended to give up her longing and settle down on the island. To occupy herself she stripped flax and wove it into a long mat. It would make a good covering for a whare floor, she said. She also spent hours on the beach collecting shellfish. She would bring the pipi and tuatua and others back with her; but she also collected something else she left in a certain place hidden among the trees."

Mary wanted to ask her next question, but Kui went on with the story so she waited.

"Came the time when Te Rongo finished her mat. It was long enough, she said, but she didn't stop working. She stripped more flax and plaited the lengths into long ropes. It seemed she was keeping herself occupied and making something useful, so her companions were happy and got on with their own work finding and cooking food. One morning when they woke, she wasn't there, and neither was her mat. They were not concerned – they knew she could not leave the island. But in the evening when she hadn't returned, they set out to look for her. She was nowhere to be found."

Kui stopped her narration and raised her eyebrows at the pair, inviting them to work it out.

"She floated off on her mat," started Mary, but Ana interrupted.

"It would sink. It's what else she collected from the beach. Pungapunga." Ana said the last word just as Mary also caught on to the secret of Te Rongo's hidden cache.

"Pumice. It floats."

"Ae. She made the mat long enough to fold it into two. Between the halves she put a layer of pumice, and tied the sides together all around."

"A mat light enough to float. It's why she needed the rope – to tie it together."

"Not only that. Remember how she threw sticks into the water?"

"To see the way it flowed." Ana had the answer but, once again, Kui's response showed it was not so simple.

"Ae, you're right. But when the tide took her out, and she was far off shore, she found the current sweeping her back toward home, not to the north, the way she wanted to go."

Mary felt her spirits sink. Kui looked at her and laughed.

"I told you she was clever, that one. Te Rongo looked up to the sky and called out for birds to come – 'manu mai, manu mai.'" In Kui's voice the words seemed to ring and reverberate. From outside on the verandah came an answering flurry as wings flapped and two distinct calls were heard. Mary's eyes grew wide as she stared at Kui. Here was yet another thing this woman could do, but Ana laughed.

"They think you're coming to feed them," she said to her grandmother.

"Te Rongo called the birds to come to her. Within minutes a cloud of them formed above her – nga parera – a cloud of ducks. She threw up the lengths of rope she had made and they caught them in their beaks. Te Rongo stretched out her arm in the direction of north, and the ducks flew along the coast towing her along below."

"She got there?" Mary knew, she hoped, what the answer would be, but she looked for confirmation of the happily-ever-after ending.

"Ae, she got there. And that's how I have the names Te Rongo-Kahere and Pokia in my ancestry. And you, little Mere, have given me something to remind me of her." Kui looked at the sideboard and gestured toward the piece of pumice. "My parera pungapunga."

Sometimes, too, I feel the presence of Hemi. I drove out to the beach and it seemed as though he was there – somewhere out in the breakers, out near Moturoa, the boards of the Marakihau under his feet.

Was he your uncle, or your cousin? I'm not sure I ever got it right in my mind. In our family we always said Aunt Marie, Aunty Cecily, and of course Uncle Elwyn. But Hemi was always just Hemi.

TWENTY-FIVE

The Marakihau

"Hemi, Kui wants you to chop some kindling for the stove."

Hemi didn't turn around as Ana spoke, and barely paused in his work rubbing the boards of the dinghy's hull. A scraper was in his hand and a pot of paint stood nearby.

"Does she now? You can tell her I've already done it. You tell her he tangata ringa raupa ahau."

"What does that mean Hemi?"

The movement and scraping sound stopped, and Hemi's head tilted to one side.

"What is that I hear? There's a tiny noise behind me – what can it be? The cheeping of another little bird? Oh now I see, it's a little white dove beside the weka. Kia ora Mere."

"Kia ora Hemi."

"Kei te pehea koe, Mere?"

"Kei te pai."

"Pai rawa. Very good. You're a good pupil." Hemi looked at Ana, cocked his head slightly to the side and raised his eyebrows. She looked away and scuffed her foot in the grass beside the upturned dinghy – the one he used when he went onto the river.

A short distance across the yard, the *Marakihau* rested on its trailer. When he went across the bar and out to sea the two craft went together, the dinghy tied behind the twenty-eight foot launch.

Once, when Mary and Ana were on their bicycles near the river, they'd seen the *Marakihau* coming down the straight toward the town. They raced to the bridge, dropped their bikes on the grass embankment and rushed across the pedestrian pathway on the upstream side till they were midway. As the two boats came near, the blue dinghy skimming along behind the larger boat, they waved down at it and yelled. Hemi's hand appeared through the side window of the small cockpit and a horn sounded out a jaunty rhythm as the craft passed a few yards beneath them.

Mary thought it was the most romantic boat she'd seen. Others using the river were shinier and more modern, with chrome railings around the side, but the *Marakihau* made her smile. The wooden hull was painted blue, with several big yellow flowers added at irregular intervals. When she asked him if they were sunflowers, he said sunflowers, sunny-flowers, whatever anyone wanted them to be – so after that she always thought of them as sunny-flowers. Even better, on either side of the prow Hemi had painted a large eye. The idea came from pictures he'd seen in a magazine, of fishing boats in the Mediterranean. He made his large and lavish, with curling lashes above, but they were not a pair. The one on the right side – starboard Hemi called it – was brown. That on the port side was blue. When she asked him why they were different, Hemi just laughed, "I ran out of paint," he said, but the way he laughed told her there could be more to the matter.

Mary shifted her gaze away from the large brown eye, and picked up a worn-down brush.

"Teach me some more." She reached out to the boards of the boat, but Hemi took the brush from her hand before she touched the wood.

"Aha," he said, "fair swap. First, did you bring anything for me?"

Mary grinned. She was ready. Since she'd pushed Georgie to come up with something suitable, she'd been rehearsing.

"Why do tigers have stripes?"

"Let me see now – why would tigers have stripes?" Hemi made a show of scratching his head. He screwed up his eyes so lines showed on his forehead, then he shook his head. "Kao. You're going to have to tell me. Why do tigers have stripes?"

"So they won't be spotted." Mary laughed as Hemi let out an exaggerated groan.

"Do you think I'll trade for that? You'd better have another one."

"Where do fish put their money?"

"Fish with money? How come I've never come across any of those? With all the fish I've caught!"

"Go on, what's the answer?" Mary jiggled on her toes, one foot to another.

"You want to go to the wharepaku? Better hurry, girl, before it's too late." Mary stopped dancing.

"Fish put their money…" she paused, waiting for Hemi to supply an answer. "Fish put their money… in… a river bank!"

"Ka pai. That's a good one. Okay little Mere, fair trade – what do you want to know?"

"What did you say before – the message for Kui?"

"Gee, I'm blowed if I remember. Ana, what was it I said?" Ana muttered something without looking up.

"He tangata ringa raupa ahau."

"He tika. That's right. So I did. Ringa raupa – rough hands, calloused hands. He tangata ringa raupa ahau. I am a man with calloused hands. I reminded Kui I'm a good worker." He laughed and displayed a fresh strip of white sticking plaster that contrasted sharply with the skin of his left hand. "Ringa raupa's right. Look at me – cuts and rough spots all over me. Did I show you where the fish hook went right through my finger last time I went out?"

"Yes," said Ana, "only about a hundred times."

"Ringa raupa…" Mary tried to make the words sound just the way he had.

"It's a saying you girls should remember. E moe i tangata ringa raupa. Hea aha, Ana?"

"Marry a man with rough hands."

"Ka pai. Good. Remember it for the future. Both of you."

"Why aren't you married, Hemi?" Hemi paused a moment or two before he replied.

"Maybe I'm still waiting for the right fish to swim my way. One of those with money in the river bank would be good, eh!"

*I loved Hemi. As much as I loved Uncle Elwyn. To
me they were equivalents. The one in your family
and mine who always had a joke waiting to be
shared, and who wasn't too tired to spare the time.*

*Remember how I got him to recite his poem about
the moa, over and over, till I knew it off by heart?*

I still do.

BACKWARDS INTO THE FUTURE

TWENTY-SIX

Hemi's Poem

Uru was a chief – an Ariki nui
Uru decided that he'd hold a hui
Many rangatira, from near and far too,
Were invited – in all there'd be quite a few.

For such a big party he'd need lots of kai
So he called his friend Hata to come – "Haere mai,
Kia ora, e Hata", he said, "e hoa,
Do you have plenty of kai in your store?

I know you had kereru preserved in its fat
And quite a few juicy kiore, the rat."
"Kao", said Hata, shaking his head
"My pataka's empty – it's all gone", he said.

"Then how many kumara are still in your pit?"
"They've all gone too – there's nothing in it!
However", said Hata after a think
"I can offer you plenty wai maori to drink!"

"Aue", said Uru, with a very loud groan
"Fresh water is just not enough on its own.
What shall I do for my guests are invited
And if there's no feast I fear they'll be slighted."

So Hata suggested "Take your waka today
And fill it with ika from out in the bay;
Then dig some aruhe, and we can at least
Have plenty of fernroot and fish at the feast."

But Uru believed that an ariki nui
Wasn't suited to mahi – only to hui.
He thought to himself "I'm a mohio man,
Surely I can think of a plan."

He thought all that ra and into the po
And round about midnight he shouted, "I know!"
Early next morning the moa and the tui
Were formally invited by him to the hui.

The moa was delighted and said he'd be there
And that he'd bring huhus along as his share
The tui, however, being somewhat shyer
Declined – said she'd promised to sing in a choir.

The feast day was fine – i whiti te ra
Many manuhiri came from afar.
Uru, the most popular host of his set
Had promised this hui would be the best yet.

The party had started, and spirits were high
When Manu the moa reached the marae;
Uru said he had saved him a space
And sat him down in the very best place.

He sat down beside him and said they'd be looking
At much entertainment while dinner was cooking;
There were haka a-plenty, poi dances too
The moa, where he sat, had a wonderful view.

The day grew warmer, he complained of the heat
Not knowing the umu was under his seat!
At last, exclaiming "Ka nui te wera"
He leapt up to find he had lost every feather.

As Uru had promised, it was the best hui
They ate moa and more till their pukus were nui;
And that's the reason, so the kuias say
There are no more moa around to this day.

Hemi called it "Uru's Hui". To me it's always been just "Hemi's poem".

I say it every year, just the way he did, with all the actions.

To remember. Every November the second.

TWENTY-SEVEN

Making Lemon Spread

"Do you know Baa Gilchrist?" Amiria didn't look up from her task. She was grating the rind off a lemon. Two others, already denuded, sat plump and white next to the chopping board on the table.

"Bar Gilchrist?" Mary thought. She'd never really been into the bar scene, but tried to fit the name with an image of such an establishment in the several places she'd lived. She came up with nothing. "I don't think so. Where is it?"

Amiria laughed. "It's not a where, it's a who. His real name's Barry, but he's always called Baa."

"No." Even with the corrected knowledge the name still didn't ring a bell.

"He works for the council – something to do with engineering." Amiria appeared to be concentrating closely on the fruit in her hand. She was using the smallest slicer option on the grater and fine strips of yellow peel fell into the clear container below the blade.

"You'll remember Johnny Lamb – you know, he owned that bi-plane. Baa's his grandson."

"Baa, as in lamb?" Mary caught on suddenly.

"Yeah. His mother called him Barry Lamb Gilchrist. What did she expect? He's always been Baaaa." Amiria's interpretation sounded so like the real thing it could have passed for a live animal had the pair not been in Mary's kitchen.

Since the first visit some weeks earlier Amiria had dropped in with increasing frequency, sometimes bringing more lemons, other times vegetables from her garden. On a couple of occasions she'd walked in the back door, taken the canister from the pantry cupboard and simply announced she needed a mug of coffee the way Mary made it. The best she'd tasted, she said. Mary didn't believe her judgment for a moment, but she'd come to look forward to the visits. Even though she was renewing past links with a number of people, there still weren't many in the district she'd be confident to call a close friend. But through Amiria she was being drawn into the activities of the town.

Today, her friend arrived holding a bucket in one hand and a supermarket bag in the other – the plastic pail filled past the brim with lemons. Mary was about to protest, saying she couldn't use so many, when Amiria swung the bag onto the table and folded it down to reveal a 3-kilogram bag of sugar.

"We're going to make lemon spread," she announced. Mary didn't question the inclusive pronoun – it wasn't the first time she'd been roped into helping.

"It'll make a lot." If it were to be divided equally, Mary saw herself eating little else for the next few weeks.

"It's for the marae," said Amiria. "There are a couple of big hui coming up, and everyone likes my lemon spread."

No question starting with 'can you?', or 'if you're not too busy…' In the city, fully occupied living her former life, Mary would have found such a situation an imposition, and moved to eject the would-be usurper of her time. In Waimamae, in her present setting, it sat well. She was amused the first time it happened, and since then she found she liked the way Amiria related to her in a manner totally open and natural.

At least, it's what she'd thought. Today however, Mary sensed some purpose beneath Amiria's question about Baa Gilchrist. If it were so, she was surprised she didn't come straight out with it.

"Is there some reason I should know him?"

"Nah, not really, I just wondered." Amiria put down another rindless lemon, emptied the container of shredded zest into Mary's biggest ovenware dish, and wiped her hands on a paper towel. "I thought you might have seen him – he drives a Zodiac car. Zephyr Zodiac, my boy calls it. He says it's a classic."

So that's all it was – just a passing comment. Amiria often mentioned things her 'boy' told her, and the subject of vehicles had cropped up before in relation to his name. Ricardo, she'd learned, was actually Amiria's grandson. The lad was at High School, and apparently something of a petrol-head. Mary measured four cups of sugar and added them to the dish. Just an idle reference, then, with no more needing to be said. But Amiria spoke again – so there might be more to it.

"It looks small now – funny how we used to think they were pretty hot, eh?"

Mary stirred the mixture, still not giving much thought to this turn in the conversation. Cars were things she drove for the convenience of having ready transport. As long as her present model was reliable and comfortable she didn't worry herself too much about details that others thought so important.

"Anyway, now you'll know who it is when you see the car. It's two-tone, green and white."

Mary picked up the lemons the other woman had scraped, cut them in half and pressed one onto the squeezer to extract the juice.

"Hey, I just thought," added Amiria in a tone tending to suggest it wasn't a random thought at all, but perhaps she'd been leading up to it, "isn't that the sort of car your uncle had?"

"My uncle?" For a moment Mary couldn't connect any uncle with such a vehicle. In the days they were talking about less than half the people of Waimamae owned a car. Besides, her family had no relatives living in the town. "I don't think so. Not my uncle."

"The one with the funny name," Amiria prompted her to remember. "Elwood? Elwyn, or something."

"Uncle Elwyn? He didn't have a car." As she spoke it came to her, jolting her with such force she stopped momentarily. There had been a car, once. The time he'd turned up, unexpectedly as usual, on the day of the school gala. Was that a Zodiac? She searched the past for a image and came up with a memory of Georgie, his eyes gleaming as he ran his hands over the bonnet, and repeating "Hot dog!"

"It could have been," Mary amended her earlier statement. "But it wasn't his. I think he must have borrowed it." She poured the lemon juice into the bowl with the other ingredients, gave it a stir, and placed it in the microwave oven. "We'd better sterilize the jars," she said.

TWENTY-EIGHT

Two-tone Zephyr Zodiac

Mary made her selection and put the three items into a shoebox. The decision had taken her more than an hour, with much switching between articles she'd pulled from the carton beneath her bed. From the signs coming from the kitchen her mother would soon call her to set the table for dinner. Sausages, boiled cabbage, boiled carrots, and of course there'd be potatoes. That almost went without saying. Every dinner included potatoes. They'd be mashed tonight, as they were whenever they had sausages, and that was all right because her mother always made sure there were no lumps and included a good dollop of butter. Sometimes she added chopped parsley and Mary liked it even better when she did. Georgie didn't.

"Why do you put this grass in it?" he'd complain, even though he asked the same question every time.

"It's not grass," Mary would start to answer wondering why he didn't remember from last time she told him, only to be stopped by Ruth.

"Just ignore him."

"Your mother's gone to the trouble of making you a nice dinner. Eat it and be thankful," his father would say. It was light-hearted conversation – everyone knew Georgie loved mashed potatoes and would eat it anyway, grass or no grass.

Mary slid the shoebox under her bed and went to the kitchen. Her mother glanced toward the table and Mary pulled out the cutlery drawer.

"Is it all right to give away Mopsy and Topsy?"

"Your upside-down doll? If you want to. Who are you giving it to?"

So it was all right. Mary couldn't remember where it came from, and just in case it was a gift from a relative who might ask about it some time, it was better to ask first.

"I'm putting it into the gala," she said.

"The school gala? Is it coming up?" asked Ruth. "When is it?"

"There's been a letter about it. You're supposed to have it."

"I haven't seen a letter."

"Georgie should have got it. They were given out yesterday."

"That boy!" grumbled Ruth. "They should give messages to you, not him, then I might get them."

"They only give them to the eldest," said Mary. She looked forward to the following year when Georgie went to High School and she'd be able to raise her hand as oldest in her family when a messenger went from class to class holding a stack of foolscap pages still smelling of duplicating ink. When her turn came she'd be sure to deliver every school circular as soon as she got home, and cement her reputation as the reliable one.

"I suppose they'll want me to make cakes again." Ruth spoke in her slightly resigned voice, but Mary knew she'd do it willingly. Her mother's baking was always complimented and among the first to go from the cake stall.

Trestle tables bearing all manner of goods were set up in a line along the verandahs of the classrooms. Mary went along the row, the half-crown spending money William allowed her for the occasion, in her pocket. Many of the stalls included goods from their own house – Georgie had taken two cartons of unwanted items on the carrier of his bicycle in the days leading up to gala Saturday. Then there were the trays of baking their mother stayed up late the evening before to produce. They'd all helped this morning to carry those along Sutherland Street then down Fergusson Street to the school – Ruth keeping a strong supervisory eye on the boxes carefully wrapped in clean tablecloths. Two more large flat boxes were strapped onto the back of Georgie's bike.

As soon as he'd been able to deliver his load, Georgie took off to see what entertainment the day offered. Last year there'd been a tall device with a low platform you hit with a mallet to test your strength. The burliest men in Waimamae – those who worked on the railways or did a fair bit of wood chopping – made the puck reach the top and ring the bell. Georgie had stood watching for more than an hour, looking on with admiration at the best attempts. His own effort fell just short of the mark lower down the pole at which primary school pupils were commended, and if the machine was there again he was determined to exceed it this year. For his last birthday he'd pleaded for a bull-worker and, contrary to his father's opinion that it would be forgotten within a week, he used it almost daily. When he displayed his growing muscles his father grumbled he could have got the same result if he chopped wood for the fire, and saved him the job; but you could tell he was pleased Georgie had stuck with something he'd started.

With the boxes of cakes delivered to the baking table and Ruth settled in her customary place behind it, William headed for the activity to which he'd been allotted to assist. Mary surveyed the grounds – transformed from their usual school-day look. So much to see and do, but she knew where she'd go first.

Increasing numbers were coming into the school grounds and once the covers were removed from the tables on the dot of nine o'clock buyers would crowd around each to make their choice from what their neighbours and a few businesses donated. Hints and rumours had spread over the days before, and each class took the opportunity to look at what their friends brought in each day and placed in the cardboard carton near the teacher's desk. Mary's upside-down doll didn't create much of a stir, though as she'd arrived at school carrying it a couple of the boys from the oldest class snatched it out of her hand, and upended it. As Mopsy flipped over, her skirt fell to reveal not a pair of legs but another face and body. "No good to us," one sniggered handing it back to her. Of course it wasn't, Mary thought but didn't say aloud. Calum Brunt wouldn't be interested in a doll, and she doubted he'd buy it to give his little sister. Fiona Brunt was in the class below hers and Mary found it hard to imagine the girl who'd earned the nickname Feisty would play with one either. The Brunts lived way down Whites Road, the area she wasn't to go into. She reached out, snatched the doll back again, and ran toward the block of classrooms.

Fenella brought for the gala box a set of furniture for a doll's house. A bed, bedside table, a chest of drawers, dressing table with mirror, and a little seat to go in front of the dresser – all in pale pink plastic. Mary couldn't understand how someone would not want such a thing, but Fenella was the girl in their class who had a choice of swimming togs when everyone else owned just one. If she didn't want the pink bedroom set, Mary did. She didn't have a doll's house to put it in, where it would be displayed like a proper bedroom, but she could improvise with a shoebox.

With her hand in her pocket holding the half-crown her father gave her, she looked along the row for the toy table. Mothers were crowding around one with knitting and sewing, fathers stood in front of another looking through other men's discarded tools. Mr Paratai stood in the middle ready to answer questions and direct people to the area they were looking for. Mary didn't need to ask.

Past the garden produce table, which held a variety of home-grown fruit and vegetables, children jostled for places in front of two long trestles. One, she knew, would be the toys table, the other for sweets. She ran to the first. Yellow, pink and chocolate coloured fudge, irregular pieces of toffee broken from a slab, pink and white cubes of coconut ice, and Turkish delight coated with a film of icing sugar were displayed in baskets made of halved tea boxes. Decorated with bands of crepe paper to cover the Bell, Choysa, Bushell's or Roma branding on the outside, the little baskets covered the table, but were disappearing quickly as she looked.

She moved on and tried to scan the length of the next trestle-top to find the pink plastic set. She knew the pieces were jumbled together in a cocoa box with one side removed, and covered with a piece of cellophane held in check by a rubber band. In front of her she saw a small girl holding the sought-for box in one hand, and Mopsy-Topsy in the other. A much taller girl, probably her older sister because she looked high-school age, was saying, "You can't have both. You'll have to choose." Mary stood still while the girl looked from one to the other. She held her breath and concentrated on the doll, willing her to select it. "Come on, make up your mind," said the older girl as the little one still dithered. Mary put out her arm and took hold of Mopsy-Topsy.

"Oh look," she said, "it's one of those upside-down dolls – they're neat!" She flipped the pair backwards and forwards. "Are you going to buy it?"

The small girl reached out to take it again. "Good," said her sister, plucking the box from her other hand and putting it down next to a set of dominoes, "here's the money, give it to the lady."

Mary reached through and picked up the discarded box. It was hers. Her fingers tightened around it lest someone else take it from her grasp. She'd been prepared to spend her whole allowance on it, but the sticker said 1/6. She'd have a shilling left. Sixpence for the candyfloss machine, the other sixpence to pull a parcel from the sawdust of the lucky-dip barrel. This was a good day already. Something to tell Ana about. Ana, who wasn't here because of some occasion at Wharemamae. Mary couldn't imagine missing the gala – it was a high point in her year – but Ana didn't appear to mind.

Ruth's job usually proved one of the shortest because the cake stall always sold out very quickly. Once again her sultana cake, baked in a roasting dish and cut into four pieces, went within minutes, and her lemon cake topped with passion fruit icing was quick to follow. She kept the caraway seed cake in a box under the table till old Mr McNaughton, Jim McNaughton senior as some people called him to differentiate between him and his son Jim, turned up.

"You wouldn't happen to have one of your…" he began as Ruth knew he would. She bent, retrieved the box and handed it to him.

"Seed cake made just for you."

"My wife used to bake me these. No one seems to make them anymore." He took the box and Ruth dropped the two-shilling piece into the chocolate box of coins on the table. None of her family liked the taste of caraway much, and she was happy to make one for the retired bank manager occasionally.

When they'd sold the remaining boxes of bran muffins, and the shortbread arranged in cardboard tea boxes cut through the middle lengthwise, she and the two women also serving behind the table with her would be free to visit the other stalls. As she handed one of the packs to a customer who arrived too late for her first choice and had to settle for what was left, she heard a male voice coming from her other side, asking what sounded like a foolish question. At home, if one of the children asked something she thought obvious, she'd respond with an answer meant to tell them so.

"What's this, Mum?"

"It's a wigwam for a goose's bridle."

"What's for dinner, Mum?"

"Bread and butter and duck under the table."

Ask a silly question and you'll get a silly answer, was her philosophy. This time, though, the voice asking the question sounded somewhat more mature in tone than either of her children's, even though it came through in a strange accent. But the query was about on a par with one of Georgie's requests.

"You don't happen to have a rainbow-cake, do you, but with only the chocolate parts?"

Ruth sighed as she lifted her eyes to the speaker, wishing she could make a satisfying retort without being impolite.

"As you can see," she started, then broke off, not knowing

whether to show pleasure or annoyance, "Elwyn! You didn't say you were coming."

Her brother seldom let them know in advance. There'd be a light rap at the kitchen door and when she opened it she'd find her young brother standing on the step grinning.

"Excuse me, madam, but would you be interested in purchasing an item of garden art?" In his hand he'd be holding a flowerpot he'd picked up from alongside the path. Once, when he'd run into Georgie and Rupena on his way down the road, he hushed them into complicit silence as he tapped on the door.

"Police, open up. Excuse me, madam, I found these young rascals causing trouble. Do either of them belong to you?"

"I thought I'd surprise you," Elwyn said now, but the surprise was on me – you weren't at home." He didn't need to say how he'd found her. Even without the signs about the gala pasted up all over town, a look down Fergusson Street at the line of parked vehicles and even more bicycles leaning against every power pole was enough to show where everyone had headed this morning.

"Uncle Elwyn!"

"Well, if it isn't little Mary. Actually," he stepped back half a pace and looked her up and down, "I may have to stop calling you that. I swear you've grown two inches since I saw you last. These two inches here," he reached toward her middle and the area he called her tickle zone. Mary twisted out of his grasp.

"Silly," she retorted, earning a frown from Ruth who believed children should not talk back to adults in such a fashion, even if it was to Elwyn who sometimes seemed little more than a kid himself, in manner if not in years.

"What is it you're eating? Your tongue is all pink."

"Candyfloss."

"Is that what candyfloss is! Do you know, I've never tried any.

"You must have. Everyone's had candyfloss."

"Cross my heart and hope to fly."

Mary pulled a portion of spun sugar from the side of her pink cloud and handed it to him. "C'mon," she said, pulling at his sleeve, "I'll show you what Dad's doing." Ruth might have suggested something else less likely to cause further tension between the brothers-in-law, but Mary and Elwyn had already turned to go and someone was pressing a shilling into her hand in exchange for half a dozen muffins.

William, together with another man who Mary recognized as the father of twins a couple of years behind her in school and the uncle of her classmate Aroha, stood beside the sandpit normally reserved for the primer classes. The surface was raked smooth and small wooden sticks were standing in a random arrangement. As he saw the pair approach his back stiffened, but his attention was diverted as someone handed him sixpence.

"Just write your first name and telephone number," he instructed, passing them a stick and the thick pencil Mary knew he used to mark names of vegetables on newly planted rows of seeds in the back garden.

"Curious," said Elwyn, regarding the sandpit and the upright sticks, "What are you hoping to grow here, Bill?" The only reply was a somewhat terse acknowledgement, "Elwyn," accompanied by a nod of the head before her father turned to see to another customer, so Mary explained the idea.

"It's a treasure hunt. There's a ten-shilling note hidden under the sand." She spoke the words ten-shilling note with a tone of awe. You put a stick where you think it is, and the person closest wins it."

"Have you had a go?"

"No, Dad said I couldn't, not with him running it." Elwyn said no more, but stood and looked at the raked sand for some time. When William was occupied finding change for another would-be winner, her uncle moved behind him and handed a coin to Mr Tamati who dropped it into a cigar box already holding others, and passed him a stick and pen. He wrote on the wooden peg and, when his brother-in-law turned away from the pit, thrust it into the sand.

"Georgie!" Mary caught sight of her brother and called. He didn't turn around, so she called again. "Georgie, look!" Georgie turned, though reluctantly, but as he caught sight of the man next to her, he gave a whoop and ran across the field. Elwyn reached out and tousled the boy's hair. Georgie hated people doing that, but never complained when it was Uncle Elwyn.

"I've got something you might like to see," Elwyn said, gesturing to the Fergusson Street gate.

"Me too?" asked Mary. She'd spent her gala allowance, the pink set of dolls-house furniture sat satisfyingly in the shoulder bag she wore around her neck, and now Uncle Elwyn had arrived the day was close to perfect – she didn't want to let him out of her sight.

"Of course you too."

They followed him out the gate and down the footpath to the end of the parked cars. Georgie spotted the last in the row and his eyes widened.

"Hot dog! A two-tone Zephyr Zodiac."

"Like them, do you?" asked Elwyn but Georgie, already

166

running his hands over it, didn't need to respond. Mary noticed tiny streaks of water sticking to some panels. Since the day was fine it must have been washed right before being driven here.

"Want to get in?" asked Elwyn, "We can run it around the block to try it out." Georgie's eyes gleamed, but after a moment's pause he shook his head.

"Can't," he said, "Dad would skin me alive." His eyes flicked from Elwyn to Mary and back again, the message clear – she'd tell.

Elwyn laughed and held up a key. "We're not pinching it." This time both the children gasped.

"Is it yours?" Georgie's voice had gone past awe.

"I just drove it all the way from Robertstown."

That's the way Mary remembered the conversation much later. Georgie always maintained their Uncle stated he owned it, and brushed off Mary's recollection of him saying only that he drove it there. Whatever the truth, it wasn't a concern on the day of the gala. Georgie flung open the passenger door and Mary climbed in next to him.

When they got back to the school Elwyn slowed behind the parked cars, then changed his mind. He drove on and pulled into the school gate, made a turn across the grass and came to a stop facing the gate again. Even as he switched off the engine, the first face peered in through the front passenger-side window, to where the children sat, Georgie's face shining with sheer ecstasy. Not only had he been in a Zephyr Zodiac – a two-tone Zephyr Zodiac at that – but his friends had seen him in it. His place at the top of the mate-stakes was assured.

As the pair slid off the bench seat, other children clamoured to get in. "How much for a ride?"

"Now there's an idea," said Elwyn, "much better than shoving sticks in sand. Shall we make these kids happy and raise some money for the school?"

An hour later when the stalls were stripped of goods to sell and most buyers were making their way home, Uncle Elwyn's hat held a collection of small coins. More satisfying still, was that dozens of children, plus a few fathers, could say they'd ridden in the classiest car in town. Even children who'd already spent their money were able to make the claim because Elwyn said all kids were welcome, whether they had the money or not, and no one was turned away.

Mary and Georgie ran to the sandpit with the hat holding the money.

"Uncle Elwyn said to put this with yours," said Mary and tipped the small hoard of threepences and sixpences into the cigar box.

"He's got a Zephyr Zodiac, a Zephyr Zodiac! He's over there," Georgie pointed, and he's waiting to take us home."

"You've got your bike," said Mary, suddenly remembering how they'd come. Georgie's face fell, then brightened again. A quarter of an hour later the car, Elwyn at the wheel with Ruth alongside him in the front, Mary and her father in the back, drove slowly along Fergusson Street and into Sutherland Street. Georgie on his bicycle rode in front ringing his bell the whole way. When they stopped at number 17 William got out, scuttled around to the back of the house and stayed there, doing something in the small work-shed for the rest of the afternoon.

"Who won the ten shillings?" asked Mary hours later, looking at her father across the dinner table. He put a fork of potato and peas into his mouth and didn't respond. Ruth looked at him.

"Yes, tell us, who got it?"

William wiped his mouth with a napkin, put his hand in his pocket and handed a brown note to Elwyn without looking up.

"You won it!" Mary's exclamation combined astonishment and delight. This day was full of wonders. She remembered him standing back and looking over the pit. "How did you do it?"

"Too easy." Uncle Elwyn lowered his voice and bent toward her as he replied in an assumed conspiratorial tone. But in the small room the semi-whisper was audible to them all, as perhaps he intended it to be.

Other questions also remained only partially answered.

"Is the Zodiac really yours?" from Georgie.

"Ask no questions, you'll be told no lies."

"You haven't done anything silly, have you Elwyn?" from Ruth.

"Silly? Me? Have you ever known me to do something silly? On second thoughts, don't answer."

"I'm not likely to have Sergeant McIndoe knocking on the door, am I?" from William. "That car is sitting outside my house. I hope I don't have any reason to be worried. I don't want this family implicated in anything unsavoury."

"Would I do such a thing to you!"

The truth, whatever it was, remained unrevealed. When the family returned from church next morning, Elwyn's blankets were folded on the spare bed in Georgie's room, and a typically extravagant note of thanks was sitting on the kitchen table, together with a ten-shilling note with instructions for Ruth to buy herself some nylons and something sweet for Georgie and Mary.

The car was gone, never to be seen in Waimamae again, at least not associated with Uncle Elwyn. Not even on that last fateful visit.

Ana – do you still remember the song we sang at school? You know, the one about New Zealand.

I've never heard it since. I found myself thinking about it a few months ago when the republic debate came up again, and people were talking about a new flag. I once asked a couple of old school friends, and other people of our age, but they didn't remember it at all. I began to think I'd dreamed it.

But then I had a memory of you and me, on top of a hill, singing it.

TWENTY-NINE

Both of Them Together

Mary lagged fifty yards behind her friend. The two had ridden side-by-side most of the way along the first easier flat stretches of the old Waimamae Coach Road, but now Ana was ahead by about the length of the football field on which Georgie, Rupena, Andrew and the rest of the school team played rugby.

Since several cuttings were blasted through the hills years ago, the road took a more direct and more level route on the latter stages of the highway linking the town with Robertstown to the south. Now traffic was light at any time on this old trail and there was a better than even chance cyclists riding two-abreast wouldn't meet anyone driving to or from the three farms that still used the road as their only access. But the gradient of the road increased once they'd passed the first two bends, and Ana pulled ahead leaving Mary to follow.

She found it hard to push the pedals on this uphill section, especially since the stones on the recently gravelled surface had been forced into ruts by car tyres. It was all right when she could keep within a groove, but if her front wheel touched the bank of the channel it wobbled, and she had to fight to keep the bike straight. To make it worse, in places where the shingle cover was pushed aside, the undersurface was rippled with ridges across, so her front wheel bumped from one to the next in a rhythm that set her teeth on edge. Memories of the dental clinic at Waimamae North School, and the surge of the drill operated by a foot pedal, came to mind. At that thought, combined with the warmth of the day and the effort required to reach their goal, she began to regret suggesting the ride. Ana, a distance ahead, didn't appear to be having the same difficulty.

Just ahead of her friend she saw a break in the deep green of the long grass at the side of the road and a gate set into the fence.

Let's stop there, she willed Ana. She didn't have enough puff to call out, and even if she did her voice, already under the strain of her uphill struggle, wouldn't carry. But Ana might hear her all the same. It was funny the way the two of them did that, putting thoughts into each other's mind. She put her head down, raised herself onto the pedals, and pushed her legs in turn till she caught up to where Ana stood, off the road in the entrance to the gateway.

"This is where we went up the other time," Ana said. "Shall we go the same way?" She didn't look to be panting. Perhaps the minute's stop was enough to allow her to recover her breath.

The two girls stood their bicycles against the fence and climbed over the wide wooden gate. Mary looked up the hill in front of them. The only animals she could see were a few sheep. She was glad she didn't have to deal with her greatest fear, or even have to admit she didn't want to go up if there were cattle in the sloping paddock. The sheep were already regarding the pair warily, and she knew they'd run away well before the girls got anywhere near them.

Twice on the way up Mary stopped and turned to look out across the flat land below, starting the climb again when she'd recovered her breath. Ana was already sitting at the top when she pulled herself up the remaining few paces.

"It's like a village for ants."

Mary dropped down beside her and tried not to let her panting breath give away the difficulty she'd felt on the way up. Once again, Ana didn't show any sign of being affected. She looked out across the network of streets and buildings laid out below them. Ants perhaps, because of the size of how things looked from here, but ants that lived in tiny houses set in pockets of green on either side of shoelace-wide streets. From up here the river was a silver-blue ribbon that cut through the middle of the network of shoelaces, with a matchstick set across it at the midpoint of the straight stretch through the town.

By following a route from the bridge, and counting the cross-streets, she located Sutherland Street first, then navigated the way toward Ruakumara Road. On what was obviously Fergusson Street a pair of dots moved down the left side at what appeared to be faster than walking pace. It's what she and Ana must have looked like as they set out on their bicycles about an hour before.

"Look," she said as something on the eastern outskirt of the town caught her eye, "it looks like a fire." A white column of smoke rose into the air, its base changing to denser grey as they watched.

"Listen," Ana turned her head slightly in her direction so her left ear faced down the hill, "it is – it's the fire siren. You can hear it way up here!"

Mary imagined Georgie, Andy and Rupena abandoning the game they were playing in the back yard of Andy's place, heading inside to the phone to find the location, and then jumping on their bikes. From their vantage point she could see the distance between the two places – the fire would probably be out by the time they got there. Ana pointed, her finger indicating the middle of the town.

"The engine's just left the station."

The two girls followed with their eyes as the red mark travelled through the streets, faster than other dots also moving.

"That's Edward Street, isn't it? Those must be the tennis courts on the corner of McKinnon Street. It's turning into Duke Street. It looks like it's down the end."

"Mrs Flint lives in Duke Street." The girls looked at each other and grinned. Each knew what the other was thinking, though neither dared speak the words aloud.

"Georgie will know where it is – he'll tell us."

Mary looked across the width of the coastal plain to the far distance. "I can see all the way to the Mangatokas." She pronounced the word the way she'd heard it, the way people in Waimamae usually said it when they mentioned the range of hills.

"Maungatoka," said Ana, "it's maunga not manga, and there's no 's.'"

"Maungatoka." Mary copied the pronunciation. She'd try to remember to say it right in future. "What does it mean?"

Ana laughed. "Maunga mountain, toka rock. Mountain of rock – it's our own rocky mountain range."

Once again Mary wondered about that day in the classroom, when Ana lowered her head and kept silent. Not knowing what to say on this occasion, once again she let the moment pass.

Ana dug into her pocket and pulled out an apple. She took a bite and passed it to Mary. Bite for bite they reduced it to a core. Ana finished it off, and they sat in silence, looking at the scene before them – mountains, river running to the coast, with the town straddling the river's lower section. A tune came into Mary's mind. She opened her mouth and started to sing.

Maunga ki moana – mountains to the sea

The sound came out in duplicate as the two girls began simultaneously. They stopped and looked at each other. Mary had given no indication she was going to sing it – she'd just opened her mouth and begun when the words came into her head. Yet the duet was precise in the timing. Not one before the other with the second joining in, but both of them together. The same words at the exact time.

"How did you know I was going to start singing that?"

"Hey, how did you know I was going to sing that?" Again they spoke together.

"Whooa, spooky," Ana remarked, and the pair laughed.

Sitting at the top of the hill, overlooking Waimamae, they sang the whole song together at the top of their voices.

Maunga ki moana – mountains to the sea
Awa me nga rakau – rivers and the trees
Putanga o te ra, to the setting sun
Te iwi, the people, two and yet the one.
Matai me te maple, pukatea and pine
Kowhai and camellia, karo, columbine.
Kotuku and kaka, thrush and sparrow too
Nehera and present, tawhito and new
Tera kikorangi, the blue sky above
Tenei taku ngakau, heart with which I love
Whenua, te Papa, this ground where we stand
Aotearoa New Zealand – yours and mine, our land.

I don't know how much you're in touch with anyone here. Perhaps you know I'm trying to find you.

Ana, I want you to come back.

More than that – Kui wants you here.

"That Ana," she says, "she is not listening to me. It's up to you to bring her back."

THIRTY

Your Basket, My Basket

It was the weekend after their ride up the hill when Kui took Ana and Mary along Ruakumara Road to the marae and explained all the carvings in the meetinghouse, Wharemamae.

"This one is Torepuku the captain of the waka – the canoe that brought our ancestors to this country." Mary noticed Ana's grandmother's use of the word 'our' – 'our ancestors', she said. She meant her own and Ana's of course, and once again Mary felt a stab of disappointment at being left out. Kui might have adopted her as another grandchild, but she supposed she couldn't be included to this extent. Her parents had told her a little about their own parents, and their grandparents who came on ships of settlers from Gloucestershire, Hampshire and Pembrokeshire – places meaning nothing to her. They were just foreign names with no images to go with them. Looking at the carved panels she felt more at home here in the wharenui, imagining the stylized figures as ancestors. Even though she knew they were not related by blood, somehow, it seemed a better fit.

"This one is Tuakai the famous tohunga who was known right around the country. He could do marvellous things, that one." Kui lifted her hand to the panel and uttered a short chant.

"And here is Hine-Toa."

Hine-Toa was sinuous, sleek, her body writhing. Perhaps the first kaiarahi, who brought the first people to this place, was caught up in the depths of her private agony as she longed for her kin back in the ancient homeland. But what Mary saw in the taniwha kaitiaki's curving shape, which curled and twisted around on itself, was the movement of the water of the river, the swirling of the currents in the Waimamae.

"Mere," said Kui as the three walked back along Ruakumara Road, "you come to me every Sunday morning. You and Ana and me – we will learn together."

Whereas before it was more the other way around, over the following year Mary spent more time at Ana's house. Sometimes sitting listening as Kui talked, telling the two girls stories from history, sharing the wisdom of sayings and proverbs.

"Nau te rourou, naku te rourou, ka ora te manuhiri. He aha te tikanga, Ana?"

"Your basket, my basket, the visitor…"

"Ae. With your small basket and my small basket, the visitors will live. That is to say, if everyone contributes what they can, there'll be enough for everyone to eat."

At other times they scouted through the patch of land that ran from behind the house down to the river. Kui called it her garden, and many of the materials for her remedies came from there, but other people saw it as a mess of trees and weeds, and some threatened to call the Council to have it cleared.

"It's her land," Mary understood her father had said, "Just as long as it's not a fire risk, it's all right."

Back at the house, they sat in the yard and crushed miro berries with a wooden club in a tin bucket, stripped the covering from kowhai branches, and pounded the bark of kohekohe. Working together, they burned branches of red manuka, and stalks of toetoe, and stored the ash in glass jars with yellow tin screw caps bearing the words *Marmite – too much spoils the flavour.*

A lot of it came from Kui's garden, but sometimes a truck or car would pause on the road outside the gate and a sack of bark or branches would be left inside the fence. Mary and Ana lugged the bags to the house and into the spare room next to Ana's bedroom. Whenever the door was open earthy smells of bush and forest permeated the building.

In the kitchen, they boiled roots of harakeke and leaves of kawakawa, infused sprigs of manuka, and steeped the inner pith of horopito in hot water.

Once, Kui chewed puwha and placed a clump of the pulverized plant on a cut on Ana's upper arm. She covered it with kawakawa leaves and would have secured it with a strip of flax, but Ana objected and fetched a bandage. She placed it over the pad of leaves and wound it around her arm. Kui looked at the white stripe against the dark skin and laughed.

"Me te makipae, nei? You remember the magpie that was here a while ago," she said to Mary.

In the urupa at the top of the small hill above Wharemamae they stood before neatly tended graves, Kui speaking to the occupants as though they were standing with them. As they left the fenced enclosure Kui instructed the girls to wash their hands, to free themselves of the tapu of the world of the spirits. "Ka pai," she smiled as they rubbed their hands together under the tap by the gate.

More often, the lessons took place around the buildings of the marae complex.

"He aha tera, Mere?" Kui asked, pointing up to the figure at the apex of the bargeboards of the meetinghouse. "What is that?"

"The tekoteko," Mary replied pleased to have remembered the term from the time before, but Kui remained looking at her, expectant.

"Ko te tekoteko," Mary said, and Kui gave a slight upward movement of her head and a flick of her eyelids. Their teacher didn't often acknowledge her pupils' achievements in words, but the characteristic movement of the head told them when they passed any test of their knowledge.

"He aha, Mere? What is it?" Kui always knew when there was a question on her mind, but Mary hesitated.

To begin with, when she first met Ana's grandmother, Mary's eyes were drawn to the rough surface where grooves were carved into her face. Black lines went around her darkened lips, and ridges and dark furrows stretched downwards from her mouth. She'd asked Ana once, years ago, about Kui's tattooed chin, but Ana didn't want to discuss it.

"It's ta moko," she'd said, "it's personal, you don't ask," and turned away.

On that occasion, following Ana's advice, she kept quiet – she certainly didn't want to offend. Since then the lines had become so familiar Mary no longer saw them as anything to be singled out for special attention. The moko was part of Kui, and without it she wouldn't be Kui. But something occurred to her now, and Kui knew, as she always did. As she pressed Mary to respond, her worn brown hand caressed the grooves set into her lower face. Still Mary hesitated, and Kui smiled.

"You're wondering about my moko?" Mary nodded. There was no point denying it – Kui had a way of seeing through any attempt at deception.

"I went to look at Hine-Toa…" Every time they went to

Wharemamae, even if their lesson wasn't to do with the carved house, Mary took the opportunity to visit the figure depicted on the tall centre panel of the back wall. It seemed she couldn't resist. If she walked toward the gate leading to the road without first standing in front of the coiling serpentine shape to pay her respects, she felt a pull in the opposite direction, as though the tide drew her back.

"Ae," Kui prompted her to go on.

"The pattern, on her tail, it's like your... it's like you've got," she indicated the chiselled chin. Mary stopped, hoping she hadn't overstepped some invisible line, but Kui's smile broadened.

"He tika! You're right. I wondered when it would come to you. And now you want to know about it. Come." She led the two girls to the long seat set outside the wharenui, where the senior men sat for the welcome on formal occasions. Ana held back a little and Mary hesitated with her.

"Ko Hine-Toa toku tipuna. Ko toku turangawaewae tenei," Kui uttered. "Hine-Toa is my ancestor. This is my place." She sat and patted the wood next to her inviting them to sit.

"My tahe had started," Kui began, "so I was a little older than you two." Mary and Ana knew what she meant – the older girls at school talked of it, and stayed in the classroom when the rest went swimming.

"The year 1900 was drawing near. Not many men were getting the ta moko by then – the old ways were being given up and they were more interested in working for Pakeha for money. And those who were having it done preferred the new way with a needle rather than the old way of cutting with the uhi. The experts who did it, the tohunga ta moko, were passing on, but some of the senior women took it up. My grandmother,

Mawehe, she became one of the best."

Kui stopped for a moment, then gave a chuckle before continuing.

"Now there was a wahine toa! You didn't get many women stronger than Mawehe. When they baptized her, the priest gave her the name Tepora. They did that in those times – gave everyone a name from the Bible. The missionaries didn't even give them a choice, just decided on a Christian name for them, and she got Tepora. Deborah, you'd say. She was only ever called Tepora when she went to church. There's a story about how the priest came to her one day and ordered her not to do her work any more. By her work he meant her mahi tohunga – healing, the ta moko, all of that. She should remember she was a Christian now and such things were not part of the new faith. Mawehe, she looked at him and said 'When I am at your church, then I am Tepora and I follow your rules. When I am here, in my world, I am Mawehe, and Te Ao Maori is my church.' I bet the priest wished he'd called her something else. Deborah and Mawehe – they were both strong women all right!"

Kui pulled a handkerchief from her pocket and wiped her eyes. "So it was Mawehe who gave me this." She fingered her chin, tracing down the ridges.

"She did it the traditional way. No needles for her – she used the uhi, like a little knife or chisel made of bone." Kui demonstrated, using the index finger of her left hand to indicate the uhi, and tapping it with her right hand. "Then she tapped dye into the cut. First we had to make the dye. A mixture of wood, kauri gum and the awheto – Ana, you know, what they call the vegetable caterpillar." Ana pulled a face and gave a shudder.

It was clear she didn't think much of the idea of it going into her skin. Kui took no notice, and carried on.

"We roasted them – the wood, and the gum and the awheto – then we crushed them into a powder. That's what this is." Again she fingered the lines around her lips and the grooves in her chin." Ana looked away and shuffled her feet along the ground below the seat.

"It took about a month to complete, because sometimes we needed to wait till the swelling went down before she could continue. We were tapu the whole time. We stayed in a hut made of nikau, in the bush out of the way of other people, and all the time she worked Mawehe sang songs and recited her whakapapa – her lineage, and mine. My mother, your great grandmother Ana, brought us food once a day – fruits and berries mashed up into a drink. We weren't permitted solid and cooked food. I was too sore to chew anyway – mine had to be poured into my mouth through a rolled up kawakawa leaf. At the end of the time, when all the swelling went down, then I looked in the mirror." Kui laughed out loud. "I was beautiful." She laughed again. "It looked even better before I got all these kuwhewhewhewhe – these wrinkles."

"The pattern?" asked Mary. "You were going to tell me about the pattern."

"He tika. So I was. This old grey head is forgetting things. You see, little Mere, this pattern as you call it is not just any design. Every moko is different – it is personal to the one who wears it. Mine tells who I am, where I am from. This mark here shows my link to Hine-Toa. I can wear it because I am of her blood."

Mary didn't understand how a person could be descended from a taniwha, but she nodded. What a great thing to be able to claim. She wondered why Ana didn't look as thrilled with the idea as she felt. Perhaps she'd heard the story many times before, while for her it was new.

Kui spoke again, continuing her story.

"It was Hine-Toa who gave our people the art of Ta Moko. Her face had marks like these and our people made them on their faces to honour her." Kui patted Mary's hand and stood to go. "That is the truth about the origin of the tattoo – don't believe any other stories you hear."

At times, Mary thought Ana kept herself a little distant from the lessons, as if reluctant to be there, and she felt torn between her friend and Kui. She wondered whether she should continue coming – perhaps Ana didn't want her there. But when they were on their own the familiar bond between them was just as it had always been. Kui must have sensed the tension in her loyalty to them both. She took her aside.

"Mere, you keep coming, and learning. Ana, she needs the encouragement."

So she kept going. Every Sunday, Kui, Ana, and Mary spent the day together. Kui the teacher, instructing the other two in te reo, waiata, pepeha and whakatauki, marae kawa – Maori language, songs, traditional sayings and proverbs, social etiquette. Together she and Ana ran their hands over the figures of the ancestors in Wharemamae, learning their names. Side by side they picked plants for Kui's remedies. In unison they chanted the verses of the karakia as they worked. On occasions Mary would notice the old woman standing and watching them. When she caught her eye, Kui would look from one to the other and nod.

THIRTY-ONE

Taniwha From Maungatoka

Mary and Ana stopped to say goodbye at the corner of Fergusson Street and Sutherland Street. Mary had walked to school that morning. Her back tyre looked flat when she went to get her bike from the garage and the pump was nowhere to be seen – no doubt Georgie had taken it again. After school Ana walked with her to the corner, wheeling her cycle.

"You're sure you won't come to my place?" Mary asked again, "Mum's given me two old pullovers. She says if we unravel them and roll the wool into balls for her, we can use some for pompoms."

"Nup," Ana said after a moment's thought, "I'd better get going. There's a tangi at Wharemamae and I should be there to help in the kitchen. And it looks like it'll rain soon and I don't have my coat." She pushed off and started to cycle away. Mary was disappointed. These days it felt empty at home after school. Now Georgie was at High School on the other side of the river he often went to one of his new friends' houses after school, not turning up till dinner time. Even though the two of them didn't usually play together, the house seemed empty until he came home.

"See you later alligator!" The sound came from down the road behind her. Mary turned. Ana was already half a block away, but she was looking back at her and waving. Mary waved in return.

"In a while, crocodile," she shouted, then skipped down the footpath toward home, keeping to the outside in order to avoid any head-high branches spreading over fences and extending across the walking space.

She'd pick open the seams of the pullovers and unwind the wool herself. When it unravelled it came out all curled and kinky, but if she wound it around a pint milk bottle, filled the bottle with hot water and left it overnight, it would straighten fairly well. Then she could wind it into balls tomorrow.

One of the pullovers was multicoloured in a fair-isle pattern. It was too small for Georgie now, but even if it still fitted he wouldn't have worn it. It didn't suit his image now he was at High School.

Sometimes Ruth gave away good garments they'd grown out of, and the children were under strict instructions never to say anything if they saw another child wearing something that used to be theirs. 'Don't embarrass them', their mother ordered – such acts of charity were to go unspoken.

"Don't bother giving it away. No one would wear it," Georgie told her when Ruth said she'd pass on the fair-isle pullover to a smaller child through the Church charity box. Then, noting the look on his mother's face, he added hastily that what he meant was everyone would recognize it as his. It was true, Ruth conceded, somewhat placated – the jerseys and cardigans she knitted for her children were often complimented. So it was put into the basket of mending, destined to be unpicked and the wool reworked into something new. Mary would use some of it to knit a hat for Ana's birthday – Ana would like the different colours. She might keep some of the curly wool and make it into a big fluffy pompom for the top.

Usually, pompoms were a similar smallish size because the same templates, cardboard tops from milk bottles, were used to make them. Ana and she used them lots of times, as did all the girls at school. They'd take two of the tops, washed and dried and with the centre hole for the straw punched out, put them together and wind wool around them. From the outside and into the middle hole, right around the circle over and over till the hole was full of wool. Then they'd cut around the loop at the outer rim and tie a length of wool between the two cardboard lids.

For this one though, Mary wouldn't use milk bottle tops. She'd draw around a jar to make bigger circles on the side panels of a cocoa box and use those. It would take longer, and more wool, but that was all right. She could imagine Ana's face when she saw the mixture of colours and the super-sized pompom. "Neat-o!" Mary heard her friend saying as she walked down the block to number 17.

The car parked outside their house looked like the council car, but it wasn't yet half-past three and her father never came home this early. She went in the back door.

"Did you see George?" asked William.

"No. Where is he?"

"He should be here," her father sounded stern, his voice louder and his words more clipped than usual.

"He doesn't get out of school till half-past three," Mary looked at the clock on the kitchen wall. It was only three thirty now. She took a biscuit from the plate on the table. Mum had made Anzacs. What a shame Ana didn't come – they were her favourites.

"The river's up," Ruth said, a tone in her voice warning this is serious, don't annoy your father.

"But it's not raining. Not yet," Mary said, puzzled. True, there was a grey sky, but it had been fine all day – they'd played sports on the field.

"It is up country. There's been a storm and the river's up. The water's close to the deck of the bridge, and high tide's at four-thirty."

It happened sometimes, Mary knew – everyone in Waimamae knew. When there was heavy rain in the high country the small tributaries emptied their engorged flow into the larger streams that, in their turn, poured into an overloaded main channel. On its rush to the coast, the increasing torrent overflowed banks, undermined the sides of valleys and pastures, taking clumps of land with it. Uprooted trees and sometimes animals were swept into the flow and carried along in the muddy swirling water. As it passed through the town the level could near, and even submerge, the deck of the bridge. Before it reached danger point, and especially if large logs jammed between the piles, word would go out for people to return to their own side before the Council closed the crossing.

Kui had another view of what happened in such cases.

"It's those taniwha from Maungatoka," she'd say, "they're always fighting." Her eyes would crinkle and the laugh lines around her mouth would deepen. "Especially that pair Maeropango and Mokowhiri. Never been able to mind their own business, those two – always going over the boundary into each other's territories and causing trouble. When those two fight they tear up the earth and it all washes down here. One day," she stopped and laughed, "they'll wake up and find they've got no land left – it's all down here."

William spoke again, both worry and irritation sounding in his voice.

"We put out a warning at two o'clock and I know it got to the High School – I saw other students on their way home as I came."

"We thought he might have gone to your school to get you," her mother added.

Mary couldn't imagine why Georgie would do such a thing. The river imposed no danger to Waimamae North – it was a safe distance from the river, and none of the pupils had to cross the bridge to go home. She shook her head.

"Perhaps you'd better take the car and go and look for him," said Ruth, and William stood and reached for his hat.

"Can I come?"

"No, you stay here. I don't want to have to worry about both of you."

"He'll be all right," said Mary as the front door slammed shut. Georgie was Georgie – nothing would happen to him. Ruth didn't share her confidence. She opened the door of the oven and scrubbed at the sides with a wet cloth and a dab of Chemico from the tin kept on the shelf under the sink. When the children were smaller she always placed it on a high shelf in the washhouse off the back porch, but now they were older such precautions were relaxed in favour of greater convenience. But their mother still worried about them – that showed in the effort she was putting into rubbing the oven walls and trays. Mary tried again.

"He knows what the river's like. He won't do anything silly."

"I hope you're right," came the response, and Mary knew the list of incidents from the past was going through her mind, particularly the most recent when just last year two brothers paddled out on a tyre inner-tube, and it overturned. The older one, about Mary's age her parents impressed upon her, disappeared under the water and drowned, while the younger boy managed to cling to the tube till someone saw him and swam out.

"How can a parent live through something like that?" she remembered her mother asking at the time, and Mrs McCaskill shaking her head and adding in an equally grim tone. "It doesn't bear thinking about."

Mary pulled out the row of casting-on stitches and wound the blue wool forming the ribbing of the pullover around a milk bottle. She heard the car pull up outside.

"Dad's back," she called.

"Is George with him?" Mary heard the fear in her voice. She went to the sitting-room window and looked out. Georgie shut the passenger side door and her father untied the rope he'd used to secure the lid of the boot to the frame of her brother's bike, which protruded over the rear bumper.

"Yes." From the look on William's face as he thumped the bicycle onto the pavement, she knew what would happen now. Georgie would be sent to his room to await the inevitable punishment.

"Where have you been? We've been so worried." Ruth's voice as Georgie came in the back door after having put his bicycle in the garage, showed a mixture of relief and residual tension.

"I wasn't doing anything." Georgie's usual first denial and defence revealed his frustration at his father's intervention.

"It's four o'clock. You were sent home two hours ago."

"I found him on the bridge." There were two strands in

William's tone also, but the earlier concern was now replaced by disbelief and anger. "On the footpath, right in the middle. The water's close to overlapping it."

Ruth's gasp was overlaid by Georgie's claim, "I was being careful," but the tone of the muttered excuse showed he knew it wouldn't be accepted, and what would follow.

"Go straight to your room. I'll be there in a minute."

Georgie left the kitchen, and Ruth held onto William's arm for a moment.

"He's home safely," she said.

"No thanks to him."

"There's no harm done," Ruth tried again, but William brushed her off.

"No harm done! What do you think we send out these safety messages for? If people see my own son doesn't take any notice, what can I expect from anyone else?"

"Don't hurt him," but William started along the passage to take the leather strap from its hook behind the bathroom door.

"Got a hiding," Georgie would tell his friends next day, with more pride than shame now the immediate pain had passed. They'd all understand, because hidings were the usual punishment for all manner of misbehaviour. The only thing that varied was the implement used.

BACKWARDS INTO THE FUTURE

THIRTY-TWO

Body of the Earth Mother

It was almost a duplicate of the time before. Not even a knock, though it wasn't necessary as the door stood open. Mary heard Amiria coming down the path along the side of the house and around to the back. It sounded as though she was carrying a load. Her footsteps came up onto the back deck and when she appeared in the doorway to the kitchen she heaved two buckets over the step and onto the floor. Three lemons toppled from their insecure perch at the top of the overfull pails and rolled across the polished wood before coming to rest in front of the sink bench.

"You start on those while I get the sugar," she said disappearing, then ducked back to say, "they'll need washing – those hoha sparrows have been sitting on the tree."

Hoha. Mary hadn't heard that word in a long while. At primary school it cropped up a lot. It was hoha when you wanted to play skipping and no one had brought a rope. Rain was considered hoha when it lasted more than a day or two and the children were bored with having to stay in the classroom at playtime. Most of all, younger brothers and sisters were hoha when they got into your things or trailed around after you, asking questions or demanding to join in your game. Georgie used to use it about her, and maybe she'd been tempted in her turn when Amiria was small. Or perhaps not, because Ana always had so much patience with her little cousin, and Mary took her lead from her in such things.

She ran water into the sink and tipped in half the contents of one bucket. Once again it seemed she'd been volunteered to help, but she didn't mind. In fact, she found she now looked forward to these visits. She wondered why Amiria didn't ask her to come to her place to do the work – it would save her having to bring the ingredients and the jars, then transport the finished product home again.

"I could come to your place, if it helps," she'd volunteered at the end of the previous session when they were carrying boxes of jars to the car, and Amiria hinted – more than hinted, stated – they'd do it again.

"There's more room in your kitchen," said Amiria, "you know that. I haven't done much to mine, except get new cupboards and give it a coat of paint." Mary wondered at the time why she should know, but let it go as her friend had her back to her, loading the boxes and buckets into the boot.

Now Amiria returned carrying three large packs of sugar.

"Phew," she said, dumping them on the table, "just as well I don't have to carry all those extra kilos around all the time – I've got enough without having more."

Mary didn't comment. Amiria wasn't overweight – she'd been lucky enough to draw good chromosomes from the gene pool, and the fact she kept herself very active no doubt helped keep her trim.

"More lemon spread?"

"Everyone liked the last lot – it disappeared pretty fast. And the tree's still got plenty of fruit. The new ones are coming on so the ripe ones need to make way for them. And Kui wouldn't like to see them go to waste. She'd probably come and prod me in the night if that happened."

Mary laughed. She could see it happening. The old lady had certainly been prodding her enough. She paused as something poked, then persisted, inside her head too – a memory from something like half a century before. She saw Kui, Ana, Hemi, herself, and a small, shiny-leaved shrub, its roots encased in a ball of sacking. She looked at Amiria as the ideas meshed.

"Are these from Kui's lemon tree?"

"Of course. I thought you knew."

"It must be more than fifty years old."

"Probably. It's huge, and always laden – never misses a season."

One of the first places Mary went on her return was Ruakumara Road. She stopped outside the house and sat looking at the place where she'd spent so many hundreds of hours. It didn't look very different. She wondered whether to go in the gate and knock on the door. What, though, if it had been transformed inside? What if it wasn't anything like the place still so clear in her memory? Someone else would be occupying Ana's room, and Kui's. But they might know how to contact Ana. After a couple of minutes she got out, went through the gate and up to the front door. No one answered her knock. She considered going around the side to the back of the house but, instead, retraced her steps to the car. She'd find out who lived there first. When she knew that, she told herself, she'd go back and ask.

"You're allowed to use them, then? The lemons?" Mary assumed whoever the house and tree belonged to now was probably well acquainted with the marae and was happy to see the fruit used for the purpose. Perhaps he or she knew the proverb Kui told them. *Nau te rourou, naku te rourou, ka ora te manuhiri.* With your small basket and my small basket, there will be enough. Mary had said it often in her mind over the years when she'd taken a contribution to a function. 'You never come empty-handed,' her friends had often noted.

Amiria looked at her strangely, amusement showing in her face. "Of course I can use them. It's my tree." As she noted Mary's puzzled look, she added. "It's where I live."

"You're in Kui's house!" So these lemons were from that tree – the one she'd helped plant so long ago.

Kui stopped and put down the covered bucket she was carrying. "Tenei," she said, pointing at a spot just in front of her feet, "we'll put it here."

"Next to the manuka?" Hemi, his feet in the cut-off gumboots he wore on the *Marakihau*, and usually when working in the back yard, held onto the spade and looked at the short distance between the two. "Do you think they'll get along together?"

"He rakau tawhito, he rakau hou, tokomaha nga tamariki o Tane." Kui pointed again at the place. Mary had picked up enough te reo by now to understand the meaning and to appreciate Kui's inclusive attitude to old and new, indigenous and exotic. An old tree, a new tree, Tane god of the forests had many children.

Hemi put the spade where she indicated. "Why do you want a lemon tree, anyway? They're sour things."

"Lemonade is sweet," Ana said, and Hemi gave a short laugh.

"Now I get it," he said, "when life gives you a lemon, make lemonade. Is that it?"

"It's good on the fish you catch too."

"He tika. That's true." Hemi dug down and eased up a first clod.

"Bigger," instructed Kui when he stood up after a few more thrusts into the earth. She held up her hands to indicate a hole more than twice the size of the root ball. Hemi gave her a look but bent to the task again. When there was a space that looked wide and deep enough for half a dozen such trees, she let him stop.

"There are different colours," said Ana, looking into the hole.

Mary crouched and examined the cut. Below the soil of the top layer, a streak of lighter earth ranging from brown to almost yellow showed through on one of the walls. Further down stretched a seam of red above richer dark loam, and below that the grey-blue shades of clay.

"Te tinana o Papatuanuku."

The body of the Earth Mother. Mary knew what it meant – Kui had told the stories of the primal parents to Ana and her weeks before. Kui stooped to look closer.

"Pakaka, kowhai, whero, puhina." Mary was glad she knew the colours too.

"Tokomaha nga tamariki o Papatuanuku, hoki." The Earth Mother has many children too. Mary related this to Kui's earlier statement about the trees, as the old woman knelt beside her at the edge of the cut.

"We, the people of the land, here." She was bending low to touch the rich brown soil. "The blood of our people," running her hand across the seam of red exposed on the newly sliced surface. "And this," pointing to the varicoloured stripe, "this is for those who came on later canoes and who are now also tangata whenua." Taking a fistful of the topsoil, she rubbed it between her fingers so it slipped through and back into the hole. "You two," she addressed Ana and Hemi, "are of the earth of your Scottish great-grand-daddy as well as the soil of this land. Remember that."

She turned to Mary and gestured toward the plant. Mary handed it to her. Kui untied the strip of flax holding the square of sacking and let the covering fall to the bottom of the pit.

"It's too deep," said Hemi, "we'll have to put some dirt back."

"Taihoa," Kui instructed, putting out a hand to stop him. She turned, picked up the bucket she'd carried to the spot, and removed the lid.

"Hey," Hemi broke out, "that's my terakihi." Kui took the whole fish and laid it on the ground near her feet.

"Tip the rest in the hole," she said to Mary. Out of the bucket came a mess of fish guts, bone and scales. It lined the bottom of the space. At a sign from Kui, Hemi covered it with two spades of soil. Kui then placed the intact fish on the surface and the shiny-leaved plant on top of it. Hemi grumbled again, but scooped the heaped-up dirt back into the remaining gap and trod it down all around.

Kui stood and chanted some words. The only ones Mary recognized were those of the deities – Papatuanuku, Tanemahuta, and Tangaroa. She guessed the Earth Mother and the gods of trees and the sea were all asked to share in the care of the little lemon tree. The four went back to the house.

"I could do with some of that lemonade now," Hemi said as he went to put the spade in the shed behind the wharepaku.

THIRTY-THREE

The Best Days For Sea Fishing

That Saturday the moon was due to be just right, Tangaroa-amua; on Sunday, Tangaroa-aroto. The best days for sea fishing.

Hemi started making preparations earlier in the week for the Friday start, cleaning the *Marakihau*, and stocking it with provisions for a two-day trip. Mary and Ana watched as he checked his long fishing rods and stowed his tin box of hooks. He was whistling and Mary recognized the tune as one her mother had picked up from the radio and sometimes sang as she baked – *Whatever Will Be, Will Be*. Ana balanced on the front strut of the boat trailer, reached her arm up at the bow end and ran her finger around the painted eye.

"Are you going on your own, Hemi?"

"No. Taking along a mate of mine." Though the *Marakihau* was small enough to be handled by one man both the girls knew Hemi usually took along one or even two others to help, and for the company. The cabin was full when there were three large men in it, but the extra company also meant more hands to share the work.

"Are you taking Joe?" asked Ana, choosing the one who went with him most often. The two men were close friends, but were rivals when it came to who caught the most or the biggest fish. Last time, when they had a bet on who would catch the heaviest, they'd come back arguing whether or not a shark counted as a fish.

"No," answered Hemi now, "not this time," adding some seconds later as Ana waited for elaboration, "I'm taking a mate called Jim."

"Jim who?"

"Ana Ihu – Ana Nosey. Is that your name now?" Ana made no response, and didn't ask again. The matter wasn't of much consequence to her anyway, and if Hemi didn't want to say, what did it matter. She and Mary left him to his work. When they walked back to the house they heard him start to sing – *Que sera, sera.*

People said it was a ten-year storm. It hit the high country on Friday night. By Saturday afternoon the river ran fast, silty, brown, with trees and clumps of vegetation sweeping downstream.

It was going on dusk on Sunday when word went out about a boat trying to get in over the bar at the heads. A group of men went out onto the sand spit on either side of the river with tractors and lights to help mark the gap. With the river in high flood, it was risky – the course of the channel could shift with little warning and sweep them away. They were relieved when the boat gave up the attempt to enter, managing to turn across the flow and head back out to sea.

In the morning no sign of any vessel could be seen. No doubt, said the people familiar with the local conditions, it was sheltering in the lee of Moturoa or one of the smaller islands off the coast.

Next morning Ana called for Mary early, and before they cycled to school they rode in the opposite direction toward the river. Though the sky was clearing, random gusts of wind made their progress slow and Mary needed to hold onto the handlebars tightly to keep the front wheel straight. They stopped on the grass bank and looked across the expanded width of the river to the bridge. The water, up to just half a yard under the span, was brown and running fast. On the upstream side the trunk of a tree lay across the flow, caught at each end by one of the piers. Smaller pieces of debris had built up behind it to form a floating mass. Someone would have to go out with a boat and somehow dislodge the log to allow the accumulation to continue on its way.

"Hemi's not home. Kui is worried," Ana said as the pair turned their bikes around and started to cycle back toward the primary school.

"He'll be waiting it out," replied Mary, repeating what William said the night before about the boat at the heads. "He can't get under the bridge anyway, till the water goes down and it's low tide."

"She keeps repeating 'Otane, bad day for everything.'"

"They don't know it was the *Marakihau* at the bar." Mary couldn't imagine Hemi being more than inconvenienced at the delay.

"Kui knows. She feels it."

A couple walking their dog saw the first sign of wreckage. When a board bearing a brown eye with curling black lashes washed up on the beach at Onepu later in the day there could be no doubt.

Hemi's body was recovered the following morning and taken to Wharemamae. Meanwhile the word went out around town, everyone seeking answers to questions.

"Was anyone else out with him?"

"Who is this 'Jim' reported to be on board?"

"Did anybody actually see another man on the boat?"

It was late afternoon on Tuesday, at a spot a further three miles up the coast, when the questions were answered. Or at least the first of them. With the second body not immediately identified by the Police and their helpers, and all the Jims in Waimamae apparently accounted for, the mystery seemed set to continue.

Mary, her eyes red and puffy, answered the knock at the front door the following evening, and called out to her father. "Dad, it's Sergeant McIndoe. He wants to talk to you."

Ruth tidied the baking dishes into the sink and took off her apron, but the men stayed on the verandah and didn't step into the house. After a quiet conversation between them, William came into the kitchen holding his hat. "Keep my dinner in the oven, I've got to go out." He left with the Sergeant in the police car. By the time he came back Mary and Georgie had cleared the table and were in their rooms. Mary heard Ruth cry out in the kitchen. She went down the passage to listen.

"It's not, it can't be. Elwyn's not in town – he'd be here. Besides, he doesn't know this Hemi, does he?"

In a place like Waimamae of course everyone knew everyone else. But Uncle Elwyn wasn't a resident – he just visited from time to time. And he wasn't here, anyway, Mary argued, echoing her mother's words, so it couldn't be him. Her father kept one arm around his wife's shoulders as he reached the other around his daughter.

"I'm afraid it is," he confirmed, "I've seen him. I identified the body."

Because they didn't know the two men knew each other, what was already a double blow came as an even greater shock to

Mary and Ana.

"They probably met at the pub," Ana concluded after the two, desperate in their anguish, considered all the possibilities. Mary dismissed the idea.

"I don't think so. Mum never let him go there. I've heard her tell him – 'You set a good example to my children while you're here.'"

Ana could come up with nothing else that helped. "I know Uncle Elwyn, and you know Hemi. They must have known each other." Try as they did though, the girls couldn't think of a time when the two were ever together. Ana was sure Hemi hadn't been at the school gala the day Elwyn turned up in the Zodiac – he'd gone with Kui and her to Wharemamae. And Elwyn was with Mary and Georgie all the time anyway. Nor had Hemi been present at that memorable Guy Fawkes party.

BACKWARDS INTO THE FUTURE

— THIRTY-FOUR —

The Worst Day of All

Waimamae, being home to Elwyn as much any place, and Ruth being his closest relative, it was decided to bury him there. Both funerals were set for Saturday. Uncle Elwyn's in the morning, and Hemi's in the afternoon.

There were not many at the church. The immediate family, two cousins from out of town – they being the only relatives not too old to travel – a few friends and neighbours, and church people. As they waited for the service to start, Mary sat between her mother and Georgie on the hard pew, her eyes fixed on the coffin, trying to imagine Uncle Elwyn lying inside. It didn't seem right. She almost expected the lid to burst open and him to jump up laughing.

"Joke," he'd say, "I had you fooled there," and laugh at the looks on their faces. Georgie told her later he'd been thinking the same thing.

Just as the organ music faded and the service was about to begin, a party of half a dozen arrived – a group of the mourners from Wharemamae. Kui, Rupena, Ana, and others Mary recognized, but not all of whose names she knew. Together they walked down the aisle and stopped in front of the casket. Kui, wearing a wreath of leaves around her head, gave a karakia, and placed a spray of kawakawa leaves on the coffin, then they moved back to take seats a few rows behind the family.

Later at the graveside, before her party left to return to Hemi and their own tangi, Mary heard Kui mutter.

"Mutu-whenua – the worst day of all."

The sitting room of the Sutherland Street house was full as visitors gathered following the burial. Mary helped serve cups of tea and passed around scones. As she handed a drink to old Mrs Gladstone she was scared in case, between her own unsteady hands and the shaky pair reaching out to take it, Ruth's favourite Royal Albert bone china cup and saucer, one of several sets left to her by Gran, might slip between them. She knew from the way her father kept close to her mother, and frequently touched her arm or gave her a smile, Ruth was only just holding things together. Any little thing would tip the balance. As it was, tears crept down her cheeks when she thanked people for coming, assuring them it meant a lot to them all.

It seemed to Mary, those present were making careful conversation, avoiding saying anything about Uncle Elwyn himself. Some of them wouldn't have known him well but, even so, she wanted them to talk about him. She wanted to hear someone say "He really made me laugh the time I saw him at...", or even "I never actually met your uncle, but I've heard about him, and what a fun person it sounds as though he was."

No one did.

Mary looked at the clock on the kitchen wall. The last of the visitors had left, the left-over cakes and biscuits, dropped in by neighbours over the previous days, were stored in tins in the pantry and, to her relief, the best cups and plates were now washed and returned to the china cabinet still intact. She could imagine Uncle Elwyn laughing at their use.

"Just an old chipped kitchen cup, or a tin mug will do me,"

he'd say, "I've never been considered polite company."

Georgie was nowhere to be seen. Mary was sure he'd be down the garden under the plum tree, probably slicing strips off a piece of wood with his pocket knife, as he did when he wanted to be on his own – usually after he'd been told off for a misdemeanour. She pushed a fresh handkerchief into her pocket, then added another.

"Mum, I want to go to Hemi's tangi." Her mother, having finally sunk onto a chair and replaced her shoes with slippers, lifted her head, giving her a look that was less than fully focussed.

"Another funeral. Mary, I'm not so sure. You've been through enough for one day. Ana, will understand if you don't go. Don't you think so, William?"

Her father paused for an instant. A similar thought, even if prompted by a sense of obligation rather than wishing to be there, had crossed his mind when Kui and her party entered the church.

"It would be polite if some of us went – they came to ours." He looked at his wife's stricken face and was torn. "You stay here." He sat down beside her, "I won't stay long," he reassured her, patting her hand. "Give me a minute," he said to Mary, "I'll come with you."

Mary went to put on her coat, then slipped out of the house on her own. Her parents wouldn't understand even if she tried to tell them. How could she explain to them that she loved Hemi almost as much as she loved Uncle Elwyn?

A group of visitors already stood by the gate when she reached Wharemamae. A woman among them saw her arrive and said, "Here, dear, you come on with us." As they stood waiting to be called onto the marae for a formal welcome she could see, across the plaza, Hemi's family sitting on the verandah, surrounding the coffin. She saw Kui motion to Ana and say a few words. Ana got up and went out the side fence making her way past a line of parked cars, and around to the gate. She took Mary's hand.

"You're not a visitor. Kui says you should come with me."

Ana led her back to the verandah where Kui settled her in beside her, put her arm around Mary's shoulders and kissed her cheek. Mary's tears mingled with hers.

"You are family, your place is here today, with the whanau."

Mary felt comforted for the first time in days.

THIRTY-FIVE

Two Uncles

The mystery about Jim was never solved satisfactorily. Most people put it down to a misunderstanding. Mary, no longer sure of her own recollection, questioned her friend.

"Ana, are you sure Hemi said Jim when you asked him?"

"It was Jim." Ana had no doubt.

"But why did he say that if he was taking Uncle Elwyn?"

Ana had obviously been thinking about it too, and come up with an answer of sorts.

"What do you think? Can you imagine Hemi calling him Elwyn?"

The more Mary thought about it the more she realized Ana could be right. Hemi was the man who didn't call a spade a spade. To him it was a ko-hou – something she didn't understand till she saw a picture of a traditional digging stick, but she'd included the word in the back of her dictionary anyway. At the same time she also entered his often-repeated term for anything he considered rubbish – writing it down as *tutaepuru* = *nonsense*. But Ana laughed when she saw it and advised her to rub it out, and not to repeat it in public.

Hemi was the one who came up with the mental picture she'd never erase from her mind, of a huge bird tricked into sitting on top of a pile of steaming stones. Years later, still no closer to solving what seemed to be a mystery that would remain forever, Mary came to a further thought. Hemi, it occurred to her, was the sort of person who would tell a little girl who still believed grown-ups knew everything, that if you pulled a certain nail in the wall of the wharepaku the can would fly out.

But now, hearing Ana's insight, a picture grew in her mind of him – a grin on his face, a slow shake of his head – looking at Uncle Elwyn and saying in the amused tone she knew so well,

"Geez, man, I can't call you that. I'll tell you what – to me you'll be Jim." Language-wise, she knew, the two names, Jim and Hemi, were the same – both derived from James. And James was her uncle's second name. Perhaps the two of them, whenever and wherever they met, recognized in each other what they were to her – equivalents. Both jokers, each with a store of jokes and stories. The most fun people to be with she'd ever met. Her two uncles.

It was a couple of weeks later when William called the children to him.

"George, Mary – I've got something to say to you."

"Yes, Dad?"

"Don't listen to any stories about your Uncle Elwyn."

Mary didn't understand. Why not? She loved hearing stories of Uncle Elwyn, and about Hemi. Having people mention them somehow let her think, at least for a moment, everything was all right. They hadn't gone. Somewhere they were waiting, biding their time till they'd make an appearance. She didn't want to forget them. Either of them. Ever.

"Why not?" she asked her father again, but no satisfactory answer to her question was offered.

"Just don't."

"But Dad…"

"I've told you. Now I don't want to hear any more about it."

Despite the fact she and Ana talked it through time after time, examining every possibility, the mystery was never solved. Reluctantly, they let it drop. In the end it didn't matter whether they ever found out how Hemi and Uncle Elwyn knew each other. The fact was, the awful fact was, they were both gone.

Every night for weeks and months to come Mary lay in bed, the same thoughts and questions troubling, tormenting, her mind.

Was it because there were no taniwha moana left? Not enough to watch over the whole Moana Nui a Kiwa? Or perhaps not one there to guard the crucial section of the Pacific coast on that November day? The old stories were legion about mariners in trouble at sea calling on the great taniwha of the oceans to come to their aid. So what happened on that day? What went wrong? Didn't Hemi know the karakia? Surely Kui taught it to him, the way she taught it to Ana and her.

E nga kaiarahi o te moana e
Haeremai, haeremai
Toia mai taku waka
Toia, toia
Toia mai ki uta
Toia toia e

"Hemi," she lay awake through many a long night asking over and over, "didn't you call for assistance from the guardians of the deep? Did they not hear your call?"

There was, though, it came to her after a time, one place where she knew the two of them, her two uncles, were together.

For her birthday after the leaflet drop, when the two of them found their lucky numbers in the Esplanade shops, Mary gave Ana a book like her own. Matching except for the cover. Her own was dark red, maroon her mother called it, so she chose a blue covered one for Ana. Though she desperately wanted the honour of being the first in it, she didn't presume to write anything before giving it to her. That was something reserved for a best friend. Ana unwrapped the little parcel while Mary held her breath, waiting.

"An autograph book – neato!" She flicked through the pages. "You haven't put anything in it." Ana sounded surprised, and Mary felt relieved as she reached for it.

Over following years they often compared entries in their respective books. Some, written by girls in their class, were similar. According to Marie, roses were red and violets blue, honey was sweet and they were too; and Janice asked to be regarded as a link in their respective chains of remembrance. Otherwise, the two books varied markedly.

People pressed to put a contribution in Mary's book, mostly family friends of her parents' vintage or older, tended to offer sage advice –

> *Help thy brother's boat across and lo thine own has*
> *touched the shore.*

> *Be good sweet maid, and let who will be clever,*
> *Do noble deeds not dream them all day long,*
> *And so make life, death, and that vast forever,*
> *One grand sweet song.*

Reverend Matthews contributed a verse from John Greenleaf Whittier.

I know not where His islands lift,
Their fronded palms in air,
I only know I cannot drift,
Beyond His love and care.

Uncle Elwyn's entry had to wait till his next visit. When she handed him the book he made a great show of scratching his head and pretending to think. He went through the pages reading what others had written, then said to leave it with him for a while. In the afternoon when she returned from school he gave it back. Mary could tell he was not very satisfied with his effort. She flipped through to find the new contribution. Elwyn had selected a blue page to pen a verse.

I'll write on this page of blue
And wish your every dream comes true
If by chance some clouds beset
They'll make a glorious sunset.

"Did you make it up?"

Elwyn nodded. "It's the best I could do. I'm not so good at writing things." He excused himself in an uncharacteristic show of self-doubt – the only time she'd seen him less than completely self-assured. But Mary was delighted. Not only did she think it a beautiful verse, but he wrote it just for her. It was original.

It took even longer to get Hemi's but finally, after being

begged several times, he came through with what she considered a masterpiece. A pencilled sketch showed a moa, its beak wide open in an almost audible squawk, perched on a fire, its feathers strewn all around. Below it, he had written

Kia ora koe Mere. Remember, never sit on an umu.
Na Hemi.

The pages in Ana's book were filled with different verses, witticisms, and small sketches. To begin with, she'd written warnings on the inside front cover.

If you steal this book you ask for strife, its owner has
a butcher's knife; and If you find this book has dared
to roam, please give it a kick and send it home.

Other contributors followed in equally light vein.

Ana is her name, single is her station,
Pity help the foolish man, who makes the alteration.

Another had them puzzling till they managed to work it out.

1 1 was a racehorse, 2 2 was 1 2,
1 1 1 1 race, 2 2 1 1 2.

An entry Ana really liked featured a postage stamp stuck on a page, accompanied by the line *By gum, I'm stuck!* There were also some Mary didn't understand but she knew made grownups, and sometimes Ana, laugh.

Apart from Georgie's verse about the billy goat, Hemi's picture of the moa, and the paw-print of Fluffy McCaskill the First added to his owner's advice *The art of pleasing consists in being pleased*, the entries in Mary's seemed to her a little dull in comparison. It was all right though, she told herself, taking satisfaction in what was most important. She had, and would always have, the honour of being the first in her best friend's book. At the time she'd been ready, and printed in her most careful lettering the verse she'd rehearsed –

> *Down by the river, carved on a rock,*
> *are three little words, forget me not.*

When the thought about a connection between her two uncles came to her months later, Mary knew that in her book there was something extra special. Far better than anything else. Something she would always treasure. The best of all.

Facing Uncle Elwyn's 'page of blue', this time on a yellow leaf, was the picture of a large bald bird, its beak open in dismay, and the line of advice, *Remember, never sit on an umu. Na Hemi.* The two pages, even though set side by side, didn't do anything to solve the continuing mystery, she knew. The dates on each showed they were penned months apart. All the same, in this place she could see the two of them together. When she closed the book, the names of her two uncles touched.

BACKWARDS INTO THE FUTURE

THIRTY-SIX

Ana Banana and Mary Peary

They were at the High School now. Every morning Ana biked to Mary's place and together they'd go on together from there – into Fergusson Street, along Rimu, over the bridge, into Anderson Avenue, and to the school grounds in Ford Street. On the occasions when one of them had a problem with their bicycle, they'd double, one sitting on the carrier behind. Georgie would look and laugh.

"Ana Banana and Mary Peary. One bike broke so they would sharey."

"Grow up, Georgie," Mary would throw back at him, her confidence boosted by their graduation to the bigger school on the other side of the river. Georgie hooted with even louder laughter.

"You're telling me to grow up. I'm more than two years older than you two. You'll never be as old as I am."

"Maybe not in age," Ana responded once, "we were talking about intelligence."

Mary laughed back at her brother, proud of her friend. Ana always came up with a cleverer thing to say than she could.

"Boys are so silly," she said as Ana pedalled off and she sat on the carrier holding both their schoolbags.

"They're more immature," said Ana, "it's a biological fact."

"I don't think I'll ever get married," Mary responded. "Can you imagine kissing any of the boys in our class. Yuk."

"Vic Wilson's not so bad." Ana put out her right arm to signal their turn into Rimu Street.

"He's in the sixth form!" Once again Mary felt something like wonder as she considered the differences between them. Ana was not only the one who could run faster, jump higher, and throw further, she seemed in advance of Mary in every way. Once again she marvelled that Ana wanted her as her friend.

Georgie was in the fifth form. Sometimes he'd bring his classmates home and, if she were in sight, dismissed her with a reference to his "little blister". A couple of them, though, were nice to her and talked to her, and from then on there was softening in his attitude.

More than that, sometimes she sensed a measure of protectiveness toward her. On more than one occasion he offered words of advice on the subject of boys. She should be careful who she went around with. In a moment of concern, such as she'd seldom seen in him before, he advised her to be "Mary Wary". If anyone asked her out, she must check with him first. Some of them, he warned, had reputations. Reputations, he repeated, with an emphasis on the word, clearly meaning it as a warning. Mary took it in, but couldn't imagine any boy asking her – anyone she'd want to go out with anyway. Mostly, she felt embarrassed in their presence – like when the fellow from Shipton stayed with them.

A visiting group of Sea Scouts needed to be billeted, and the Scoutmaster asked if they'd take one for a night. At William's insistence, Georgie had been a scout in the past, but dropped out at the end of the previous year. He pleaded that in the fifth form he'd need to spend all his time studying for School Certificate. It was hard to argue with his ploy, so William agreed. Now, though, Georgie didn't spend any more time with his books than before – just the minimum he calculated he needed to get a pass mark. Since Mr Owens, the Scoutmaster, worked with William, there was no question of refusing the request for a billet.

On the due date Georgie was sent off to the Scout Hall to bring home a lad called David – lean, gangly, with a well-scrubbed face more than a little pimply. Because he came without context it was the first time Mary had looked at a boy as someone in his own right. Not as Ana's cousin, or Janice's older brother, Sandra's little brother, or some other appendage attached to friend or family.

Georgie and David arrived home on Saturday afternoon an hour before dinner. William was having a cup of tea after working in the garden, so poured one for the two boys. They sat in the kitchen talking – David explaining how his troop spent a weekend on a navy frigate in the previous school holidays. To the surprise of both Georgie and Mary, he called their father "Sir" and their mother "Ma'am". Respect for grown-ups was always insisted upon by William and Ruth, but hearing their parents addressed in that way was weird.

An hour later they were sitting at the dining-room table starting their meal, David sitting across from Mary. Though she kept her eyes on her plate, not wanting to look at him, she saw from the way he fidgeted and moved on his chair he was uncomfortable. As the plates were passed around, the visitor became more and more restless. He turned to William and spoke in a lowered voice, but which, given the confines of the small room, was audible to everyone.

"Sir, can you please tell me, where's the heads?"

Mary wondered about the reason for the query, but no doubt it had something to do with the Sea Scouts' programme over the weekend. William, in the act of spooning carrots onto his plate, was also surprised – but pleased to oblige with the answer. At least, the answer to what he understood was the question.

"From here you turn left at the second corner and go down Rimu Street. Over the bridge, and along Lancewood Avenue to the end. It's a good distance, about ten blocks. Then all the way along Beach Road..."

David looked bewildered, then even more concerned. "I mean, the lavatory," he blurted.

Their father got up and showed the young man into the hall. As they left the room, Mary caught Georgie's eye. On her own, she might have managed to hold onto her mirth, but her brother's eyes bulged with laughter. Ruth reached out and pushed the door closed as they both let it out. After that, Georgie often referred to 'going to the heads' when setting off along the passage, giving Mary a wink as he said it. It was enough, he knew, to make her break out into a fresh fit of laughter and, even better, to annoy their father by the reminder of the embarrassment.

Mary had already added the term, meaning the area at the mouth of a river, to the others in her dictionary. Now she recorded a further definition.

— THIRTY-SEVEN —

Just the Two of Them

Back in the grounds of the primary school after a time away it didn't feel the same. When Mary and Ana looked around though, they found it just as it was before. The swimming pool, the primer's sandpit, the jungle-gym – all exactly as they'd been when they were pupils there, before they'd left at the end of the year before last. Not even a coat of new paint showed time had gone by. Mary could still just about skate blindfolded across the concrete slabs of the paved area in front of the classrooms. She knew when to swerve to avoid a wider crack and when to give a little jump because one slab stuck up higher than the others. If anything had changed, it must be them rather than the place.

Alison was new to Waimamae and didn't know the area, including the school, which is why they were there on Saturday morning. Alison came from Shipton, and had been revealed as one of the new neighbours in Sutherland Street a few days earlier. As the moving van pulled away after off-loading enough furniture and boxes to refill the house left vacant since old Mrs Horton passed on, Ruth insisted Mary go with her along the street to number 11. The full casserole dish was handed over, and the promise made that any further help would be forth-coming – any time, just ask. And Mary had been volunteered to show the new girl around the neighbourhood. It wasn't an offer Mary welcomed at the time, and she resented the fact it had been made on her behalf.

The new girl was in the third form, a year behind where Ana and she were now but her manner showed that Alison saw herself as more than their equal, and favoured everything in Shipton over Waimamae. Mary looked at her as she stood poised on the front part of her sandal-clad feet, aiming at the basketball hoop over her head.

Such extraordinary sandals, Mary thought, unlike anything she'd ever seen before. The footwear in question was simply a sole of blue rubber, held onto Alison's feet by a pair of straps originating from between her two largest toes and anchored, one each side, mid-foot. Jandals, Alison called them, adding everyone in Shipton wore them. The way she said it, with the exaggerated emphasis on everyone, made it sound as if Waimamae lagged way behind the times. When she'd first seen them, Mary stared. They looked ridiculous. She was sure everyone here would think the same way, but Ana gave a broad grin.

"Can I try them?" Ana took a few steps, letting the soles flap on her heels. "Neat-o! I'll have to get me a pair of these."

Alison threw the ball. It arced just over the hoop, brushing the top, then dropped through. A lucky one, thought Mary, but the next one went straight through too, followed by the next.

"A. B. C…" Alison stated the appropriate letter on each occasion. "H. I. J…" The next one went up without any attempt to steady her stance or even aim – as though she didn't care if it made it through the ring or not. It bounced off the side of the hoop and dropped into Ana's hands.

"J," Alison stopped and pretended to think for a moment, "Julian. I'm going to marry someone called Julian."

Mary felt a twinge of annoyance, though she couldn't have explained why. John, Jimmy, James – there were enough of those around. Even Jacob, she knew one of those at school. Why did Alison come up with Julian? No one in Waimamae was called that. The only one of those she'd heard of was in the Famous Five books. Besides, she suspected Alison missed the shot on purpose.

"Do you know someone called Julian?" she asked.

"There's one I know in Shipton – he goes to the school I went to."

"Is he your boyfriend?"

"He's in the sixth form. But you never know what'll happen, do you?"

Ana raised the ball. She hardly even glanced upwards when she threw goals, and often did it with one hand, but she rarely missed. By now she stood taller than Mary by half a head, and the extra height helped. She sent the shot through cleanly and Alison started her A B C chant again.

The irritation increased as Mary heard the letters progress. On their walk to the school Alison had prattled on about the messages on conversation lollies – though she'd called them love lollies – giggling over *kiss me* and even more at *if you love me, prove it*. When Mary looked at Ana, her friend's eyebrows lifted in a wordless expression revealing she wasn't impressed by the new girl so far either, but an amused look went with it, which Mary didn't share. Georgie was in the sixth form now. The two hadn't yet met, but she hoped Alison wouldn't latch on to him when they did. G was even easier to get to than J.

"K. L. M…"

Mary knew Ana could go on for as long as she liked. She'd made the junior basketball squad and was sure to be in the first team next year.

"Q. R. S…" A growing tone of admiration showed in Alison's alphabetical count and a sudden moment of panic swept through Mary's mind. Ana wouldn't follow the new girl's lead and miss on purpose, would she? Once she'd said she thought Vic Wilson wasn't bad. "T. U…" Mary held her breath, then let it out in relief as V and then W passed without mishap. Ana completed the set of 26 and stopped.

"That's enough. Come on," she said addressing Alison, "it's almost lunchtime. We've shown you around, now we'll take you back home."

They left Alison at number 11 and walked on, past the Poole's place, McCaskill's, and through the gate of number 17. Ruth gave them a questioning look as they entered the kitchen.

"We did as you asked," said Mary, "we showed her around." She was aware of the tinge of grumpiness in her reply – intended to give the message that she'd complied with her mother's request. Complied even though it wasn't her choice of how to spend a perfectly good Saturday morning, and she wanted the deed added to the credit side of her account. If Ruth noticed, she gave no hint of it.

"Good. Did you like her?"

Mary paused. If she told the truth it would cancel the credit. Ana stepped in to rescue her, as she so often did.

"She's all right. For a third-former," she added in a lower tone, grinning at Mary.

"Yeah, for a third-former," repeated Mary. Ana might like her jandals, but Mary was pretty sure she wouldn't suggest taking Alison along with them in future. It would be just the two of them, as it would be tomorrow at Kui's. Nothing had changed, so everything was all right.

THIRTY-EIGHT

Black Sheds

The whole time Amiria and she had been chatting, something niggled at the back of Mary's mind. The very back, deep down. She tried to isolate it, wherever it was hiding, so she could draw it to the surface and pluck it out, but it proved elusive. Every now and again, when Amiria reached across the table or flicked her hair away from her face, something flitted by, tantalizing her by almost making it into her consciousness. Almost, but not quite. The sensation remained unidentified. The word wouldn't come. So infuriating.

Amiria looked at her watch.

"I suppose I'd better go home. The boys are painting the back sheds, but they'll be wanting lunch." She picked up her coffee mug and stood.

The back sheds. She'd mean the garage. The part that was Hemi's whare. And the two small rooms behind it – if they were still there. The connection niggled even more now – demanding to be picked up. The back sheds. The black sheds!

They were still black when she'd looked at them last year. Ana's house was one of the first places she went when she came to the town a year ago – when Kui's call grew so persistent she made a visit to Waimamae in the hope it would satisfy her. It didn't, of course, more like the opposite, and after staying two days and looking around she'd come to her decision. At the time, she walked and drove through the town where she used to cycle. Sutherland Street, Fergusson Street, Rimu and others. Then along Ruakumara Road to Ana and Kui's house, and Wharemamae. She stopped the car outside each place that held significance to her, and sat for a minute or two, comparing the present views with her memories.

Her old home, 'number 17' as she and Ana used to refer to it, retained the same basic appearance, though the inverted V-shaped structures that used to form decorative shelters over the side windows had been removed. The front section enclosed by the verandah was painted duck-egg blue in contrast to the light grey of the rest, with the roof charcoal – a change from the buttery cream colour and green roof the house was in her time. Kui's house, Ana's home, still kept to its scheme of white with a red roof. The view down the driveway at the side showed the boards of the sheds were still painted dark, with the corrugated iron roof and the facings the same red as on the house.

"Are they going to be black again?" In any other situation she'd wonder why on earth anyone would want to paint a building black, but on this one occasion she hoped the answer would be positive.

Amiria nodded. "I wanted them white, to match the house, but that damned stuff on them. It's so hard to paint over – keeps coming through, so we're going with it again. Geez, the smell gets into everything – up your nose, into your hair. I thought I'd get away from it for a while – your coffee's a lot better!"

That was it – the sensation eluding her. She'd been looking for an image or a word to provide the clue, but it was the trace of the smell Amiria brought with her. Mary plucked up the memory, a recollection of a day before the worst day of all, and breathed it in.

"There's a man holding a spade…"

"Not me. I've got a paint brush." Hemi waved his right hand to show her.

"No, not you! It's a joke."

"Ah, a joke. I didn't get it, little Mere. Tell me again."

"I haven't told you yet. Not properly. Listen! Whakarongo!" she added to emphasize the necessity.

Hemi grinned, came down three rungs of the ladder and stepped onto the path. He wore cut-off gumboots, khaki coloured shorts reaching to his knees, and an old red checked shirt that had obviously been employed on several painting jobs before, because spots and smears of different shades showed on the sleeves and front. When Hemi wasn't home or out fishing, Ana often said he was at someone else's place – helping them paint their house, dig up or plant a garden, break in a new horse.

"There's a man holding a spade. What is his name?" Mary jiggled with the anticipation of supplying the answer while Hemi took a long swig from a soft-drink bottle then gave a loud burp.

"Doug!" Mary gave the answer and Hemi feigned a look of annoyance.

"Hey! You didn't give me time. I was just coming to it."

"I haven't finished." Mary had the next part ready. "You can answer this. There's another man who doesn't have a spade. What's his name?"

Hemi reached his hand to the top of his head and adjusted the handkerchief knotted at each corner, which served as a head covering. "Let's see," he started, "no spade…"

"Douglas!" She made it sound more like dug-less, the way

227

she'd heard Uncle Elwyn tell it.

Hemi laughed. Ana was standing a distance away, near the verandah.

"That paint stinks," she said.

"Creosote," said Hemi. "It preserves the wood. This shed will still be standing when everything else has fallen down."

Mary bent to look at the tin where Hemi had laid the brush across the top. The fluid inside was thick and dark. It looked like treacle.

"Don't touch it," Hemi warned. "That stuff's pretty strong. You get it on your skin and it can burn."

"You've got some on your hands."

"Yeah, but I'm tough."

"And your legs."

"So I have. Perhaps it will preserve me too."

As Amiria stepped from Mary's kitchen onto the porch and waved a hand in farewell, it was there again. Now Mary knew what had jostled her thoughts, demanding to be identified. The smell – an aroma once smelt always remembered. And with it remained a voice, also never to be forgotten.

"It'll preserve me too. No rot, no borer in me now. I'll be around forever."

THIRTY-NINE

The Great Hine

On Sunday Kui didn't eat lunch with the girls. Mary tried to tempt her.

"Have a curried egg, Kui. I made them because I know you like them."

"Not today, Mere."

"A sandwich then. I'll make one. What do you want in it?"

"I don't need anything."

"But you've only had a cup of tea."

"It's all I need now."

"Then I'll put the eggs in the cupboard for you – you can have them later for your tea."

"Ae, thank you Mere."

Mary didn't think much more about it, but on Thursday Ana spoke to her when they sat together at lunchtime on the benches outside the assembly hall.

"I haven't seen Kui eat all week. She only drinks tea."

By the next Sunday Mary saw she was weaker, and Ana fretted around her as she sat, hands clasped in her lap, her eyes often closed.

"E Kui, what do you want? Mary and I can pick whatever you need and make it up for you."

"There's no remedy for my condition."

"There must be – tell me and I'll get it."

"Not this time." Kui paused a moment then continued. "Hine

Nui has been here. She has visited me."

The meaning didn't register with Mary immediately. Who had visited, and what did it have to do with Kui's sickness, whatever it was? But her thoughts didn't have time to get any further. Ana stood immobile for a second or two, and as Mary looked at her it seemed she had changed. Never had she seen her friend look like this. Though brown skin still covered her face all the colour beneath was gone.

"No, no! Kui, you are not going."

Kui looked calm, strangely peaceful, the lines in her face eased. She shook her head at Ana's response.

"I have seen her, the Lady of the Night. First off at a distance, now drawing nearer."

"Then I will chase her away. Haere atu, haere atu. Hoki atu ki te po..." Ana started to utter a chant, and a chill went right through Mary's body. She stared at her friend. Ana looked like someone she had never seen before – no longer the girl with whom she'd spent so much time over the decade they'd known each other. She was transformed. She stood taller and something sizzled and spat within. After all those years it was as though Mary didn't know her at all.

"Kaua e korero! Don't speak!" Kui held up her hand to stop the words coming from Ana's mouth. There was no anger in her tone, but a strength and firmness coming from a lifetime of knowledge. "Do not challenge Hine Nui. It is dangerous. She may take you instead."

"Then let her," Ana hissed the challenge. "E Hine! Ko ahau tenei. Haere mai. Come on, I'm here, waiting for you."

"Kati rawa! That will do! It is not your time. There is nothing you can do."

Mary stood silent, stunned, as she watched. Ana seemed to deflate. The fight eased out of her and left her friend standing there again. But not the same. The same slim figure, the face as familiar to her as her own – but she was strangely empty.

The following week Nanny Peka came and looked after Kui. Nanny also ignored Mary's entreaties.

. "If Kui sees the great Hine coming for her, nothing can be done. It is time to call the family."

Mary stayed away for a day or two. The family needed their own time, their own space, advised Ruth, and because Mary felt powerless to help when she was there, it came as something of a relief to comply. But Ana called.

"You have to come. Kui wants you here too."

Kui sat in her armchair. Her face and arms narrower than Mary had ever seen them, and the skin of her face fell in new folds from her cheeks to her chin, but her eyes were bright.

"E Mere, give me your hand. And Ana, yours too. There you are, my two mokopuna, my grandchildren, the brown and the white. You two stand together."

Later, as they all sat on the back verandah enjoying the late afternoon sun, Kui pulled Mary close to her and pointed. "Can you see her, over there, by the kawakawa?"

Mary knew she meant Hine Nui. She looked into the gathering dusk, out over the scrubby back garden where the three of them spent time collecting leaves, bark, wood and flowers to make remedies for others' ailments, but which did not work against time and fate. She wasn't sure what to look for. No figure was discernible, but she fancied she saw a strange shimmer in the light, right where the pointing finger led. A shiver passed through her as she spoke.

"No. I don't see her."

Kui's laugh rang out, the way Mary had seldom heard it before – full but somehow thin at the same time. She'd never been able to keep anything from her. Kui held her hand and patted it.

"Ka pai. That's good. She hasn't come for you."

The following day when Mary arrived she found, close to where the *Marakihau* once stood, a tent was erected on the lawn. Two men eased Kui's bed out the doorway. They took it across the lawn and set it down in the shelter. After Mary greeted her, Kui walked herself down the steps, Nanny Peka and Aunty Tui holding an arm each. She walked to the tent, paused to raise her hand in the direction of the kawakawa, and entered. From then on she drifted in and out of sleep, always watched by a number of people.

"Stay over," Ana said on Saturday night. She and Mary stretched out in sleeping bags on airbeds on the verandah, close to the opening of the tent. The first fingers of dawn streaked the horizon when Ana woke. She reached out her hand and shook Mary.

"Kui is calling."

The two girls sat up. In the early morning light they saw Kui propped up, leaning back on her pillows, beckoning with her palm. They threw back the sleeping bags and went down the two steps to the lawn. The aunties in the tent who had been dozing in the chairs beside the bed also woke.

"Haere mai, haere mai. Come to me, I'm waiting."

Mary started forward, but Ana put out her hand to check her. She was standing, stiff and pale, staring at a place to their left, where Kui's gaze was focussed. Ana let out a small cry and Kui looked their way.

"Ah, there you are. Both of you. Always stand together."

And she was gone.

It was never the same after that.

Those special Sundays and their learning were over. She who was descended from Hine-Toa, the taniwha, had gone. And with her something Mary couldn't then name but which she recognized as central to her own being, was lost. On top of her own sense of loss, she ached for her friend. For all the pain she experienced herself, she knew Ana's agony was so much greater.

BACKWARDS INTO THE FUTURE

FORTY

Part of the Family

Mary felt desperate. She'd asked Ana over and over to go with them, but her friend shook her head.

"It's only two weeks. We've got the bach again – where we went last year. You liked it then." Ana remained silent and spun the pedal of her bicycle with her foot.

"Won't Nanny Peka let you?"

"She wouldn't mind." Apparently that wasn't the reason for Ana's reluctance. Mary tried again to persuade her.

"You loved the beach, and the hot pools. Why won't you come?"

"Just don't want to."

"I want you to. Mum and Dad want you to – they say it'll be good for you to get away for a while."

"We'll have to come back." Ana turned her bike around so it faced back down the street.

"Of course we'll come back. It's just two weeks. So, you'll come? Say you will."

"Nope, it's better if I stay here." Ana pulled herself onto the seat, her legs stretching easily to the ground to keep the bike steady as she sat.

"Even Georgie wants you to come." Mary hadn't actually heard him say it, not the words exactly, but she knew he didn't mind. It might be the last annual holiday he'd share with the family because he was leaving school at the end of the year.

Besides, it had been accepted for years past that Ana was part of the family – she'd come with them each summer wherever they'd gone.

"Yeah, I can imagine that." At least it raised a small smile on her face.

"Come with us, Ana. Please, don't say no."

"I just don't want to. I'll stay here." She put her foot on the pedal, pressed down, and pulled away. A few metres on she raised her right hand in a brief wave, and Mary heard her call out, "See you later alligator," as she continued along the street toward home.

"Perhaps it's for the best," said Ruth, "she's gone through a lot in the past couple of years, she probably needs some time on her own."

Mary didn't agree. It wasn't for the best. Ana should be with them. Now, of all times.

"It's not as though we're her family," her mother said, "she has her own, and she probably wants to spend the holidays with them."

Mary stared at her, not believing what she was hearing. "How can you say that?" she challenged. "We are her family. Especially now."

Ruth looked at Mary and sighed. "Yes. We are – as much as she wants us to be. Tell her we want her to come."

But Ana didn't go with them.

When the family came back, Mary got on her bike and cycled to Ruakumara Road. Ana stood on the grass at the back of the house with her hula-hoop circling round and round her waist. She made it drop over her hips then rise again.

"Hey there," said Ana, as though they'd seen each other just the day before, "look, I've put my record up to thirty four minutes." She stopped and let the plastic hoop fall around her feet. "It gets boring after that."

Mary noticed the area of lawn where the *Marakihau* used to stand was almost grown over.

Mary had got it wrong about Georgie. She often did, she thought more and more these days. Their mother always said he was unpredictable – usually just before she shook her head and said he'd be the death of her. William stroked his chin, looked thoughtful, and agreed their son was a complex character that was for sure.

She'd been certain that when her brother left school and had a job he'd be a pumped up version of what he was before. He'd be even more of a know-all, ready to argue and correct everything she said. It wasn't something she looked forward to. The way he would make fun of her and her friends would be even more infuriating than in the past. It would be better, she thought, if their parents agreed to letting him go to Robertstown, or somewhere. Anywhere else. It's what he wanted. But even though they couldn't really have stopped him, William's voice prevailed, and father and son sat down at the table in the dining room.

"What are you interested in?" William asked, and Georgie rolled his eyes.

"I'm almost seventeen years old and you don't know what I'm interested in!"

Ruth motioned to Mary to join her in the kitchen, and shut the door between the two rooms. The pair must have come to some agreement over the next hour because the following day, after a talk to Stu Watts at his radio shop on the Esplanade, they were both smiling. At dinner that night a bottle of lemonade sat on the table, rather than the usual jug of water. William made a formal announcement of the planned apprenticeship, though they all knew the news already.

"It's appropriate I suppose," he said, holding up his glass, "considering all he's broken over the years."

"Will," Ruth started to protest, but Georgie laughed with the rest of them. The following week he began his training as an electronics technician.

On his first day he set out dressed in a white shirt, the new blue tie Mary gave him for Christmas, and a pair of dark coloured trousers rather than the familiar grey shirt and shorts of the school uniform. He looked different. With his long legs covered, rather than displayed between mid-thigh and mid-calf, he wasn't the gangly boy he'd been throughout his High School years.

Perhaps it was that, or maybe the signing of the apprenticeship papers and being under the watchful eye of 'Sparky' Watts, which brought about the change. When Georgie brought home his first pay packet he fished out five shillings and gave it to Mary, telling her to shout Ana to the pictures. Within a few weeks her fears faded, Ruth and William relaxed – the reality had contradicted all their predictions. Despite the fact she'd thought it would be better for them both, all of them in fact, if he'd moved away from home, Mary knew she'd have missed him.

It was even better when, for her birthday the same year, Georgie came home with a transportable radio for her to use in her room rather than having to listen to the large set standing on the sideboard in the sitting room. She knew it wasn't new, and the fact pleased her even more because Georgie said it was thrown out but he'd made it work for her. She placed it on her dressing table knowing it would all be good between them from now on.

BACKWARDS INTO THE FUTURE

— FORTY-ONE —

Guess What

"Guess what!" The news she had to share wasn't earth shattering, but Mary hoped the effort to use her imagination would help Ana out of her uncharacteristic silence.

She loved the way her friend always came up with inventive ideas when challenged by such an opportunity. They'd played this 'guess-what' game for years. When Ana did the same to her, she could never respond with such ingenious ideas off the cuff. Her guesses seemed to limp along while Ana's took off and flew. She used to worry in case she'd be thought dull in comparison, and one day she'd be on her own, replaced by another best friend. So she found a way to make up.

It was a secret she'd never divulge to anyone – not even Ana, and she always told her everything. Sometimes, in the early years of their friendship, before she went to sleep at night Mary would push herself, stretching the bounds of her inventiveness in order to produce suitably fantastic scenarios as Ana did apparently spontaneously. She'd go over and over them in her mind, refining and practising, so they were ready the next time she was challenged.

In her imagination Ana would look at her, her dark eyes shining the way they always used to do, and say, "I bet you can't guess what!" Then she, Mary, would pretend to pluck a series of fanciful ideas out of the air. Except, in her case, they were prepared ahead and rehearsed.

"The Queen is coming to Waimamae and she specifically asked to meet you and me."

"Miss Prudey Purdey got locked out of her house with nothing on and had to go next door to Mr Jervois for help?" It was completely unlikely, because even in Mary's wildest imagination she didn't believe Miss Purity ever got completely naked, even in the bath, but it did conjure up a picture she hoped would keep them laughing for several minutes.

"Johnny Lamb went flying and found he'd left his plane behind. He was as high as a kite!" She had a joke made by Georgie to thank for this one.

Then, again in her contrived fantasy, Ana would laugh and tell her she was funny, and that would be Mary's reward. Ana was naturally funnier, she knew – she didn't have to work at it as Mary did.

The game always made each other laugh, and right now, Mary thought, Ana needed something to take her mind off the previous weekend.

"Guess what!"

"Don't tell me you saw a U.F.O., and I wasn't there?"

"No, not so exciting, but almost as scary." As she said it, she realized once again the breadth of the differences between them. Some years earlier they'd gone to the Majestic to see a film about an invasion by aliens and she'd been scared all the way through while, next to her, Ana sat on the edge of her seat repeating "Neato!" If a flying saucer did come to rest on the grass of Waimamae Domain, Ana would be the one to walk right up and ask the little grey men if she could go in and take a look through. Mary would be the one moving at light speed in the other direction.

"I know! Elvis Presley's coming to New Zealand."

"Nope."

"Connie Francis?"

"Nope."

"Roy Orbison?" Ana named her favourite artists.

"No, sorry, not even close."

"Okay, what is it?"

"Mr McCaskill chopped off another finger."

"Eeww!" Ana wrinkled her face in distaste, then after a moment asked, "How many is that now?"

"How many does he have left?" William had asked, more practically, the night before, no doubt concerned their neighbour wouldn't be able to work any more.

When Mary and Ana first rode down Battle Road to the shop at the front gate of the freezing works to pick up an order of meat for Ruth, they looked in awe at the butchers behind the counter. Not one of them still had all their fingers, especially on their left hands. In some cases just tips were gone, but more often the finger ended at the first joint. Others were missing altogether. They watched as the men, standing in white gumboots on the sawdust-strewn floor, sliced cuts from lumps of red flesh with razor-sharp knives, and slid carcasses across the blade of an electric saw. No wonder none of them boasted a full set.

Now Ana turned her revulsion into a giggle. "I wonder if he took it home for Fluffy." The two of them often looked at Fluffy McCaskill the Second barely managing to waddle across the lawn at number 15 and decided he was in imminent danger of exploding. They suspected Fluffy McCaskill the First had met the same end a couple of years before.

Ana giggling – that was better. Mary didn't want to dwell on the gory thought about the finger, but if it helped shake Ana out of the quiet mood she'd been in for the last few days she could almost believe it was worth it.

The previous weekend, Mary had tried to stay in the background, helping in the marae kitchen at Wharemamae – setting out hundreds of plates on the long trestle tables in the dining hall, clearing them when one lot of diners finished eating, and replacing them for the next serving. Then working at the sink benches that formed half of the long kitchen, washing the plates, bowls and cutlery, stacking the dishes in tall piles ready for the next meal.

It was Ana's place, not hers, to be outside and in the wharenui, talking to the visitors. Mary recognized many of them who had come for Kui's tangi a year before – some of them from a distance as people travelled to pay their respects. Now they'd come again, twelve months later, for the unveiling of the headstone. For a person who didn't travel far herself, at least not in the years Mary knew her, Kui was certainly well known.

Every now and again, when she managed to get away from the ever-present 'aunties', Ana came looking for her and took her outside to keep her company.

"So you're Ana's friend," people said, reaching out to envelop her in lavish embraces, and kissing her on both cheeks. "Kui used to talk about you." Mary didn't ask what she'd said. She expected it would be something gentle – she'd never known Kui to speak an unkind word about anyone else, so trusted it would be the same in her case.

Then, as soon as she could, Mary slipped away back to the

kitchen, the kauta, to plunge her hands back into the washing up water or pick up a tea towel, and listen to the talk around her.

She knew from all the times she and Ana helped on other occasions called for a variety of reasons, this was the place to hear stories. As the cooks, their assistants, the servers, and those who dropped in to do their share peeling vegetables or cutting up sides of meat, worked at their tasks, a constant buzz of talk filled the room. Most times there'd be frequent outbursts of laughter as one of the workers told a story that made the others crack up and stop to wipe their eyes. In the past, it was most often Hemi at the centre of the kitchen chatter, entertaining the others as he worked.

Sometimes he'd tell a tall story, elaborating on each part of the tale and taking his audience along with it till he finished with a twist or pun that made them collapse in laughter.

"Did I tell you about the time I was out on my boat, up the coast a bit? I couldn't pull up my line of crayfish pots – I reckon one got caught in something on the seabed. So I jumped into the water to check out the rope. All of a sudden I found myself surrounded by sea lions. These were pretty mean-looking creatures – every one of them coming at me, mouths open. I thought, this isn't going to end well for me, I'd better try to do something about it. So I put up my hand to stop them. 'Wait,' I said, 'there's a lot of you and only one of me. Which one of you is going to eat me?' Well, I could see that made them think. They started to turn on each other – no doubt having a korero about which one should have me for dinner. While they were arguing, I climbed up the ladder back onto the boat. I looked over the side and all these angry faces were looking up at me – furious I'd got away. 'You've got flippers,' I said to them, 'next time don't stop to argue – flipper coin!'" He burst into a loud guffaw and everyone else joined in, not stopping for many minutes.

Often someone would beg him to recite one of his poems – "the one about the man who took his pet octopus to the foot doctor", or "what about the fellow hitchhiking to Cape Reinga" – in which case, after an initial show of modest reluctance, he'd put down his peeler, the dish-mop or the broom, in order to give the verses his full attention. There was another very popular one too, but Mary never heard it. If someone asked for the poem "about the woman who bought a tin of antiseptic salve from the Rawleigh man", Hemi cast a glance in her and Ana's direction and said that one had to wait for another time. Everybody said there was never any shortage of volunteers to lighten the work in the kauta when he was in session.

On such occasions Hemi avoided the forms set outside the meetinghouse where the senior men sat – the ones who made the serious speeches. Twice Mary noticed Kui motion to him with her head, telling him to join them, but Hemi shook his in response and went back to his work behind the scenes.

"Me nga pukeko ratou," he once remarked about them to Mary as they scrubbed potatoes and kumara, "They're like pukeko – all show and noise, those birds."

For a similar reason Mary was pleased to be able to do what she saw as her job on this special weekend. Ana had to be with the guests, for Kui's sake. For her part, she followed Hemi's lead – staying behind the scenes where he chose to be. Mary wanted to be there for him, in the place on the marae she'd seen him most, because this was his occasion as well.

The unveiling of Hemi's headstone had been delayed till now. Each time anyone raised the subject in the year after the accident with the *Marakihau*, Kui dismissed the thought with a gentle shake of the head.

"Taihoa," she'd say, "not yet. The right time will come."

She knew all along, people said now – she foresaw she would follow soon afterwards. She always intended there'd be a double unveiling, for the two of them together. Ana shrugged when Mary asked if she thought it was true.

"Who knows," she said, and left the matter there.

BACKWARDS INTO THE FUTURE

FORTY-TWO

Their Brilliant Career

Then they were in the sixth form. Broomsticks and paint tin lids had led to some success for Ana in the High School sports. Mary clapped her hands red when her friend was called onto the stage in the hall to accept yet another prize. Every time Ana's name appeared in the *Waimamae Guardian* because of a further win, she cut it out and pasted the clipping into her scrapbook.

Apart from pinning some of the certificates and news reports on the wall of her bedroom along with pinups of film stars and singers, Ana never drew any attention to her successes, and didn't like them being talked about.

"Hello Ana," Ruth greeted the girls as they came in after school. "How did you get on in the sports?"

"Oh, all right."

"Tell her, Ana," urged Mary, but Ana pretended to examine the china swan on the mantelpiece. They'd learned years before in Mrs Flint's class modesty was a virtue to be praised, and skiting one of the deadly sins, to be punished by one's peers with scorn. It was all right to boast on someone else's behalf, though, so Mary added the elaboration herself. "She got three firsts. And a second, but only because she twisted her ankle near the finish line."

Mary had won a few prizes too over the years. The best one, the one she treasured most, was for an essay on the set topic of

A Waimamae Story in which she retold the story of Hine-Toa. When the subject occurred to her she encouraged Ana to tell it but her friend passed the idea back to her in favour of her own choice of subject – the first person from the district to compete in an international athletic event. So Mary wrote the tale herself, after checking with Kui first.

"Of course you can use it, Mere. The story belongs to all Waimamae. It should be remembered. We should always remember the past," Kui added, "it is how we go forward – by going backwards into the future."

However, her successes came nowhere near the number Ana could report, if she'd wanted to do so. Hers used up four pages in the scrapbook while Ana's took eleven, but she didn't mind.

It was just as well they planned to leave school this year Mary sometimes thought. Even though Ana was selective, the number of certificates and photographs of her receiving some award or other didn't leave much room on her wall for more. There could be no doubt of her place as star performer in the local area, but by now the girls knew the chances of either of them making it to the winners' dais in international games was minimal.

Consequently, they'd rethought their ideas about the future, and now the form of their brilliant career was decided between them, but not before Ana toyed with a variety of ideas. At times she talked of how neat it would be to be a vet, a model, radio announcer, and several other professions that all sounded to Mary as scarily exotic as a trapeze artist. And just as hard to imagine achievable for a girl from Waimamae, even Ana. For her part, Mary had never been sure – besides, she'd learned to keep her mouth shut about her aspirations, particularly in front of Georgie.

Her parents weren't much better. For a reason Mary was never able to fathom, either at the time or ever after, her mother kept up her hope Mary would go to teachers training college, even though it meant she'd have to travel a long way from home, which she knew Ruth wouldn't like. It was an idea Mary refused repeatedly to consider. She suspected Ruth had something to do with the same expectation held by some of the staff at the High School.

A few months earlier Mrs Williment called Mary to the office she occupied when filling the additional duty of Careers Advisor. When Mary seated herself on the opposite side of the desk, the teacher slid a document in front of her.

"This is the form you'll have to fill in," she said.

Mary didn't know what she was referring to – there'd been no discussion about a need for completing any forms.

"For teachers training college," came the explanation in response to Mary's blank look. The tone was matter-of-fact, brisk, efficient. It compounded the shock Mary felt as she heard the words.

"I'm not going to be a teacher." She was aware as the instant denial emerged it might be regarded as rude, being directed at one of the profession, and particularly given the negative stress she put on the last word. But Mrs Williment didn't appear to take it personally. She simply looked puzzled.

"You're not?"

"Me? Be a teacher – I couldn't."

"Yes, you can, there's still time. But you need to apply right away if you want to get in next year." Mrs Williment obviously didn't understand. "You'll make a very good teacher," she assured her, tapping her finger on the top edge of the form.

Mary had a vision of a classroom, an overbearing teacher stuffed into a tight woollen dress and bulging shoes, a leather strap coming down hard on the outstretched hand of a boy with callipers on his legs. Then of the same figure, her mottled face frowning as she advised the class, "If Mary ever gets a job in a shop, don't go in there." She stood, needing to get outside, away from the situation.

"I couldn't do it. I can't. I won't!" The back of her legs knocked the chair so it toppled over behind her as she ran out of the room, but she hardly noticed. She didn't believe that these people, who had known her now for at least four years, some of them for most of her life, thought her capable of such a thing. Ana was waiting for her outside – she would understand.

Ruth didn't. Perhaps her mother had wanted to be a teacher herself, Mary wondered from time to time over following years when the memory came back to unsettle her. But then, thinking further, of the stories Ruth told about the way she grew up, Mary decided it was probably another legacy of the years of the great depression her parents had lived through. Schoolteachers stayed employed even when large numbers of others lost their jobs. William, when pressed by his wife to support her, said merely her mother was right – teaching provided a steady career, but it was up to her.

Years later, when Mary remembered the depth of revulsion she felt at the time, an even more disturbing idea came to her mind. Was her reaction really caused by the thought the teachers believed she could be the sort of person that persisted, disturbingly, in her mind as a model? Or was it fear that, if she tried, she might find out they were right?

In the past week, however, Mary had finally made up her mind. What a relief to at last have a plan she was happy with, but she wondered how Ana would take the news. She couldn't remember a time when the two weren't together most days, when they didn't share everything – their possessions, their thoughts, their secrets. Now it looked as though this time was coming to an end. She was going away, leaving Ana behind. For the first time she remembered, she didn't race to share news with her best friend.

"Let's go to the primary school," she said, picking up her basketball and tossing it into Ana's hands. These days they almost always worked at her house and Mary seldom went to Ana's. Things were changed there now. Nanny Peka occupied Kui's bedroom, and the one next to Ana's that used to store bags and boxes filled with leaves, bark and lichens for their medicine making was cleared. Now it was often inhabited by one of Nanny Peka's relatives who came and went at will. Ana pulled a face whenever she mentioned him. It wasn't so bad when he sat on the verandah to smoke the strong acrid-smelling cigarettes he preferred, but at night he puffed away in the bedroom next to hers. Even though she kept her door shut, unwanted fumes crept in.

Today the two girls put in more than an hour on their biology notes – summarizing a section of the course each, discussing what was likely to come up in the exam, and deciding on a plan to cover the work between them. The few blocks walk to the primary school ground and a half-hour spent shooting goals would do them good, and she'd tell Ana the news as they played. Now the time had come.

Ana stood under the metal post, her right arm over her head

with the ball balancing on her hand – just as Mary had seen her hundreds of times before.

"I've decided."

"Decided what? Whether you prefer licorice allsorts or chocolate fish? Or whether to go out with Ferret-face or not?"

Mary knew the reference to Fred Dubble wasn't meant as a judgment, from Ana at least. It's the way Georgie referred to him after he came home to find Fred talking to her at the front gate. Fred was in the sixth form too, and after school delivered groceries packed into a carton carried in the wide frame attached to the front of the bicycle belonging to the Rivervalley Farmers Co-op. Mary thought he was good-looking, but Georgie would find fault with any boy who showed interest in his little sister.

"I've decided what I'm going to do next year." She paused for a moment. Ana didn't ask, but she delayed taking the throw aimed at the metal hoop on the goalpost.

"I'm applying to go nursing."

Ana looked at her, then back upwards at the shot in her sights.

"Yeah," she said, "that sounds neat. You'll be good at it." She threw the ball up to the goal post where it curved downwards into the hoop in a perfect fit. Taking a step back she repeated the move. Once more it fitted through with precision. "I could do it too."

"You'd come with me?" The thought hit Mary like a blow. It hadn't occurred to her in all the time she'd been thinking it through. Ana, her dreams on other things, always seemed destined for something else. More glamorous things. She'd always imagined her in costumes of shining silver or gold, a glitter-covered plume on her head, not in starched white cotton topped by a stiff hat held on by a pair of bobby-pins. But this solution was perfect. Her mind raced as she rushed to absorb it.

"We'll have to go to Robertstown for our training. But Mum says I'll be staying – we'll be staying – at the Nurses' Home. It's not far by train. We can come back whenever we have a couple of days off."

"Sure."

"You will?" Mary stood stunned. After the worrying, despite all the concerns, it had worked out. Ana was going with her. Her fears of leaving home, of going to Robertstown, of starting work, dissolved. With Ana there with her, it would be easy. And she wouldn't be leaving her best friend behind.

The days and weeks that followed were filled with joy. At the end of the year she and Ana were going to the city. Both of them, together.

Ana, as soon as I came back to Waimamae I walked around the cemeteries. First, the one on North Road. My mum and dad are there now. Uncle Elwyn of course. Mrs Rosen, Mrs McCain, Mr and Mrs Wilson together – you'll remember all of them. And many others we knew. Every row has so many familiar names. Hey – you'll like this one, Ana – I spotted Miss Purdy's grave, and right behind it in the next row, Bottler Bob's. Their headstones are back to back. I wonder if Miss Prudey is resting in peace, knowing that.

Then I went to the urupa at Wharemamae – especially to visit Kui's grave, but there were the others too. Hemi's, of course. Rupena, Uncle Matiu, Nanny Peka, and so many others we knew. I talked to them all.

But it was Kui who talked to me.

FORTY-THREE

As They Had Always Been

At the end of the year loomed the hurdle that for so long seemed far in the future – University Entrance. For a month before the school exams that preceded the national event, the two girls spent all the time they could spare swotting together.

"What are the major rivers and land forms in England?"

"TOTTS. Thames, Ouse, Trent, Tweed, Severn." It was a memory prompt they'd come up with.

"Pennine Mountains, mainly carboniferous limestone. I don't know why we have to learn this stuff. We should study New Zealand geography." Ana dropped her pen on the small desk in Mary's bedroom. "I'm sick of this. We're never going to use any of this, anyway." Her hands fidgeted and she looked as though she was about to get up and go.

"A bit more, there's so much we need to go through," Mary pleaded.

"Why? You're going to pass. You'll be accredited. You can't miss."

"So will you. Our marks are way good enough."

"Then why are we bothering to swot? We've already been accepted into nursing training."

"Just in case. And we want to do well in the school exams, to make sure."

"Let's go and throw goals." Ana still wavered, tapping her feet.

"Test me on biology first," Mary asked, picking Ana's best

subject. "We need to do well in it, because of our nursing."

"Okay," Ana sighed and picked up an exercise book. "How many hearts does an octopus have?" She snorted. " I don't see how that's going to help us. We're not going to have any of those in the hospital as patients, are we!"

The Monday morning they were to sit the first of the school finals Mary stood waiting at the gate, holding her bicycle. She hadn't seen Ana over the weekend – there'd been a phone call to say Nanny Peka wanted her help with some things, then she'd study at home. That was all right – Mary intended to spend every minute she could with her books, and after this week they'd have all the time they wanted for other things. She looked along the street – no sign of her friend. She cycled to the end of the block and checked the length of Fergusson Street. Ana was still not in sight. Mary waited till the last moment possible then had to pedal hard to get to Ford Street in time. Even though she'd gone through her notes over and over, she felt nervous about the exam. Perhaps, she thought on the way, Ana was concerned too, and just rode by. But how could she? They'd been going to school together as long as she could remember.

Ana was not in the examination room. For the first hour of the three-hour exam Mary expected her to arrive late, even though it wasn't like her, but Ana didn't come. Something unexpected must have happened. As soon as they were released, Mary cycled to her friend's house. Nanny Peka met her at the back door.

"Ana is in hospital. I took her to the doctor on Friday afternoon. She is having an operation this afternoon."

"Why didn't she say?" Ana in hospital. About to undergo

surgery, and she didn't know. This was unbelievable. She looked at the woman standing on the kitchen step. "You didn't tell me!"

"She needed to rest," said Nanny Peka. She didn't volunteer any more, and gave simple answers to any further questions – Mary could see her when she was better. "Why don't you phone me tomorrow," she offered as Mary stood on the verandah, "I'll tell you how she is."

Mary picked up her bicycle and pedalled back along Ruakumara Road. She should be going over her notes for tomorrow's exam, but she knew she wouldn't be able to keep her mind on them even if she tried. She crossed back over the bridge, rode past the school in Ford Street, and up the slope of Gordon Road. As she parked the bike in a steel stand against a long low building set at a right angle to the main block of the hospital, she thought of the time she'd come here to have stitches in the back of her head. Now Ana was somewhere in there, apparently cut open and sewn up again, and she didn't know why.

The woman behind the reception desk picked up the phone and made two calls, then smiled at Mary.

"Your friend has had her operation. She's all right, but she's still sleeping," she said. "She'll be very drowsy for the rest of the day. Come back tomorrow afternoon."

Ruth was as surprised at the news as she was. "Ana didn't say anything to you?"

"Nothing."

"Maybe it's something she doesn't want to tell you about. Something private, that she wants to keep to herself."

Mary dismissed her mother's suggestion without a further thought.

"We don't have any secrets. Not from each other. We share everything." But the idea rankled within her mind. She hadn't known about this. Ana hadn't mentioned anything of the sort. Ana was her best friend, and here was something about her that she didn't know.

Mary found it difficult to concentrate during the next morning's exam. This was usually her best subject, so she hoped her past work would pull her through. As soon as she could, she ran to pick up her bicycle.

Inside the hospital she stopped at the entrance to Ana's room and looked around the doorframe before she went in, afraid of what she might see. But Ana was propped up in bed reading a magazine.

"Ana, you're all right."

"Hey, it's about time you came to see me. They took out my appendix."

"You never told me. Was it sudden? Did you have a lot of pain?"

"No, I had nothing beforehand." Ana winced as she shifted in the bed. "It's a bit sore now though."

"I thought appendicitis was painful. Why did they take it out?"

Ana shrugged. "Nanny Peka said I needed to go to the doctor. He said my appendix had to come out. Look." She pulled down the elastic waistband of her pyjamas. "See – they made the cut right down here – on the hairline where it won't show. So I can wear a bikini, they said." She laughed. The girls had looked at pictures of women in bikinis in *Pix* magazine, and wondered if they'd ever find the nerve to wear such a thing. The two pieces covered the essentials, but they were a far cry from the one-piece suits they'd always worn. They doubted anyone in Waimamae would ever wear something so daring, leaving their puku exposed to view. Now, telling her about the comment made by the nurses looking after her, Ana was laughing, and Mary joined in with relief.

At that moment, and for the next few days while Ana stayed in hospital, it seemed nothing had changed. They were Ana Banana and Mary Peary as they had always been.

BACKWARDS INTO THE FUTURE

— FORTY-FOUR —

Picking the Alstromeria

Ruth looked at Mary as she got up from the breakfast table and picked up her plate and cup.

"You're not dressed."

Mary looked down at her full-gathered cotton print skirt, white blouse and red cardigan, but she knew what her mother meant.

"It's junior sports. We've got a study day." She'd told her mother about it earlier in the week, but wasn't surprised she hadn't remembered – given the date.

William, a zipped-up leather portfolio case in one hand, his hat in the other, came into the room, kissed Ruth on the top of the head and said he'd be off. Ten seconds later the front door closed behind him. Georgie had left a quarter of an hour earlier.

Ruth reached for the teapot, then put it down again.

"Shall I make a fresh pot?" Mary offered.

"No, I'd better not. Later."

"I'll come with you if you like." Mary knew where her mother would be going today, even though they hadn't discussed it.

"Would you? He'd like that."

"Of course. Shall we pick the alstromeria?"

Mary realized years ago why the best of the blooms Ruth always nurtured in the front garden were cut on this day. In the morning there they were, in a variety of bright colours with

263

their stripey markings, but in the afternoon when she came home from school few were left. She remembered Uncle Elwyn once looking at the border of flowers, remarking he liked the cheeky faces of those ones, and asking their name. "Alstro-mary-a," he'd repeated the word with the emphasis on the mary, "no wonder I like them," and Mary glowed with delight.

"What about...? Are you and Ana...?" Ruth left the questions unended, but it didn't matter, once again Mary understood what she meant. Even after these years, her mother found it an effort to say Hemi's name. Whether or not she blamed him for her brother's death wasn't certain. She'd never said so in so many words but, after all, it was his boat the two of them were on.

"We went to the urupa yesterday, after school."

Ana had taken a packet of seeds, and they'd loosened the soil around the plot and scratched them in. Sunflowers, sunny flowers, which would soon stand tall and bright around the grey of his concrete slab and stone. Two weeks earlier, on October the nineteenth, Kui's assumed birthday, they'd done the same for her. This time with aster seeds – mixed pink, purple, blue and white, as she liked to put together in a vase. Each time as they left the fenced enclosure they washed their hands at the gate.

"Ka pai, ka pai," she heard Kui say in approval.

Mary left her mother on her own for a few minutes. They had scrubbed the headstone, pulled out a dock growing through the grass in the plot, and placed the flowers in the hollow made in the base of the headstone to hold a vase. Now she walked up and down the rows nearby, looking at the wording on the memorials at the heads of the plots, but with her thoughts fixed on Uncle Elwyn. She knew Ruth came up here on other occasions on her own, and was glad she'd come with her today. Ana would have come too if she'd asked, but Mary didn't suggest it. The cemetery was a two and a half mile ride from their place – even further from Ana's, and at the end they needed to push their bikes up the hill. The day before, on the path from Wharemamae to the urupa, Mary walked slowly on purpose. Ana maintained she'd healed after her surgery but there wasn't the usual buoyancy in either her step or her spirits, so Mary went ahead on the track and took the longer but easier route. Ana followed, rather than bounding up the shortcut between the two as she usually did.

Ruth was sitting on the grass. Mary went back along the row and sat beside her.

"Do you remember how he called them alstro-mary-as?" she asked. Of course her mother did, but Mary wanted to say something – to share a story, to show she remembered too. Ruth nodded and wiped her eyes.

"He loved you," she said.

"We loved him too," Mary responded. "Georgie adored him." Her brother would never tell his mother himself, just as William, for all his good qualities, couldn't give his wife the emotional support she needed at these times. To do that was her role, she understood.

When the pair stood and walked back along the grass aisle between the rows of graves, Mary steered her mother away from where they'd propped their cycles against a tree, and toward the tap mounted low down on a post.

"Let's wash our hands – they must be dirty." She held her own under the flow, then waited as Ruth followed her lead. Ka pai, she thought to herself – the dirt and the tapu associated with the place were washed away together. She fancied she heard a small chuckle from somewhere behind her.

"Mum and I went to the cemetery today," she told Georgie as he came in after work. "It's the anniversary. Five years."

Georgie glanced at her, then looked away. Mary saw he was having trouble dealing with the fact.

"What a waste," he muttered, "what a bloody waste." He went into his bedroom and shut the door. Mary knew it wasn't the trip to the cemetery he meant. Ten minutes later he came out again and walked along the hall to the front door.

"I'm going out. Don't worry about my dinner," he called back toward the kitchen, and left the house.

"I saw George going down the road," William stated as he came into the dining room a few minutes later, "where's he off to?"

"I don't know," Mary said. Strictly, it was the truth, but she did have an idea. Everyone knew there were backyard premises men went to after the bars closed at six o'clock, and they didn't have underage rules in those places either.

It was after eleven when the telephone woke them all. Mary heard her father go along the passageway and lift the receiver.

"Keep him there," he said after a short conversation. "If he's stupid enough to do that, he deserves it." He listened a moment more. "No, keep him in a cell all night. It'll do him good." The handset thumped back into place and his footsteps trod their way back to the front bedroom.

FORTY-FIVE

Touching the Mauri Stone

"Sorry about the coffee. It's not up to your standard." Amiria poured two mugsful from the plunger and put them on the scrubbed wooden table in her kitchen.

"Thanks. It'll be fine." Mary had no trouble reassuring her. She couldn't count the number of inferior brews she'd consumed over the years, often being grateful when the cup proved at least warm and wet as she worked through yet another night shift, or when she took a short break from a makeshift clinic by a steamy river. And on too many other occasions when she fought to keep herself awake and the nightmares at bay.

It was good to have the mug to hold as she sat and looked around the room. Amiria had said several times over the past weeks she should return the hospitality, and Mary really must come to her place one day – when she had a day off work and nothing at Wharemamae demanded her attendance.

Mary let the invitation lie there till it felt more comfortable. She wasn't sure how it would be, coming back to Ana's home, Kui's place, after all these years.

The verandah at the back of the house where she entered, the way she always did in the past, looked much as it did then – the deck a darker colour if she remembered correctly, and no cages with recuperating birds. Down the garden the lemon tree spread for metres in each direction. The manuka was gone, along with much of the rest of the old garden. Now lawn surrounded the few trees and shrubs. Where Mary remembered the spot the *Marakihau* occupied, and the bare patch that replaced it for a time, a trampoline sat – the grass around it once more patchy and worn.

Inside, the kitchen layout was much the same, but the units were new. A refrigerator replaced the wood-burner stove, with a dishwasher squeezed into the space where a shelf used to hold boxes of vegetables from the garden. Picture frames with colour photographs of weddings, graduands, children and family groups covered a new sideboard.

Amiria sipped her coffee, allowing Mary time to take it all in.

"I told you we haven't done much to the place," she said, sweeping her eyes around the room.

Mary pointed to the dishwasher. "Kui never had one of those! Or a fridge. It's fifty years now."

"You said Kui told you to come back?" Amiria's question was an open invitation, and she waited till Mary thought about how to reply.

"You remember *Te Maori* – the exhibition of Maori art?"

"Remember it. Didn't go. It didn't get to Waimamae." Amiria grinned. "I haven't been far away – I'm happy to be a small frog in a small pond. Not like –" she checked herself then carried on a second later, "not like you, and just about everybody else we were at school with. Almost everybody moved away. Not me – I'm the one who stayed."

"It was in Wellington. I went more than once. At the entrance to the exhibition there was a big rock – the mauri stone." Mary looked up, and noted the nod of recognition. "It's a stunning thing – huge, full of different colours. People were touching it. You couldn't resist. I ran my hands over it." She paused, wondering if she should share with Amiria what she hadn't disclosed to anyone else. Of all the people she knew now, she would understand.

"It felt as though there were others, other hands along with mine, touching it at the same time. People from the past. Kui, Hemi, Nanny Peka, my parents, Uncle Elwyn, Georgie." She paused. "And Ana." Mary stopped, waiting to see if Amiria would respond – an invitation, perhaps, for her to comment on her including the living with the dead. If that turned out to be the case. There was silence, but it was comfortable. She began again.

"When I went through the exhibits it was as though I felt a hand, Kui's hand, on my arm, drawing me to some of them, the ones that looked familiar. She's been with me ever since."

"What does she say?"

"The same message. Always the same. She tells me to find Ana. She says Ana has to come back."

Amiria shook her head. "She hasn't, not in all this time."

The notes of a tui sounded close by, then other calls – the whistling chirp of a thrush, and a rasping of a magpie. Mary's head jerked toward the door. They were right outside, on the verandah.

"What is it?" Amiria looked at her, questioning.

"The birds." Mary glanced at her friend. Amiria was staring at her, a curious expression on her face. A searching look, perhaps one of puzzlement, minus the element of doubt there'd been before.

"I didn't hear anything," she said.

There's so much I have to tell you. When you come back it'll take us weeks to catch up.

You'll remember Georgie joined the army. That's where he met up with Rupena again.

FORTY-SIX

Like Before, But Different

"Guess what!" Mary knew there was no way Ana would guess the news she had to share with her today, but after all these years she still loved hearing the inventive ideas that came from such a challenge.

Ana rode alongside her on Rimu Street, her summer school uniform hiking above her knees as she pedalled. A slight difference between the colour of most of the skirt and the lower two inches still showed where, weeks before, Ruth had helped her take down the hem. With only a short time to go before the girls finished school for good there was no point, they agreed, in paying for another uniform if this one would do. Now the remaining term time had whittled to a few days, and Ana was bare headed. She'd arrived at Mary's minus the white panama hat regulations decreed must be worn with the blue cotton dress.

"Where's your hat?"

"Didn't bring it."

"Why not?"

"It's in the garden." Ana grinned at the look on Mary's face.

"Why?"

"Nanny Peka said we should make a scarecrow – birds are eating her strawberries. That hat's ugly enough to scare away anything, and I'm never going to wear it again. I put my winter gym frock on it too." She shook her head as though to draw attention to her hatless freedom, and her long plait swung across her back, its tip just touching the top of the saddle. Mary knew how much Ana hated their hats, but there were still four days of school to go.

"Don't you think..." Mary started to say, but Ana spoke over her.

"Take yours off too. Go on. They accredited us both, we've got no more exams. What can they do to us now? It beats me why we're even bothering to go this week."

What Ana said was probably right, but Mary still hesitated. In the past Ana would have laughed as she'd said something like that – but lately a tone of rebellion often came through in the way she responded to things she didn't like. On the other hand, since they were both prefects they were supposed to set an example to those in the lower forms. At her friend's further insistence, though, Mary took off her own panama as they rode along Sutherland Street and a distance down Rimu Street, but when more uniform-clad cyclists came into view she put it back on. Ana shook her head again as she saw her do it, her attention diverting from the question Mary put to her a moment earlier.

"Guess what!" Mary repeated.

"I don't know. The McCaskill's cat exploded?"

Mary grinned. "Not yet. Guess again."

"I give up. Tell me." It wasn't like Ana to stop so soon. She'd given in too easily. Perhaps Ruth was right, and she still had some pain from the operation. At Mary's mother's concerned enquiry, though, Ana denied it and insisted on her fitness – of course she felt well enough to ride her bicycle. Mary could insist and push her to make more guesses, but it might annoy

Ana if her mind was occupied elsewhere.

"You'll never guess anyway. Okay, the news is, Georgie's joined the army."

"Really? Nah, you're kidding. Not him. He wouldn't."

"He has. He's going to Waiouru, starting after New Year."

"Straight up? What about his apprenticeship?"

"I think he can transfer it, and carry on with it while he's training in the army."

"Was it his own idea?" The doubt in Ana's voice showed she still found it hard to accept.

"Dad wanted him to do it. He thinks Georgie will benefit from the discipline."

"He'll get plenty of that all right. He should have asked Rupena." Ana pondered a moment longer. "I'm not sure Georgie will take it, though. Is it because of the trouble he got into?"

"I think so. Dad's been encouraging him ever since."

"What does your mother think?"

"She doesn't like it."

After the initial shock of her brother's announcement, Mary accepted his decision. Not only was Georgie excited about going into camp for training, but she knew that over the past weeks he'd been jealous of the fact she'd be leaving home before he did. He'd made no secret of wanting to leave Waimamae when he qualified. Now it appeared he'd beat her after all. And he'd be going further – Waiouru was twice as far as Robertstown.

When the hands of the clock set high on the wall of the bach pointed to midnight, the four of them raised their glasses and wished each other happy new year.

Mary sipped the dark liquid as she'd seen her mother do very occasionally, on special occasions – just a bit at a time. So that was sherry. It was the first time she'd tasted anything stronger than lemonade. She looked at Georgie and he raised his eyebrows at her giving his 'I'm only doing it for the oldies' look. Given his choice he'd be somewhere else, with his mates, and the small glass would be replaced by a bottle of beer.

Ruth was smiling, but quiet. Several times over the past week she'd offered the remark that this might be the last time they'd all be together over Christmas and New Year for a while. The last time here at the holiday bach where they'd spent their summer breaks for years.

They weren't all together though. Ana wasn't with them. Mary had taken it for granted she'd be with them as she usually was.

"But you always come," she'd pleaded.

"Not always. Two years ago I didn't." Ana was right, but Mary didn't want to remember that year – just after Kui died. She'd had no fun the whole time they'd been away. She sat on the beach with a book most of the day, but at the end of the holiday she still hadn't finished reading it. And she couldn't help thinking about Ana being there, back in Waimamae, without her. And without Kui. Now this year it was like that all over again. Mary tried once more.

"Mum says it might be the last time for ages all the family will be together."

"All the more reason for you to be on your own."

"You're part of the family," Mary insisted as she'd done the year before last, but Ana remained unswayed.

"Thanks," she said, "another time, though."

Mary felt let down. Her mother could be right, and there mightn't be another time. Georgie was off to army camp and they were going to Robertstown to start their training. "Mary Care-y" Georgie called her now, adding once after checking Ruth wasn't within earshot, "When I step on a landmine I'll know who to crawl to." He wore his hair longer than she'd ever seen it – copying those scruffy boys in the Beatles band, William said, adding the warning it would all come off once he got to Waiouru.

When they returned from the beach it was like the time before. And it was different.

Mary took her bicycle from the garage and pedalled to Ruakumara Road. Now she was back and the disappointment of Ana's absence from the holiday bach was behind her, things were back on track. Schooldays were behind them, and the future stretched ahead. In two short weeks they'd be starting their careers and the next big part of their lives. Together, as they'd always planned.

Ana was kneeling on her bed taking down the pinups she'd collected over several years.

"I hope we're allowed things on the walls in the nurses' home," Mary said, wondering how strict the rules would be. Ana took the thumbtacks out of a photo of Elvis, a Hawaiian lei around his neck, standing in front of a surfboard with the words *Blue Hawaii* in wavy letters.

"I'm not going to the city," she said without turning around. "Not right now. You go on first – I'll let you know when I'm coming."

Suddenly, after everything seemed so good, so full of

promise, it was starting to fall apart again. Ana wouldn't be going with her – they wouldn't be sharing this new part of their lives after all. At least not for a while. She said she'd come later, but where did it leave her nursing training? At best, the two of them would be in different intakes. When Mary asked why, Ana shrugged – she didn't appear to have an answer.

Worse than that – not only had Ana changed her mind and wouldn't say why, but on his last night at home Georgie let something drop, and made their mother worry again.

It mightn't be long before he got the opportunity to go a lot further than to Waiouru, he claimed. In the army there was a chance of even going overseas. Mary saw Ruth's face turn quite pale.

"Not to Vietnam!" she gasped, turning around to face William. "I hope you don't come to regret this," she said to him.

FORTY-SEVEN

The Only Thing That Made Sense

They all came to regret Vietnam. Even though Georgie came back. To begin with, his letters home were entertaining and full of chatter.

> *Still stuck here in Comms. Our CSM's not a bad bloke. He reminds me a bit of Mr Gladstone, if you can imagine him about 40 years younger – tough, I know. I think it's because they talk the same way.*
>
> *I told you about Paul, and there's another fellow I've made friends with. Everyone calls him Ginger. He's from near Dunedin. They've both been out on patrols and they tell different stories about what it's like. Ginger goes on about 'Charlie' hiding in trees ready to shoot at any of our troops on the road. Charlie's from Victor-Charlie – VC – Viet Cong. Get it? Dad will understand. Ginger also calls the VC gooks.*
>
> *Paul's been here longer. He says when he first toured around, the country was beautiful, with neat farms and fields, and lush greenery. But he said the roads were pretty rough. Just like up home, he reckons – he's the one from Ruatoria. Now though, it's different because whole areas have been sprayed to kill the*

vegetation so there's nowhere for Charlie to hide. Ginger's always itching to go out again, but Paul says what he's seen is more than enough for him. He's ready to go home.

I suppose I'll have to wait to make up my own mind. Good news, I've been told it might be in a couple of weeks.

The letters got shorter, terser, till they hardly said anything.

Still here. So far.

Ruth cried over that one. Mary took the railcar back to Waimamae whenever she had time off training, in order to support her mother – even when she could stay only overnight.

On each of the short visits she tried to contact Ana. The story was always the same – she was away somewhere but would be back soon. None of the letters Mary wrote, telling of the training, the other nurses, the mistakes they made, were answered.

The message about Georgie being in the army hospital at Nui Dat had Ruth overcome with worry, and relieved at the same time.

"Let's hope it's not bad, but enough to bring him home."

Georgie's next letter told the family that Rupena had turned up in the same ward.

"It's a fairly minor wound to his right leg; he'll be out again in a few days."

It arrived in the letterbox at 17 Sutherland Street at the same time as the news of Rupena's death reached the town. The day after he'd got out of hospital and rejoined his platoon, they'd run into an ambush. They entered a village they'd been through before, to find it had been taken by Viet Cong, and they were hit by heavy fire.

When Rupena's body came back to Waimamae the *Guardian* ran a full-page article, with a picture of the platoon with Rupena in the centre. Two others were also marked as dead as result of the encounter, with the report stating eight Viet Cong were killed.

"That's some consolation at least," said William.

"It won't help Mrs Rawiri," said Ruth, "or ten other mothers."

Mary had a week's holiday at the time, but was due back at work the day before the funeral. She thought about asking for more time and staying for it. No one answered the door at Ana's house. It looked closed and empty, Kui's garden overgrown. Nanny Peka moved to her daughter's home, a neighbour told her. Mary went there, but Nanny was away – up north, her daughter said, but she'd come back for the tangi. No one Mary asked knew where Ana was. Or they wouldn't tell. All she could find out was that she had gone. Mary caught the railcar back to Robertstown.

At the end of his term of overseas duty Georgie came home. Ruth, all smiles, went around singing, and made his favourite orange-chocolate cake.

"The *Guardian* wants to run a story on you, George."

Georgie turned away. "I'm not interested."

"Local boy comes back. How I fought the Viet Cong single-handed." Mary tried to lighten his mood. She too felt relieved, for more than one reason. She had just passed her nursing exam and was a step closer to being eligible to wear the red, white, blue, and gold star-shaped medal she'd set as her goal.

"I told them to call you this afternoon." Ruth dismissed her son's disinterest. She'd gone into the newspaper office herself and talked to the editor. It was a good opportunity, they agreed, to run a more positive story after the coverage of Rupena's tangi.

Georgie turned back to face his mother and thumped the table with his fist. "Then you can tell them I don't want anything to do with it."

The only ceremony associated with his homecoming was a very private one, involving Mary, Georgie, and Rupena. At the urupa at Wharemamae, in front of the bare earth of the grave, Mary saw her brother as she'd never seen him before.

> *E Rupena, taku hoa, taku tuakana*
> *Kua hinga koe ki te po*
> *I a koe e ora ana*
> *he tangata rongonui*
> *Takoto i to waka*
> *Takoto, takoto, takoto.*

She had no idea Georgie could speak te reo. She guessed he learned the chant in Vietnam, so far from Waimamae. As she stood there, a series of scenes passed through her mind. Rupena and Georgie under the plum tree swinging a golf club, lighting the touch paper on fire-crackers and throwing them, on their bicycles racing to follow the fire engine, disappearing into the hole in the ground of Puketapu. Though Mary knew the pair hadn't served in the same unit, she saw them in her mind's eye, uniform-clad, marching together over war-ravaged land a hemisphere away.

Over the next few years she and her brother didn't see each other often. A year after she qualified she moved from Robertstown to Wellington, and when Georgie left the army he went north to Hamilton. For both of them, visits back home were much further apart, and Mary saw her brother on television more than she did in person. The first time was when a group of protestors occupied a government building in Auckland. She recognized Georgie holding one end of a banner that read,

MOBILIZE AGAINST THE WAR.
END WESTERN INTERVENTION.

The news showed the protestors being carried out, limp in the hands of the police, and people in the crowd outside heckling.

"Peacenik hippies – why don't you get yourself a job," a man hurled at them, a companion following it with "Bloody commies."

He took up flying helicopters.

"Why this now Georgie?" asked Mary, when for the first time in three years they'd both managed to make it home at Christmas. "You know it'll make Mum worry even more."

"You can ask, Mary Care-y." He grinned, then became serious. "It was the one thing in 'Nam that impressed me – the chopper pilots who risked their lives flying into battle zones to rescue people." Georgie paused, his voice dropping as he carried on. "It was the only thing in the whole damned place that made any sense."

For some years he seemed to be in the thick of every dangerous situation in the country. Hovering above burning buildings, over trawlers out at sea winching up wounded fishermen. He received an award for taking rescuers into a stranded party on Mount Cook in conditions other pilots wouldn't consider.

"Why do you do it George?" After one news item on what was reported as an exceptionally risky manoeuvre, Ruth made a rare toll call to plead with him. "I get sick with worry about what you're doing."

Georgie tried to calm his mother, though he knew nothing he said would allay her fears.

"Why do you do it?"

He could only answer her question with another, "How can I not do it, when I can?"

It was a simple test flight on a helicopter repaired after a minor accident when things went wrong. An enquiry showed the rotor blade had been repaired instead of replaced. The chopper burst into flames when it hit the ground. The firm responsible would have to stand trial and no doubt faced a heavy fine.

"That's some consolation," stated William, placing the report on the kitchen table.

"It doesn't help George. Or us," replied Ruth.

Georgie didn't have a grave. After Vietnam he talked of cremation, saying he'd decided it was the way he wanted "to be disposed of" as he put it. At the time Ruth, horrified at the idea, objected. No one in Waimamae had ever been cremated. Everyone was either in the hillside cemetery on the southern edge of the town, or in the urupa at Wharemamae.

"Don't talk like that," she remonstrated with him when he mentioned it, "and when my time comes don't you dare burn me up like unwanted rubbish."

William was also at a loss how to reconcile the wishes of his son with those of his wife. Mary called the friends Georgie flew with, and found he talked about cremation to them too.

"Perhaps we'd better do as he wanted," said William, though none of the family was at all sure.

So it was Georgie's ashes that came back to Waimamae. Ruth shrank when she saw the urn.

"So little of him left. I don't want the jar in the house always reminding us."

Mary thought back to the other family funeral – the one almost two decades earlier, but still so clear in her memory.

"We could put it in Uncle Elwyn's grave."

No. Not there. It wouldn't be suitable. William shook his head and Mary noted how grey his hair had become – he'd altered even over the past few months. He talked more and more about retirement – he was just waiting, he kept repeating, till the political parties finally agreed on the eligibility age for national superannuation.

"Then we could put the ashes in the river," suggested Mary, remembering the times Georgie used to swim there. In Wellington, she knew, people sometimes sprinkled such remains into the harbour.

"What, just drop him off the bridge?" Ruth's voice showed her horror at the suggestion, and Mary herself was already having second thoughts. She doubted whether Tiaki Hou would welcome ashes of the dead into his domain. She remembered times rahui, periods of ritual prohibition, were placed on the river after a death in its waters. No, when she thought about it, she was sure that idea wasn't at all appropriate.

In the end they decided, mainly through lack of a better alternative, to sprinkle the ashes on the sand at the heads. As the three of them drove there, the urn held upright between cushions beside Mary on the back seat, she imagined Georgie enjoying the situation. She could almost hear him saying as they passed through the streets,

"Down Rimu Street, across the bridge, and all the way along Lancewood Avenue. Ah, that heads! What a relief. I thought for a moment you might drop me in the other one."

— FORTY-EIGHT —

A Small Red Book

Mary took the small dark red book from where she had placed it in the kitchen along with her cookery books awaiting Amiria's next visit. A few days earlier, she'd pulled it out of one of the last cartons to be unpacked. She passed it across the table.

This time the two women were tying tiny bows of narrow aquamarine ribbon Amiria brought with her, onto wishbones sprayed silver. Aquamarine and silver to match the bridesmaids' dresses and shoes, she explained. One wishbone for each place at the dinner tables, for guests to pull to wish the happy couple luck. Mary didn't want to dwell on how many chickens had been sacrificed to provide the bones. Not lucky for so many birds, she couldn't help thinking, but didn't say so aloud. No doubt they were collected after many hui at Wharemamae – probably over years because, as they cut and tied the ribbon, Amiria chattered on about how couples these days didn't go in for big flash weddings anymore. Most often they just lived together, and her grandniece's celebration on Saturday would be the first big such do for ages. She'd volunteered to decorate the tables and, she promised with satisfaction, they'd be something people would remember.

The first half of the finished decorations now filled a two-litre ice-cream container, and the women stopped for coffee before completing the job.

"There were two hundred and fifty at my wedding," Amiria

285

volunteered, then added looking at Mary, "I guess there were a lot at yours too." It was her usual way of extracting personal information – coming at it from the side rather than asking directly. Mary appreciated the approach – it was easier to switch to another subject if she didn't want that one pursued. It wasn't as though her life hid great secrets, but throughout her career she'd learned to be careful of what she said regarding personal information about those she came into contact with; and the policy had extended to include her own life.

Her wedding! That was an age ago, or more than half an age anyway, and the facts wouldn't satisfy a lover of lavish affairs. She knew Amiria to be in her element when Wharemamae brimmed with people – for a wedding, tangi, or hui to discuss politics, local policy, land rights, whatever. Even when school parties were in residence for a two-day marae experience, 'Aunty Amiria' was always at the centre of the proceedings.

"No," Mary responded, keeping her eye on the coffee pot as she poured a stream into her mug, "my wedding was very small." Should she elaborate? Tell of the almost spur of the moment decision when David told her his plan to join a volunteer medical team in Papua New Guinea, and followed it with the remark that nursing staff were desperately needed too? They'd made the arrangements within two weeks and picked her thirtieth birthday for the event – a matter of convenience that suited them, rather than for an attachment to the date. She didn't feel like a big occasion, even if it had been possible, or they could afford it, and she knew her parents wouldn't either. They were all still raw from Georgie's death on that day the year before. Perhaps the choice of date might help Ruth and William, if that were possible – give them something positive to connect with it, to balance the other. While getting away, out of the country to something so different was good for her, she knew her absence would be a double loss for them. But she'd keep in touch, she promised herself.

At the time, no one mentioned her past experience with birthdays. William wasn't likely to remember and, even if he did, wouldn't bring up the subject. It was too closely connected with Georgie. Any time his son's name came up he left the room. It was his way of coping, Mary and her mother understood, but Mary saw Ruth's pain. It brought back her own when Uncle Elwyn went, all those years before, and she wanted to keep him alive by remembering and talking about him, sharing stories.

On the day, as they walked along the corridor to the hospital chapel, she and her mother side by side and William behind a pace or two, Mary was sure her brother walked with them. The presence she felt on her right side was Georgie's body close to her, the voice in her ear his as it said, "It's Mary's doooom-day." She laughed. Ruth looked at her, wondering.

"I just heard Georgie say, "It's Mary's doooom-day."

Ruth's hand grasped hers and held it. The two of them walked on, taking a son and a brother along with them.

It was a four-year contract the couple signed up for, but they hadn't quite made three. David didn't survive the virus and her own long convalescence after being evacuated meant there were months of her life she didn't remember. In the years, stretching into decades, which followed, she often found herself thinking that all the drama in her life was concentrated into the first half of it. The second part consisted of long hours of hard work, further study, building and extending her career – not so much out of ambition but because keeping busy kept her from thinking of other things.

"No, my wedding was very small." She didn't want to talk any more about it now. Instead, she stood and picked up the little book from the shelf and opened it where a small piece of paper marked the place she wanted.

"I bet you don't remember this!"

Amiria took the book, looked, and shook her head in wonder.

"Is that me? I wrote in your autograph book?" Amiria looked at the up and down letters making up her name. "I must have only just learned to write by the look of it." She continued to shake her head as she went through the rest of the pages, reading words written more than half a century ago. Exclaiming as she remembered others whose entries appeared. Though she paused at the spread containing the verse by Elwyn and the picture drawn by Hemi longer than she did for other pages, she passed no comment.

At the page where Kui had written, she stopped and read aloud.

"E Mere. Haere atu koe. Kia kaha to ako. Ka hoki mai ki te mahana o te kainga. Do you know what it means?" Amiria asked.

"I do now."

Amiria nodded and carried on reading.

"There're not many people in here who are still around," she concluded, "still alive. Just me..." She left the sentence hanging as she flipped back through the leaves, back to front. Mary felt a surge of fear pass through her as she considered what might be to come. From time to time it occurred to her Ana might be among the many who had gone, but if that were so, surely

Kui wouldn't be pushing her in the way she was. She would know, wouldn't she? All the same, it had been a relief to find no marker bearing her name in the urupa.

"And Ana?" she asked.

Amiria put down the book. "Ae. And Ana," she said, picking up the spool of ribbon and a wishbone from the pile still to be done.

Do you remember, Ana, all these things, the same as I do? The way I do?

Mary Peary and Ana Banana who, without being prompted, would burst into song with the same words? At the same time?

The route between Sutherland Street and Ruakumara Road, and the grooves we must have made in each side from our comings and goings between the two?

The bridge over a river that spoke of past and present pain, the swirl of the water where a taniwha lived, and a boat with painted eyes?

The sound of fireworks, and a man who didn't want to grow up?

The smell of creosote, and a man who said he would live forever?

Two boys, who went underground and diced with fire?

A woman who could look with her eyes shut tight and see?

And a girl. The best friend another ever had. The first and the last in my autograph book.

FORTY-NINE

We Used to Have a Plum Tree

"Plums for a change," Amiria announced as she dumped two full flax bags on the table. "Kia ora, Mere," she said when her hands became free, and kissed her on the cheek.

Mary put aside the packets of seeds she intended to sow in the border she'd cleared the day before. There was no point resisting. Besides, she'd learned from the other occasions they'd spent together that a day with Amiria always brought a few laughs. It was good to have such a friend. Though some of the family names she remembered from five decades ago remained in the town, there were few of her generation still around – those she recognized anyway. And Amiria's social knowledge of the town eclipsed any digital database, plus the volunteers at the Citizens Advice Bureau, and library history records rolled into one.

Furthermore, Mary still hoped the contact between them would prove to be the key to learning what she wanted to know. Perhaps at one of the hui at Wharemamae, while the people ate the jam she'd help make, or pulled one of the silver wishbones, someone would volunteer something about Ana, and she'd get to hear of it.

"So what's wrong with lemons all of a sudden?"

"Nothing wrong with them," Amiria replied, "but they keep. These plums are all over the ground, and they won't."

"So what are we doing this time? More jam? Chutney?"

"We'll preserve them. I've brought my big boiler, and the jars for bottling." Amiria disappeared out the door to fetch the next load.

Mary pulled out a dark red plum from the kete. She looked out the doorway to the rear of her garden. She could see the back fence between shrubs planted along the width of the fence-line. The tallest was about the height of the boards and she could see the green roof of the house behind. It didn't used to be like that.

Fruit like these used to drop on the ground down there. Georgie and Andy, Rupena and others, used to have plum fights under the large spreading tree, twisting and ducking beneath the laden limbs as they fired off a fleshy bullet then dived for cover. Once, long ago, two little girls rigged up a trapeze on one of its branches and spent hours upside down, swinging from their knees or ankles and dreaming of fishnet tights and tutus covered with sequins.

Amiria reappeared lugging a large stainless steel pot, set it on the stove, extracted bags of sugar from its interior, and dumped them on the table.

"We used to have a plum tree," said Mary as she washed half the fruit from one of the bags in her sink. "Someone must have cut it down."

"Maybe not. That could have been cyclone Samuel. A lot of trees didn't survive that. Trees and other things."

The tropical cyclone had cropped up in their talk on other such days, but each time the conversation was diverted by another matter more essential to the moment, and Mary didn't know whether or not to go back to the subject with a comment or question. Remnants of trauma relating to the time remained in the town. This time, though, she shouldn't let it pass lest she be thought indifferent to what happened.

"What about you? Was it difficult for you?"

Amiria didn't reply right away and Mary wanted to take back her second question. Of course it must have been difficult. How many times had she clucked her tongue in exasperation hearing a news reporter asking a witness or victim what she considered a silly question under the circumstances? 'How did you feel when you saw the dogs coming at you?' 'What was it like to have to jettison your main parachute?' She remembered the look on Georgie's face years ago when a well-meaning neighbour asked if he'd found it hard to see his friends die in Vietnam.

No one in Waimamae could have been unaffected by the cyclone even if their home hadn't been one of those flooded, even if their roof stayed on, or they hadn't needed to be evacuated.

"I'll tell you what," said Amiria after what seemed a couple of minutes but was probably much less, "I've never seen rain like that, before or since. Three days of it. The middle day was unbelievable. The *Guardian* said sixteen inches of rain fell up at Maungatoka – it was bad enough here. And the wind…" she left the sentence unfinished as though no words could describe it adequately.

Mary weighed the washed fruit kilo by kilo and added them to the pot, putting one plum aside each time to keep track of the tally. Now they'd started on the subject she wanted to hear more.

"Did you know the people who died?" A difficult area, but she had to ask.

"Sure." The single word reply was clipped, matter-of-fact. Amiria drew a breath and continued. "The two killed in the car on the Old Coach Road – the one the bank collapsed on and buried – were relatives of mine. They weren't recovered for three weeks. The road had to be remade so the graders could get up as far as the slip. And a man I knew who lived in Ranfurly Street suffered a stroke, and there was no way to get him to hospital in time."

"Because of the bridge."

"Yeah."

"It must have been hard for everyone with it down."

Amiria filled a two-litre milk container with water from the tap and added it to the boiler. "Not easy, that's for sure."

At the time, Mary kept up with the news reports. For some reason she'd felt guilty about not being there, on the spot, not going through it and doing her bit to help. It didn't make sense – she'd been away from the area for more years than she'd lived there and none of the family was left in the town. William had passed on years before and lay in the hillside cemetery in North Road. Ruth moved into a retirement village in Robertstown where one of her cousins was already settled, making a final journey back to be with Will when her time came.

In lieu of giving hands-on help, Mary wrote a cheque for the disaster fund, and stared at the news photos of the river in flood. They showed the main stretch of the bridge washed away and a wide expanse of water flowing between the end piers, effectively cutting the town in two. The closest alternative route – a round trip of 62 kilometres over a stretch of rough unsealed road – also experienced washouts.

"It must have been a huge relief when the new bridge opened." Mary recalled it had taken close to two years before transit to and fro got back to normal.

"Yeah," Amiria replied, then added the curious rider "mostly." Mary looked at her. How could it not be a great improvement to have the crossing rebuilt?

"Of course it was," Amiria corrected herself, "it's just, when it was down there was a different feeling in the town. The army came, and set up a punt. They ferried people from one side to the other. If you wanted to go across you walked or drove to the crossing point and waited for the punt to come to your side. While they waited, and crossed over, people talked to people they'd hardly seen in years. Everyone had got so busy, so involved with their own lives they'd got out of touch. Now they weren't in their cars they found time to talk. After Cyclone Samuel, with things so bad, we were all in the same boat." She stopped and laughed at her own expression. "It felt like it used to be years ago – you know, back in our time."

Mary did know. When she'd told people of her plan to return to her old hometown she saw the dubious looks. You can't go back, they said, it's never the same. They were right too. It wasn't the same – and could never be. For one thing, she herself was not as she'd been then, a gauche immature girl living in a time of hard 78-rpm records and washing machines with wringers. When milk was delivered to the gate daily in glass milk bottles, and pogo sticks the closest to high-tech toys they had to play with. She didn't want it that way now. But, all the same, there was a sense of loss for some things that were no longer – the best parts.

"I know how it was," she agreed.

The two didn't say any more for a minute or two. Amiria stirred the plums with the longest wooden spoon Mary had ever seen, and she put the preserving jars into the oven to warm.

"Never seen weather like that before. Never want to again." Amiria shook her head in wonder at the memory.

"Kui would have said it was the taniwha up in the hills fighting," said Mary, and Amiria laughed.

"Must have been a ding-dong battle."

"She said Maeropango and Mokowhiri always caused trouble, and one day there'd be no land left up there – it'd all be down here." Mary saw Kui, her eyes twinkling, the laugh lines around her mouth merging with those of her moko.

"What did you say their names were? Those taniwha?" Amiria was looking at her strangely.

"Maeropango and Mokowhiri," Mary repeated. The piercing gaze Amiria gave her made her wonder for a moment if she'd got them mixed. No, that was right. From the first time Kui mentioned them they'd been fixed in her mind, and with them two images. One of a dark coloured scale-covered beast with eyes glinting as brightly as the inside of paua shell, the other a long green lizard-like creature with a body that twisted and coiled at will.

"You remembered them? Their names? For all these years?"

"Yes. I think I remember just about everything she taught us – Ana and me. There was something about Kui – when she looked straight at you and told you something, it went right inside you, and stayed there."

"Into your head?" Amiria stopped what she'd been doing – her look was probing, challenging. Mary paused a moment, assessing how to phrase her response.

"Perhaps," she allowed, considering whether to elaborate on how it felt. Of all people, Amiria might understand. "Not so much te mahunga," she indicated her head, "into te ngakau." Mary put her palm onto the middle of her chest.

Amiria remained still, observing her for half a minute, then turned back to the stove. Mary placed a further half-dozen preserving jars into the sink and ran the hot water to wash them. If Amiria didn't want to discuss the matter any further, it was better to leave it there. After all, Kui was her relative, not Mary's, not by blood anyway, and she understood there might be mixed feelings about Kui teaching what she knew of the past to someone outside the family.

The two women worked for the next hour, ladling hot plums and syrup into jars, pressing down the seals and tightening the screw caps. With the first batch of preserves lined up on the table, and the ingredients for the next added to the boiler, they sat at the table for a short rest.

"You use the internet." Amiria made the words into a statement, rather than a question. On occasions when they'd talked about other things, Mary had mentioned the net as a source of her knowledge on some subject or other. "Have you looked for her on that?" There was no need to ask Amiria who she meant.

"I have." Mary had made searches on Ana's name many times over the years in the hope something had been added since the last occasion she'd checked. "Nothing's come up."

Nothing useful, anyway. Old records appeared from time to time now, as sites added information from archived material. A year earlier she'd been excited when, finally, in answer to her repeated searches, a page of results came up on screen. But when she went through them she found they were all from the same source. Past issues of the *Waimamae Guardian* had been scanned and there, recovered from history, were all those results of long gone triumphs. First place for the 100 yards at Waimamae North School sports two years running; first place for high-jump Waimamae High School the next year; more firsts for sprint, cross-country, discus throwing in following years. Even once, a grainy black and white picture of Ana holding a trophy and shaking the Mayor's hand. Good as it was to see them, they didn't help. Mary already had those in the scrapbook kept over the decades between, with the pasted-in clippings recording the events of half a century earlier.

Amiria pulled a piece of paper from the small pad Mary kept next to her telephone and wrote two words. She put it on the table without speaking, and turned back to the stove.

The name itself meant little to Mary, though she felt sure she'd heard it before. There was certainly a familiarity about it, as with those connected with figures people talked about but who were beyond her sphere of personal interest. That was no worry – she'd run a search online. No doubt she'd find all the clues she needed there.

She folded the paper in half and slipped it into her pocket. As she did so, she fancied a tingling went through her fingers and Kui's chuckle sounded in her ears.

It's taken me a long time to find you, Ana. On my own I might have given up. Except for Kui – all the time she's been driving me.

Just last night she was with me, those eyes of hers looking into me and asking, "Where is Ana? She should be here." It was as though we were sitting at your kitchen table, and she was stirring a pot on the stove.

"I told you always to stand together. E Mere, you make sure Ana comes back. Soon. You tell her, though Waimamae is the place of her pain, it is the only place with the remedy to heal her.

Tell her to remember Hine-Toa. Tell her to remember Te Rongo-Kahere. She is of their blood. This is what has made her, and this is where she should be.

You say to her from me, E Ana! He taima. It is time!"

There are so many changes back here now, Ana. You will find that when you return.

No more stories of squirrels and badgers. Waimamae and Waikato and Waimakariri are our rivers – not Thames and Trent.

Remember when the teacher asked our class who spoke Maori and no one would say they could? Now people want to learn the language – it's not the pupils but the teachers we need. Our generation, and the one before – so few understood. And the kuias who knew have all gone.

Ana, as children we ran together over the same ground, learned side by side in the same school, traced our fingers over the same carvings in the wharenui.

Come back now. Then you'll see what our country has become, and we can share those things again.

You and I can march side by side over the land.

We can select the herbs and make the remedies.

We can sing the same song.

We can run our hands, yours and mine, over the variegated mauri stone.

Together we can pull out our fingernails and set the land on fire again.

Thank you for taking time to read Backwards Into the Future. *If you enjoyed it, please consider sharing your thoughts about it by posting a short review on Amazon (www.amazon.com) Goodreads (www.goodreads.com) or other review sites.*

You can also tweet about it, and please tell your friends. Reviews, either printed or word of mouth, are an author's best friend and much appreciated.

Grateful thanks to all those who have assisted the production of this book in some way, including: Aaron, Candy, Christine, Merilyn, Ollie, Rewa, Susannah, Tannis.

ABOUT THE AUTHOR

When carried away on a flight of fancy, Bronwyn Elsmore might say that if she'd been gifted with a better voice, she might have chosen to be an opera singer. Sadly for her, that wasn't the case, but luckily she found she could write. A good list of awards for short stories, plays, and children's verse confirms that.

Throughout her long writing career Bronwyn has written over a wide variety of genres – articles, short stories, poetry, stage-plays, fiction and non-fiction. Since that didn't pay many bills, along the way she spent many years as an academic.

Currently, though, she spends most of her writing time on fiction – particularly novels. She also reviews theatre.

When she's not writing? You might spot her feeding neighbourhood and stray cats, or possibly adding to the list of countries visited to date. And reading, of course.

You can also meet Bronwyn at

Website – www.flaxroots.com
Blog – www.flaxroots.com/blog

Amazon Author page – www.amazon.com/stores/Bronwyn-Elsmore/author/B001JSAPRA
Goodreads – www.goodreads.com/author/show/436327

Facebook – www.facebook.com/writingfromNewZealand
Twitter – www.twitter.com/@flaxroots

RECENT BOOKS BY BRONWYN ELSMORE:

Every Five Minutes

"We are proud to announce that EVERY FIVE MINUTES by Bronwyn Elsmore is a B.R.A.G. Medallion Honoree. This tells a reader that this book is well worth their time and money!"

Book Readers Appreciation Group

A woman, a man, a white dog. The woman calls herself Gina, but it may not be her real name. The woman calls the man Mr Chipzenburger – definitely not his name. The dog is less complicated and is happy to answer to Electra. Their story will make you laugh and cry.

Readers say about *Every Five Minutes:*

"Bronwyn Elsmore has crafted a beautiful story in a unique way."

"A very unique read to be sure, but her writing brilliance showed on each page."

"A five star read! I hated the story to end. Read it and you'll see. It's a lovely, lovely book."

"A masterpiece! To find that it is perfect in its style and delivery has left me a little breathless."

"Thank you for the opportunity to read this wonderful story! I love, love your book!"

"This is a love story, NOT a romance, and it's beautiful."

"A feel good read. A joy not to be missed."

"It's an ingenuous way to tell the story, and it's exciting to discover a whole new approach to writing."

Further reviews can be seen on Amazon and Goodreads.

BRONWYN ELSMORE

Seventeen Seas

Is there really a stowaway in one of the life-boats? And what's the truth about Germans and deckchairs? On a cruise ship full of passengers from a variety of countries there's bound to be plenty of fun. *Seventeen Seas* tells their stories through ten countries, fifteen ports, across seventeen seas.

Fiction, non-fiction, humour – *Seventeen Seas* is all of these. Some would class it as creative non-fiction. The Author likes to describe it as a travel book with a difference.

For all who have taken a cruise, think they'd like to, or are certain they never would!

Readers say about Seventeen Seas:

"...everyone will see portrayed someone they know or have met. A great travel book."

"I have recommended the book both to my friends who cruise as well as people who have never cruised and would like to. This book gives a realistic view of what cruising is like in a fun and fictionalized manner."

"I enjoyed the wry humor of this book. And while the subject matter seems light, there is a depth in the characterization and a hidden seriousness that gives the text more depth, and makes it a more fulfilling read."

"The descriptions of different experiences in the ports, their ambience and what they offer make it both factual and informative, as well as engaging equally to those who have been there, and those who would like to visit the ports in future."

"It's the total cruise experience, including sea time activities to port visits, tours, and tourist traps. Having read Seventeen Seas, I feel as though I took the cruise and enjoyed it from my comfy reading chair."

Further reviews can be seen on Amazon and Goodreads.

These Islands Here – Short Stories of the South Pacific

A B.R.A.G. Award book.

Literary fiction inspired by life in the South Pacific. *32 tales* reflecting life, events and conditions in the islands and nations of the South Seas-Polynesia, particularly Aotearoa-New Zealand. Together they present the varied facets of living in this region of the globe –pleasure, pain, calamity, comedy, fun, misfortune, loss, triumph – indeed, as in any part of the world, of being human. Most have been published previously, in magazines, newspapers, anthologies, and broadcast on radio. Several have won or been placed in short story competitions.

Readers say about These Islands Here:

"*I have just finished reading 'These Islands Here'. I enjoyed reading your book very much from start to finish. There are many surprises in terms of style and topic in your stories and it is easy to see why so many are award winning pieces.*"

"*I love this collection of short stories. These Islands Here gives an engaging sense of the people of New Zealand; some of the tales are wonderfully memorable. The story of the little Protestant girl who sees the Virgin Mary is absolutely delightful. I look forward to reading more of Bronwyn Elsmore's work – every time I need some reading that is gentle and wise, which is often.*"

"*A little of everything. Funny, empathetic, insightful, historic, sad, uplifting, inspiring, nostalgic, fantastic, Just about any adjective you could think of would apply to at least one of the stories in this amazing collection! I recommend it to all readers.*"

Further reviews can be seen on Amazon and Goodreads.

www.ingramcontent.com/pod-product-compliance
Lightning Source LLC
Chambersburg PA
CBHW060850250626
47159CB00008B/2677

* 9 7 8 0 9 9 2 2 4 9 1 4 4 *